I0608065

HERE & Now

A NOVEL BY

MARY A. WASOWSKI

This is a work of fiction. Names, characters, places, brands, media, and incidents are either the product of the author's imagination or are used fictitiously. The author acknowledges the trademarked status and trademark owners of various products referenced in this work of fiction, which have been used without permission. The publication/use of these trademarks is not authorized, associated with, or sponsored by the trademark owners.

Copyright © 2019 by Mary A. Wasowski
Cover Design by Francessca's PR & Design
Editing by Joe Marron
Formatting by JT Formatting

All rights reserved. Without limiting the rights under copyright reserved above, no part of this publication may be reproduced, stored in or introduced into a retrieval system, or transmitted, in any form, or by any means (electronic, mechanical, photocopying, recording, or otherwise) without the prior written permission of the above copyright owner of this book.

First Edition: December 2019
Library of Congress Cataloging-in-Publication Data

Wasowski, Mary A.
Here and Now / 1st ed
ISBN-13: 978-0-9969605-9-5

HERE & *Now*

PART ONE

Lawson and Renee

PROLOGUE

PRESENT...

Lawson

Slinking out the door before the alarm went off was not typical for me to do but lately, I haven't done anything that's my norm. Maybe I'm in need of a vacation. I guess when you can't remember the last time you actually took one that's a sign you need one.

My 50th birthday is fast approaching and all I want to do is forget that I'm actually fifty. My wife and kids want to throw me a huge birthday celebration and although I have been adamant about not wanting one, I don't think anyone is listening to me. It's been like this for a long time now especially with the kids now grown and out of our house. My wife completely and perfectly manages us in a rhythm only she can explain how it works. The rest of us just follow and fall in line.

Is it wrong to not want that anymore? I want to just throw responsibility out of the window and just be free for one fucking day with no worries to come home to. My therapist wife would disagree with my plan and list all the reasons why that's not a good idea. So, I avoid and internalize my feelings while plastering a smile on my face.

When I got to my office it was quiet and I took a moment to myself. I dropped my things on my desk and walked into my en-suite to splash some cold water on my face. Staring back at me was not the same man I used to be. Keyword: used to be. Time has been kind and according to the women in my life, I'm devilishly handsome in a distinguished way. I smile when my daughter reminds me that I should be happy I have a full head of hair and in good physical shape. Rubbing my hands down my face, I didn't feel any of those things, just the opposite.

"Excuse me Mr. Douglas, are you here?" my assistant called out.

"I'll be right out, Alison."

"Of course, sir, your coffee is on your desk." I deeply sighed and then manned up and began my busy workday, but first, coffee.

"Sir, I'm leaving the office for an appointment. Is there anything you need before I go?"

"Yes, book me on a one-way ticket to paradise." I wanted to say and be funny since that was the song playing on my way to work this morning. No, instead I kept it simple. "No thank you, Alison, I'm fine." Instead of working, I closed my eyes and got lost in thought.

PAST...

The late day sun was hanging on with a bit of cool air threatening with rain. I wanted to take the bike out for one last ride before I leave tomorrow but dad encouraged me to take my Jeep. This way I had a roof over my head if the sky opened up and rained down on me.

1983, the best summer of my life, and one spent with the love of my life, Renee Canton. I've been lucky enough to be stationed close to where our families still live and can visit my girl when I'm not on shift. It's not a bad deal and with my girl taking summer classes before she begins college in the fall, she didn't have a lot of time on her hands to miss me. After today will be a different story.

I leave for my overseas deployment in the morning and wanted today just for us but I got delayed with last minute packing and taking care of some family commitments. I just hope when I'm gone, her father doesn't give her too much of a hard time. Yeah, he kind of hates my ass with a passion. He has this misconstrued idea in his head that I am just not the right guy for his only daughter.

I can respect and appreciate how much he loves her and wants the very best for her life, but he doesn't have to worry. My girl knows how much I love her and will take care of her for the rest of our life.

I gathered my keys, wallet, and what I wanted to bring to Renee's when my father appeared in my doorway.

"You about ready son?"

"Yeah, Dad, I'm about to leave."

"May I offer you some advice?"

"You're asking? This is new."

"Don't think you're not too grown up to smack. Listen to me. I'm going to give you the same advice my father gave to me on the day I said goodbye to your mother. He's a wise man, your grandfather and it helped me a great deal."

"I'm listening."

"When you see your girl, just say what you have to say to her and get out of there before she breaks down in front of you. She will try her best not to but times like these wears heavily on the heart. For your own peace of mind, you don't want that image of Renee looking broken while you're on the other side of the world. You need to focus on your job and stay alive. You need to come back home to us, and to your girl in one piece. You understand me?"

"Dad, we've been over this. I'm going to be fine. You don't have to worry about me. Between you and grandpa preparing me for all I need to know, it's all good."

"Do not get overconfident there, son, your sergeants will eat you alive if you do."

"I survived basic and a year in the sun and mud, not to mention all the long hours I worked this farm. This tour? A piece of cake."

"Okay, I see you don't need me to tell you anything else. It's all there in your eyes. Go find your girl. I'm so very proud of you son."

"Thank you, Dad. I am too."

As I made my way out, he pulled me in for a strong hug and patted me on my back. He wasn't always hands-on when it came to affection, but he didn't have to be, I knew. I parked my Jeep and there she was waiting for me on the porch and looking so beautiful.

"Hey baby, you have something for me." She blushed slightly and smiled looking down at the ground. I loved when she did this.

"Come here," I said. I didn't need to repeat myself as Renee practically leaped off the top step wrapping her arms around my neck and pulling me into a tight hug.

I tapped my lips with my index finger showing her what I wanted. She never disappointed. I could feel her body warming as she fused her mouth with mine and poured all her emotion behind that kiss. A kiss I would feel for days.

"I'm going to miss you so much."

"You can't imagine how great that makes me feel knowing that, baby. Please don't cry, not today. My father warned me to make this visit quick just in case you did cry, but I'm not going anywhere until I know you are okay."

"I'm trying but this is hard. All the time I've had to get ready for this moment and now it's here and I can't help but to feel all torn up inside."

"I know. It's the same way for me but you are going to be so busy with school and finishing up with your degree, you won't have time to miss me."

"That's not true, I think about you all the time."

"I'm happy to hear that because you are always on my mind too. I love you so much, but I can't be worrying about you while I'm away. You need to promise to stay on track with school and get that degree. Once you do, I'll be home and then we can begin our life together."

"What if something happens to you? Where will that leave me?"

"I won't let that happen. I promise you." I was going to say more but her father interrupted our moment. Renee's arm tightened around my waist bracing for another confrontation with her father but that didn't happen, taking us both by surprise.

"Lawson," he said.

"Sir."

"Despite our differences, they don't seem as important as they once did when I have to see the pain in my little girl's eyes saying goodbye to you. She loves you and I know you love her too. Understand that I want the best for her and no man will ever be perfect in my eyes, but you come pretty close to that and I know you have made her happy. So, I'm no longer going to stand in your way. You take care now."

With his hand extended, I moved Renee aside and shook her father's hand for the very first time I truly felt welcomed by him. He said nothing more and gave me time with Renee, but not before my girl hugged her father and thanked him for being nice. He didn't say anything back, just returned her hug and went back inside. We saw her mom smiling at us from the window and we knew she had something to do with this surprising gesture. He wasn't a bad man, just wanted the best for his daughter and I intend to do just that and more.

"I have to go but I want to give you something first."

"No, you've given me way too much already. I love my promise ring."

"Just wait here, it's something else and not what you're thinking."

I opened up the passenger side door and reached for my backpack, inside my bag was what I wanted to give to Renee. "Here, this is for you." I handed her the items.

"A calendar? Why are you giving me this?" she asked.

I pulled out a red marker from my back pocket and handed it to her. "When do you want to get married?"

"Lawson, it's impossible to choose right now. We don't have any way of knowing when you will be home."

"Not true. My papers are for one year and then it's my choice where I choose to serve out my remaining contract. Once I return home, I will have less than six months and then I can begin to process out."

"What if your father makes you change your mind?"

"Not going to happen. Do I have to worry about yours while I'm gone?"

"Nope. He knows I will choose you over him."

"Good. Now pick a date."

"I can't."

"I can see the doubt in your eyes but baby, you have to trust me, trust us and what we have."

"I trust you. I just don't trust the Army."

"What if I pick a day and month and we miss it because you're not home yet?"

"Then it's Vegas baby and we get married by Elvis." She laughed and made her choice.

"Halloween? You serious?"

"Yup. Just like the conniption fit my father is sure to have when I tell him our plans."

"Very well. Halloween or Elvis."

"Deal." She crushed her mouth to mine and kissed the ever-loving shit out of me. I didn't want to let her go but I had to leave. I wanted to tell her one more thing before I did. I cradled her face in my hands and whispered these words to her.

"I know your father still has his doubts about me, but his feelings are not going to stop me from loving you. He may be your first love being a daddy's girl and all that, but I intend to be your last. You've marked the calendar in red because I wanted it to be visible for you to see and remember what this means. Look at it every single day so you don't forget that I am coming home to you. I love you, Renee Canton, and I plan on making you mine forever. You won't forget, right?"

"Never. I will be counting down the days until you return. I love you, Lawson. You have my heart, body, and soul, always and forever."

"And you have mine." I took her hand and kissed the ring I had given her. A declaration of my love for her.

"I have to go. What do you say?" I asked and then kissed her one more time.

"See you soon." I waved as I drove off promising I would be back no matter what.

CHAPTER
One

PRESENT...

Renee

What a week it has been planning Lawson's surprise birthday party. He's turning the big 50, and all our friends and family will be here to celebrate my amazing husband. I always wondered why milestone birthdays are referenced in terms as big, or bite my tongue, over the hill which he is not.

Lawson has managed to stay in shape all these years we've been together and what kills me the most is he eats anything he wants and there is not one love handle on his body to be found. In my case, I've always been a work in progress when it comes to my battle of the bulge. We don't use the word hate in our home but I use it quite often when I'm standing in front of a dressing room mirror. Those things are rough on a woman's self-esteem when she's trying to find the perfect black dress. Notice I didn't use the word, little.

My husband always says I am my worst critic when it comes to my body image. I've always been a curvy gal but as I get older, I'm left wondering where my curves have gone. I'm currently between a size 14 and 16, more on the 16 these days. Thank you, retail gods, for creating all the secret treasures women wear to hide the lumps and bumps. Again, Lawson would be so angry with me for thinking like this. He loves all parts of me and never has complained about my weight. The running joke is since I am a Psychologist and specialize in family psychology and developmental psychology. So, in other words, I am the last person who should be worried about body image, but when you have a husband who looks like Hugh Jackman, can you really blame me?

I decided to finish the last of my dictation while I was at the office so I could leave my work here and concentrate on Lawson. I've always been career driven, and now with our kids grown and out of our home, I work more now than ever before. I slowed down when they were little because I wanted to be supermom I guess, but I never had to be because I had Lawson to help me. We shared everything when it came to our son and daughter and I never felt alone like some of my girlfriends did.

Back then it was just me and Lawson against the world, and then we became a family. And now, it's just us two again. My mind spins when I think of our life together and everything we've shared and built hence this is the reason why I want this birthday to be the best he has ever had. Lawson deserves nothing else. Our kids, Rogan and Emily are spending the weekend at the house, another surprise for Lawson.

The kids are very busy with their lives but make every attempt to stay close to us. I have it easy with Emily, I see my daughter every day since she has joined my practice as a wellness life coach, along with her fiancé, Augustus, who prefers Gus. He jokes that his parents loved raising their family in Augusta, GA so much that they had to name their child to something they had a special connection to. I love it, it's old school and I haven't met too many men named Augustus. We like unique names in our family.

I can't wait to see the look on Lawson's face when Rogan tells him that he has taken and passed his final exam and has earned his master's degree in Biology. As a child, he loved getting his hands dirty especially when it came to working with his father. Most boys want to grow up to be baseball players or a firefighter, our son wanted to work in the dirt and the water. I smile at that memory because after all his hard work he is now an environmental engineer and he can officially join his father's team at Douglas ECO Systems.

Yes, this is going to be an amazing night.

"Knock, knock. You asked me to kick you out of here by six, and it is now closing in on seven." My assistant, Jeanie reminds me from the doorway.

"I know and I've been done. I guess I've just been sitting here re-flecting on the past."

"You okay?"

"Sure, I'm fine. I just can't believe how fast time has gone by and my husband is fifty and fabulous. Do you think he will like his party? He's not much for the big gatherings anymore unless it's with our kids."

"He will love it because he loves you. He knows your heart is in the right place and once he pushes through your front door, he's going to be incredibly appreciative of all the thought and love you put into giving him a special night and surrounding him with family and friends celebrating him."

"From your lips to my ears, I hope you are right. He's been off lately and very quiet. He says it's work and new projects covering his desk has him crazy. He only had Rogan be an apprentice until he achieved his master's and now he has. Rogan can join Lawson full time and be the perfect team like Lawson was when he worked with his father. I know it's something he's wanted for a long time and now it's here. I just want everything to be perfect."

"And it will be. You need to follow your own advice sometimes. Go home and enjoy your family. Take tomorrow and enjoy all the pampering I have arranged for you and Emily during your day off, and then tomorrow night, you can party your asses off."

"You'll stop by, right?"

"Yes, I will be there. Now go!"

"Okay, Ms. Bossy. Thank you for managing my life the way you do."

"You're welcome. See you at the party."

"Yes, you will."

As I drove home from my downtown office in Augusta, my mind once again drifted to the lifetime of beautiful memories shared with Lawson. When I think of the first time my father met Lawson Douglas, he just chose to hate him on sight, which only pushed me closer to him. My mother was always on my side and after she forced him out of their bedroom for three full nights, he decided hating Lawson took up too much energy and the back pain he endured was not worth it. So he went from hating to strongly dislike but ultimately waved the white flag for the sake of peace in our family.

When Lawson was given his deployment orders and seeing how strongly it affected me, that was the day he was welcomed into our family as my future husband. I waited every second of every day for his safe return. He kept his promises and in turn, I kept mine.

"Where is he? do you see him?" I asked my parents as I stood on my tippy toes through the crowd of excited people waiting for their loved ones to step off the plane. "There he is, mom, oh my goodness, he looks so good."

"I see him, darling. You need to take a breath before you fall over."

"Mom, I can't help myself. It feels like forever since I last saw him."

"Well baby girl, there he is and he's on his way. Go get your man." I looked over my shoulder at my father and thanked him for his support—finally!

His arms were already opened and I was calling his name as loud as I could. "Lawson!" I screamed and my body was lifted off the ground and in his arms. I wanted to wrap my legs around his waist, but my mother made me wear a dress.

"Miss me, baby?" and then he kissed me madly.

CHAPTER
Two

PRESENT...

Lawson

I tapped my fingers along the Cherrywood finish of my twelve-seat conference table. I feel as if I've been held hostage all day with these investors trying to stall the deal that will make my company a great deal of money. I don't like my time wasted and in about two seconds I'm going to lose my fucking mind. 1, 2, and—my secretary's phone buzzes. Yeah, saved by the literal bell.

She gave me a suggestive look and then discreetly took her call. I let out a frustrated sigh and then finally ended the chaos around me and silenced the room. "Gentlemen, enough with the dancing around and let's make a deal or get the fuck out of my office, it's that simple."

"Excuse me?" I heard from the end of the table as my eyes found the ones that matched mine—my father, Roman Douglas.

"I apologize but what choice did you all leave me here?" I asked and then I turned to address Winston Lockhart of Creekside Orchards, and landowner of the biggest orchards in the state of Georgia. "Winston, what's it going to be? If you read over those contracts one more time, you're going to go blind. What's the problem?"

"Lawson, the problem is you want a piece of what I got and I don't play nice with others, especially when they are trying to steal my land from under me."

"Now wait just a minute," my father roared from where he was seated. I raised my hand with respect and wanted to show him that I could handle Winston. He sat back down and let me do what I was good at.

"Before another word is spoken, I think we should clear the room because I don't believe you want me embarrassing you in front of your entire board, now, do you?" He remained silent and looked around before finally waving his hand and one by one his team vacated their seats and Alison was back to escort them to the waiting area.

I took off my suit jacket and loosened the tie while I was at it. Removing my cufflinks and rolling up my sleeves, I was now comfortable to tell Winston exactly what I thought of him and his usage of improper words.

"First of all, let's get something straight. The Douglas Company does not steal, never has nor will it ever. There's only one thief in this room and I'm looking at him."

"How dare you!" he got up to get in my face. I rose with my bigger frame towering over him and then he stepped back before sitting down.

"No, how dare you?" I retorted. "Ten years ago, Lockhart bought up thousands of acres that had gone deserted. Land that was once prominent farms until the market crashed along with bad weather destroying everything in its path and leaving the farmers to fall on hard times. You swept in and bought it all not even close to market value. I want that land back and you are not leaving this room until I get it. You know we have the money and our offer is a very good one that has been presented here to you. It's a deal over a year in progress. The filtration systems that Lawson will install will make that land prosper

14

again and bring back those farming families."

"You saw an opportunity to collect and you ran with it. You made a lot of money benefitting from the less fortunate. I suggest you take what has been proposed to you and run with it because the clock is ticking and I won't be so generous again if you don't sign today, hell, I might just lose my fucking mind and kill the deal completely, but then we would both lose."

"And, why is that? You holding out on me?"

"No, Douglas does their business the honest way. Let's just say I have some pull in all the right places and hell will freeze over before that land becomes another fucking shopping mall."

"You can't do that!"

"Yes, I can and I will if I have to wait another five minutes for your answer. What's it going to be, Winston? Sign on the dotted line or pay taxes on dirt that will never see structure on it."

He huffed in frustration and then asked for those five minutes to speak with his team. I gave it to him which gave me time to collect my thoughts and deal with my father who has had his reservations about this matter from the very beginning. The door closed and I braced my-self for a fight but that didn't happen. He tapped my shoulder which he always did when he was proud of me and then the words followed.

"I am in awe of you son. If I didn't see it or hear it, I might not have believed it. You have that guy pissing his pants right now. Tell me this, is it true?"

"Yes, it is. I already have killed it if he doesn't sign."

"Mind telling me how?"

"Yes, I do. You made me CEO for a reason, let me do what I do best."

"You're right, son. You asking me here today meant a great deal to me."

"Dad, you taught me everything I need to know to be able to do this job, and I hope I have passed that knowledge down to Rogan."

"You have, and that boy of yours is so smart. I have no doubt when I'm gone, I can die a happy man."

"You're not dying and certainly not anytime soon." I was about to say more and then Winston returned.

"You win, Lockhart accepts your proposal and is going to sign off on it today."

"Good choice, Winston, a very good choice. Here, use my pen."

My team along with my father raised their glasses up in my honor and took a sip of the chilled champagne we held on ice for most of the day.

"Well done son, you are amazing. Your grandfather is smiling down on you today and I know is very proud too."

"Thank you, dad, I appreciate it." I topped off my glass and gulped it down like it was water. It should have been scotch on account on the day I just had. My father seemed to be in the mood to chat but I was not.

"What's on your mind?"

"At the moment, not a damn thing."

"Try again."

I looked over at Alison and strategically avoided my father and his questions. "Has everything been filed?"

"Yes, sir, everything is good to go."

"Perfect."

"Okay, if there's not anything else you need, I'm going to call it a day." I silently counted to five and just when she was almost home free, I called her back.

"Oh, Alison, one more thing."

"Sir?"

"The phone call earlier. Is there anything I need to know?"

"Oh, no, it was just one of our distributors confirming a delivery date."

"Really? Which one?"

"Son, what does it matter? I'm sure Alison handled it." I gnashed my molars together.

"Thank you, dad, but I wasn't asking for your input."

"And, that's my cue to leave. Talk to you later, Lawson."

Fuck! "Yeah, goodnight." My father was not the one I was pissed at, no that honor went to my assistant here, and one other person I've yet to accuse until I confirm what I think I know.

"So, the distributor? Which one was confirming?"

"Pittsboro," she muttered. "You know how they are, always double checking."

"You know, maybe I should call over there and get Jim on the line just to put his mind at ease."

"No! You can't do that."

"Why not? I'm the CEO, I can do whatever I want."

"And, I am your administrative assistant which is so much more than a secretary. I have it handled."

"You're right, and I know better to question you when I know you are the most honest and efficient and trusted person I have here on my staff. I mean, what would I do without you?" I knew I was being an asshole questioning her when I rarely did, but my reasons had not one thing to do with business. This was personal.

She was biting the shit out of her lip and just when I thought I had her, my phone buzzed in my pocket, giving her the opportunity to escape. She called out, "good night" and was out the door faster than I could blink. I pulled out my phone and didn't look at the number before answering.

"Douglas" I curtly answered.

"Hey babe, are you coming home soon?"

"Renee," I deeply sighed. There was silence on the line for a minute and then I felt like a total dick.

"I'm sure you're busy, I was just calling to ask if you were making it home for dinner? I'm running late myself and wanted to see what you were in the mood for?"

I thought, how about a new life? "Sorry, it's been a long day. I'm leaving here in a few."

"Great. I'll see you soon. I love you."

"Yeah, me too."

Fuck. Fuck. Fuck! I sighed and then poured myself a scotch. "Happy Birthday, Asshole!"

CHAPTER
Three

PRESENT...

Renee

I'd been home for more than an hour since disconnecting with Lawson. I know my husband vehemently told me his reasons why he didn't want to make a big deal about his birthday but I wasn't having it, and the kids agreed with me. They wanted their father celebrated and begged me to overrule what Lawson wanted and just do what we want for him. Judging by the tone he used while he was on the phone with me, I think he is on to us.

My timing was completely off when I called Alison earlier to see if Lawson was still in his meeting. She was supposed to call me when he wrapped up his meeting but it was taking longer than expected and I called her back interrupting her in the middle of it. Now I was screwed because she doesn't lie well and knowing how Lawson's mind works, I'm sure he drilled her with his incessant questions.

I don't understand why he's behaving like this. What is the big deal about having a party and celebrating with people who love him?

The kids don't get it either but I assured them all would be fine but now I am doubting my own good intentions.

It's no secret he has been distant since losing his mother. His father expected it for a while now but not Lawson. He never gave up faith and held on to all the hope he had. He was devastated when his father had phoned him in the middle of the night with news of her passing. Her only wish was not to die in a hospital or anything resembling a hospice. After talking with her family and making sure they all understood her wishes, the decisions were made and she signed herself out. Lawson spent every minute he could with her and the night before she died, we all had dinner together and laughed about every story Lawson and Roman could fit in a short amount of time before she tired and asked to go to bed. We all gave her a hug and told Becca we loved her never knowing it would be the last time we would hear her voice or see her smile.

She fought her cancer to the very end, so brave and strong. When Roman called us to tell us the news, Lawson got up without saying a word to me and drove over to his parents' home. It would be a full day before he came home to me. I knew where he was but I never understood why he would just coldly shut his family out. We always leaned on one another and never went to bed angry. It was a rule we made very early on in our marriage. Both our parent's marriages were loving and strong, we always vowed to be better than both of them put together. Lawson said our love was invincible and we would always be happy. It's what I've been trying to do for him every day since his mom died but I feel as if I am failing at every turn.

"Mom, are you home?" *Perfect timing! Emily's here.*

"Hi honey, I'm in the office."

"Mom! Come on, Cosmos on me."

"Can I get a hug first?"

"Yes, you can." Emily wrapped her arms around me and squeezed as hard as she could. We've always had a close relationship and she is the perfect remedy for my mood tonight.

"So, I thought we were meeting at the spa tomorrow morning? What brings you by tonight? Not that I'm complaining because I love that you're here."

"Ugh! Gus is studying and kicked me out telling me that I was a distraction. I didn't even get mad because he said it in such a sweet way and then kissed me all over and begged me to go or he would change his mind and fail his test."

"He's sweet, one of the good ones. I'm happy I have such an understanding daughter when it comes to her future husband's priorities."

"When's his exam?"

"Tomorrow morning at nine."

"He's going to pass it with flying colors and then I can officially bring him on board at the wellness center. You two have worked so hard in school and in your internships. I am so proud of you."

"Thanks, mom, we just fit, you know?"

"Yeah, I know a thing or two about that."

"Ice cream?"

"Yeah, and lots of it."

"Okay, I'll fill the bowls, you pick the movie."

"I'm on it." I looked down at my watch and deeply sighed. *"Where are you, Lawson?"* I thought and then pulled my phone from my pocket and called my missing husband only to get his voicemail. I ended the call and decided not to stress over it. *"He'll come home."*

Emily had gone to bed way before the closing credits had begun. I told her I was right behind her but wanted to wait up for her dad. When she caught the time she was taken back by how late it was and questioned why her father hadn't arrived home yet.

I assured her that all was fine and he had a late meeting. Our daughter was very smart and I knew she wasn't buying the bullshit story I was trying to believe myself, but with a hug and kiss the subject was dropped and she went to bed.

"Lawson, it's me, again. Where are you? Because I know where you're not and I'm worried. Emily is here and Rogan will be here to-

morrow. Please come home to your family. We love and need you. Okay, I'm going to go to bed now. Please wake me up when you get home."

After the clock struck two, I went to bed without Lawson by my side and left to wonder if he would come home at all.

"Mom, coffee's on," Emily called up from the bottom of the stairs.

"I'll be right down," I called out and then closed my bedroom door sliding down to the floor. I hugged my knees and fought back the tears that would fall if I wasn't so strong to hold them back. I was worried last night but now I'm angry that Lawson hadn't returned my calls or messages, and I still have no idea where he is. The kids are home and it's his birthday, so I am going to refrain from flipping out and ruining this weekend that our children have been looking forward to. When it's over and it's just us two again, Lawson Douglas has some explaining to do.

"Good morning, Emily, how did you sleep?" I asked my daughter before giving her a hug.

"Slept great and then I was so energized this morning, I went for a run and as I was coming in, I nearly crashed into daddy on his way out. He's always telling me to take my headphones out but I never do."

"So, dad was home?"

"Um, yeah, where else would he be?"

"I guess I was just curious because I waited until two and he hadn't come home yet."

"Well, he was dressed and leaving for work when I saw him, so I'm sure he came home. I wouldn't worry. Now, are you ready for our spa day because I know I am."

"I wouldn't miss it for the world. Let's go." *Yup! Like I was saying, Lawson Douglas, you have some explaining to do.*

CHAPTER
Four

PRESENT...

Lawson

I listened and re-read all of Renee's messages she had left for me. By the time I sobered up enough to drive home, it was way beyond late. I know I fucked up royally by not coming home like I was supposed to, and I feel like a selfish jerk for making my wife worry.

I knew our daughter was home and a very early riser. After managing a couple of hours asleep on the couch, I grabbed a shower and changed before I was caught where I shouldn't be. I thought I was home free and then by dumb luck, I run into one of the two people I was trying to avoid for at least a few more hours—Emily.

"Daddy! Oh, my goodness, what are you doing up so early and dressed for work?"

"And good morning to you too," I said and then she practically jumped into my arms for a hug. "I was trying to be quiet and not wake the house. I have a few meetings this morning before our family weekend begins and wanted to get a jump on it." *Liar! Let's hope she buys it.*

"This is perfect. You go into the office and finish up what you have to do, and mom and I will be at the spa. We should be home after lunch and then Rogan should be here and we can all catch up."

"Sounds perfect, honey. I've missed you so much. Step back and let me take a look at you." I smiled and couldn't believe my little baby is this amazing woman standing before me.

"Dad, you just saw me last month and you will probably be seeing a lot more of me now that I am joining mom's practice, and Gus too!"

"One big happy family," I said, feeling like a selfish bastard for shutting my family out and behaving recklessly with my excessive drinking binge I did last night instead of coming home to my family.

"You know it. Okay, I need a shower and you have to go. See you later!" a few air kisses and she was gone. If you had any balls, you would march yourself up to those steps and talk to your wife. I'll call her once I get to the office and apologize. I gave Alison the day off knowing she was up to no good with my wife and daughter. I told Renee that I didn't want a party but that's exactly what she did behind my back.

I stopped at a local Starbucks on my way into my office and grabbed a light breakfast. I knew the office would be quiet since it was a holiday weekend, but I never expected to see my father waiting for me and sitting behind my desk with his feet up.

"Make yourself at home why don't you?"

"Oh, I have. I love this chair. Italian leather?"

"I don't know, Renee decorated my office."

"She has wonderful taste in furniture, too bad her judgment is off in husbands."

"Excuse me?"

"What? Do you have a hearing problem? You mind telling me what in the fuck is going on with you?"

"Stay out of it and if you don't mind, will you please get out of my chair."

"No and no. Now, why did you spend half the night here in your office when you should have been home with your family? Secondly, this bottle was full when I left here yesterday." My father held up the bottle of scotch that I had tossed in the wastebasket.

"Dad, I'm just working out some stuff right now and I am not in the mood for a lecture."

"Too bad, you're going to get one. Now, it's no secret that my lovely daughter in law is throwing you a 50th birthday party tomorrow night at your home, and it's also not a secret that you didn't want one. The bigger question is, why not? It's a party to celebrate you, and the best part is that you are going to be surrounded by people who love you and have been working really hard to make you smile again. What is the problem?"

"If I tell you, you're just going to be disappointed and hurting you is the last thing I want to do."

"But hurting your wife is okay?"

"I didn't say that, dammit, you're twisting my words."

"Renee loves you so much and you going off without returning her calls just disappoints me and hurts her deeply. I know you son. You would never deliberately shut your family out. What's going on with you? And I want the truth."

"No, you don't. You, Renee, and everyone in my life just want to hear what you want to hear. No one is listening to me and what I fucking want!"

"I'm listening now, and I can probably guess one reason why you don't feel like celebrating this year but something tells me there's so much more to your bad mood than I realize. Will you talk to me, please? I want to help but I can't unless you give me something to work with."

"You won't understand."

"Try me."

"Dad, to the outside world, I am a man who has everything. A beautiful wife. Two amazing kids. A home and a successful running business."

"And? What's the problem?"

"I can't breathe. I'm tired and I'm fifty years old and I look around to everything I've built and I'm just not sure if I want it anymore. And I know that makes me sound like a selfish sonofabitch but it's the truth. I wake up every single day in this robotic life and most days are good because I know at least in my professional life I feel like I'm doing good work and giving back. It's my personal life that's a mess and here's the big riddle, no one knows the wiser, just me because I'm afraid to tell Renee how I feel."

"Son, she's your wife. What the hell is wrong with you? She loves you more than life itself and those kids? My grandkids? I couldn't be prouder. You got damn lucky being as blessed as you've been. You have two grown children following in each of their parent's footsteps because they idolize you both. Emily is just gorgeous, probably could have been a model but she chose to be book smart and wants to help people with their problems. And Rogan? You name it with him. He excelled in every sport he ever played in. A straight-A student which is rare considering all his time was spent out on the field, and don't even get me started with all the girls chasing after him. But what does he decide to do with his life? Follow his father, get his hands dirty and make a god damn difference in this world, just like his great-grandfather before him."

"Yes, Lawson Douglas, you are a selfish asshole, not a sonofabitch because that would mean your mama, god rest her beautiful soul. You are all twisted up inside and it's going to dismantle you if you let it. I'm not going to sugar coat it for you, grief sucks but there comes a time you need to not get over it because I would never ask you to do that."

"Good, because I am nowhere near ready to forget mama."

"No one asked you to. And by the way, you look like shit. Get your head out of your ass and man the fuck up. Yes, losing your mother hurt us all, no more than me, but life goes on and she would want all of us to do that. I still have a lot of living to do and I plan on enjoying it. You are too old for me to worry about. Get your shit together and go home to your family."

"What if it's not what I want anymore? What then?"

"Then? You are a damn fool and the house that Lawson Douglas built is going to burn up in flames all around you and all that will be left is a big pile of ash. Don't be that man. Happy Birthday, son."

"Dad, please don't go."

"I've said my peace. I'll see you at your party, that's if you're decent enough to show up."

After my father told my ass off in his usual colorful manner, I called my wife and apologized for my assholery behavior. Being the understanding person she is, graciously accepted my apology and told me she loved me.

She didn't come clean about the party and talked right over me. I decided to just give in and not be the asshole my father accused me of earlier and suck it up. Some would say I should be thankful they care at all but I didn't see it that way. I didn't want a party and it should have been respected but parties are never really for the intended. They are meant for the people throwing it and the invited. You want to show them your best and give them your best. I'm just the reason they all came together.

I punched the code to open the gates to our property and as they slowly opened, my stomach felt knotted inside. I wonder where all the cars were parked. I almost expected to see a valet service at the top of the driveway but knowing Renee, she had all her bases covered and stay true to form with making this the big surprise she wanted for me.

I climbed the seven steps to our big open porch where I used to sit to watch the kids play. I loved those times and then the other times just sitting out here with Renee watching a storm come through on a hot summer night. We don't do that anymore.

My hand touched the doorknob and I exhaled a deep breath before turning it and stepping inside. Once I crossed the threshold, I was greeted with a boom of applause and the happy cheers of my family and friends wishing me a happy birthday. I played my part although I felt the urging feeling to flee as fast as my legs would take me. My eyes roamed around the room to find Renee smiling and then she simply shrugged and winked, sending me the clear message that although I said no to a party, she went ahead and did it anyway. The next person I saw was my father. He stood tall with a drink in hand but glared at me with his icy eyes. Yeah, he was still angry at me for being an ass.

Before I could speak, our Emily ran over to me and practically leaped into my arms. "Happy Birthday, Daddy! Are you surprised?" she happily asked.

"Yes, I am surprised," I said and then lovingly kissed her cheek.

"Liar! Oh, Daddy, you are so cute. Don't be mad. I helped plan with mom and all we want is to make you happy. So act like it, okay?"

It hurt me to ever disappoint my daughter. Her eyes were practically sparkling. She looked so happy and just wanted me to feel the same way. "I promise."

"Thank you. Now be good and go say hello to your guests. Rogan is running late but he has a very good reason, so don't be too petulant when he does arrive."

"You spend too much time with your mother." Knowing I was right, she stuck out her tongue and then made her way through the throngs of guests in our home. I said hello to our friends and then made my way over to my father who just placed his drink down to the bar.

"Hi," I greeted him.

"Hello. I see you decided to grow back your balls and show up. It's nice to know you haven't completely lost the good sense God gave you."

"Gee, thank you for that warm sentiment. I'm here because it's where I was expected to be. Don't fool yourself into believing that I actually want to be here. It's not a crime for not wanting a party. Just once, I wanted a little peace and quiet and again, not a crime."

"Fine! You're right. Having said that you don't always get to have your way. It's something you signed on for when you married Renee and made a family with her. It's called compromise and a lot of give and take. You see your daughter over there looking at you as if you are the only man in the room? Her hero. Her dad. Stop this bullshit already. It's a party for crying out loud, not a funeral." He finished off his drink and waved down the bartender.

This was not the place for a scene. I turned toward my father and quietly said, "The fact that I'm here at all should be enough for you, so please spare me any more lectures. And just so we are clear, I know the difference between a party and a funeral. I've recently been to one." Yup, I knew that did it because my father muttered under his breath and called me the exact word that fit my behavior—asshole. At least I was consistent. "Bartender, I'd like a double Knob Creek, neat."

"Right away sir."

I downed my drink after he stormed off and ordered another. I wanted to say leave the bottle but that would probably earn me a punch to my mouth, so the drink would have to do. I enjoyed the slow burn down my throat as it successfully chipped away at the tension I felt. I'm three for three in the asshole department fighting with my wife and two rounds with my father. I pushed the empty glass away and then my wife finally made her appearance at my side.

"Happy Birthday, Lawson. I love you." She wrapped her arms tightly around my shoulders.

"Thank you, Renee." She pulled back studying my face.

"No love back? I guess you're really mad."

"Sorry. I love you. I'm not sure I can say anything else to you right now without hurting your feelings." I turned away and reached over the bar to grab the bourbon and poured myself another double. Her happy expression fell and I knew I was the cause of it.

"Okay, Lawson, you're angry with me, that much is clear since you're hell bent on getting plastered tonight. I'm sorry I disrespected your wishes and threw this party for you, but can you do me a favor and try to enjoy it? Whether you believe it or not, this is a big deal and it means a lot to your children."

"Fine. I'll comply."

"Thank you. Rogan has arrived and is waiting for you in your study. He wants a few minutes with you in private."

I said nothing more and walked through my house smiling all the way to my study. I felt my father's eyes burning holes in my back as I passed him. *Fuck!* I entered the room and saw his back to me as our son was facing the huge built-in bookcase that housed hundreds of my books. A vast collection of favorite works of art from authors I have followed throughout the years. It was a great escape from stress and reading always cleared my mind.

"Rogan, hi, it's nice to see you son." And I meant every word because it was the truth. I didn't know how much I missed him until now.

"Happy Birthday, it's good to see you too."

I gave my son a long drawn out embrace taking my time since it's been a while since he's come home.

"I have a present for you."

"You didn't have to give me anything. You coming home is enough."

"Thank you for saying that but this is something that I believe is going to make you very happy. A gift you've been wanting for a while."

"You certainly have me curious. Okay, let me have it."

He handed me a gift-wrapped box with a perfectly tied bow gracing the top. I slowly unwrapped my gift and peeled back the multi-layers of tissue paper. Inside was a leather book of some sort. My eyes didn't catch the gold embossed writing on top until I took a second glance. My eyes became glazed over with so much pride and adoration for my son because now I knew what this gift was.

"You did it. You really did it."

"I don't know, you tell me." He winked.

I opened up the book and there was a smooth blank paper covering what I would see next. It was my son's degree of completion for his master's in environmental engineering and ecology. "Come here, son," he walked back into my arms and all I could do was to hug him. "I am so proud of you."

"Thank you, sir. If you'll have me, I would like to officially join Douglas ECO Systems and work side by side with my father, a man who I look up to and admire so much. You and grandpa have literally given me all the knowledge that no textbook could ever do, and although it took me some time to get my degree, I now have it and want to put it to good use beginning with the land we just acquired back. It's going to need a lot of testing and care to reach a level before we even can begin to think about installing new water systems. It's been neglected and polluted by industry for too long now and with me and the team I have already in place, I know I can restore it back to as it should be."

"Rogan, you don't have to sell me on the sales pitch, I know how hard you've worked in school and the love and passion you have for the farmers in need of our help. I would like nothing more than to have you join me."

"I'm sensing a but in there somewhere. Dad, right what you are holding is what you said you wanted. I've done my part and now it's time for you to do yours. I'll start on Monday."

"Rogan, for the past two days all I have heard are reminders of my promises and commitments that everyone seems to enjoy holding me to. I have no room to fucking breathe and all I want is to do that and take a moment to catch my breath. Yes, you earning this magnificent degree has made me immensely proud and so honored that I am your father. I am not going back on my word; it never crossed my mind. I just need a minute here and then once I'm back in the office, I will work out a plan that will best suit you."

"Okay, fine. Let me be clear before you make any decisions. I mean no disrespect here, but my place is not behind a desk. If that's the plan you want for me than I respectfully decline your offer. My place is out there working that land, making it better for our local farmers, and preserving it for future generations. My choice is you but if you can't give me what I want then I have to choose my backup plan and move forward."

"Wow! How did giving me an amazing birthday gift go from elation to demands? I mean, seriously, Rogan? Did you practice that speech all the way over here?"

"No, I just always have to be prepared when it comes to you. You say one thing and then do the other. I had to cover my bases and be ready."

"Fine. If you want an answer right now, I don't have one for you. Congratulations Rogan, I wish you well." I slammed the box down to my desk and walked out of my office.

"Hey, hey, hey, where are you going?" Renee called out as she tried to catch up to me. "Lawson, why don't you look happy? I thought talking to Rogan would put you over the moon."

"Dammit, Renee, I was happy and so proud of him, but now I'm not and I am going to go back to my birthday party you so perfectly put together for me. Isn't that what you want me to do?"

"Lawson, I don't know what has you in this foul mood, but this is neither the time or place to have this meltdown. Please calm yourself."

"Spoken like the true therapist you are."

"Lawson, what has gotten into you?"

"You know, I'm not sure but seeing how you always have the answers, figure it out and let me know. I have a bottle of Bourbon with my name on it."

CHAPTER
Five

PRESENT...

Renee

*O*kay, just breathe and remain calm. He's having a moment and I will allow him to cool off before we sing Happy Birthday to him. I let out a few breaths and then Rogan stepped out from his father's study and looking like someone just kicked him hard in the shin.

"Rogan," he put his hand up to stop me.

"Dad will make the right choice, I know he will. I threw too much at him all at once and I should have just been happy with his reaction to my degree."

"You worked incredibly hard to earn it and why shouldn't you talk to your father about working with him."

"Because mother, it's his birthday and I should have known better just by the look on his face. He's tired mom, don't you see that? He doesn't need me or anyone else coming at him in all directions."

"We're just being the family that loves him. I don't understand

33

why you would say such things."

"He didn't want this and we should have listened to him for once. Look, I don't want to fight with you too. I'm sorry. I'm going to go in and say hello to Emily and grandpa and then eat because I'm starving. It was a long drive."

"Okay, I'll join you in a minute."

I made my way back to our grand living room where our guests were happily engaged in conversation. The band I hired was playing Lawson's favorite selection of Jazz he enjoyed. I looked around the room and spotted my husband sitting at the bar and waist deep in Bourbon. *Come on babe, hold it together for a little while longer,"* I said quietly under my breath before joining him.

"The band is playing our song. Care to twirl me around the dance-floor?"

"Sure, why not?" he knocked back his drink and took my hand in his.

"Lawson, I'm—"

"Shhh, don't talk. Let's just move with each other and enjoy the dance." He pulled me closer to the point of pain with his fingers digging into the small of my back. My husband has something tearing him up inside and he won't let me in. I'm not for silence between us and I desperately wanted to push him to talk to me. I remained quiet and allowed him to move us across the dance floor until the song reached an end.

He stopped but didn't let me go and then there was a roar of applause with Emily wheeling out her father's birthday cake. He pulled away in confusion almost lost in our moment and then he tried awkwardly smiling as she pushed the cake right in front of us. Friends and family gathered around us urging Lawson to blow out his candles and make a wish. He let me go and looked over to our children and then to me before deeply inhaling and successfully extinguishing all fifty of his candles.

"Whoo-hoo! Way to go, Daddy! Did you make a wish?" asked

Emily, as she smiled happily standing by Rogan who was clapping along.

"Speech. Speech." More demands from our friends.

Lawson looked as if he was going to throw up, I mean chunks and everything. I was praying he would keep it together for a few more minutes.

"First off, I would like to say thank you to my wife, Renee, and our children, Rogan and Emily. Surprising me is no easy task this I know, so thank you for keeping me in your hearts and giving me this great night."

Happy applause rang out as I watched Emily hug her father. Rogan smiled politely and then Roman stepped up to shake his son's hand. Lawson returned the gesture and then made his discreet exit from the party. He was done and I knew he would not be returning. Our guests enjoyed a lot more champagne, cake, and then said their good-byes letting me know what a grand time they had.

"Whoo, I'm tired. Another successful party."

"You think so?"

"Sure, why not. Everyone had a good time."

"Yeah, everyone but your father who looked like he wanted to be anywhere but here."

"Oh, mom, that's not true."

"Listen, do me a favor. Please stay in the guest house tonight with Rogan. I need to speak with your father and I don't want an audience."

"Mom, you're scaring me. What's going on?"

"I don't know baby, but I intend to find out. Please do this for me."

"Okay, I will. Rogan is already over there. If you need me for anything, just text me and I'll be right over."

"Thank you, but no need to worry. I am just going to speak to your father privately and hopefully, he will open up about what is bothering him."

"Is it nanny dying? I mean, I know they were close but not even grandpa looks sad anymore."

"There's no timetable on grief and just because your grandfather doesn't show it, doesn't mean he's not sad. I think that's one of the reasons why he went back to work. He needs to keep busy and I can't imagine him wanting to stay in his big house all alone."

"I'm sorry, mom, I shouldn't have said that. I miss nanny too. I guess we've all been busy in our own way and with nanny preparing us the way she did, it's been easier for me to cope with."

"Well, and being a therapist in training helps too. You learn so many coping mechanisms that sometimes it's just easier to flip the switch and manage your feelings better than some can."

"If anyone is an expert at that is you, mom. I'm tired and I'm going to go to bed. I love you."

"I love you too, so much." As I hugged our daughter, I saw Lawson at the top of the stairs shooting me cold daggers that had the ability to pierce my soul. He shook his head and walked away before our daughter noticed him.

I took my own shot of Bourbon before climbing the stairs to our bedroom. It appeared Lawson was even more in a mood than what I first believed. I didn't know what I was in for tonight but hoped we could find a resolution. This is not how I wanted this evening to go and I still haven't given him his birthday present yet. Would he even want it? One way to find out. We need to have a talk whether he likes it or not.

CHAPTER
Six

PRESENT...

Lawson

Listening to Renee with our daughter infuriated me on a level I have never felt before. My hands were white knuckling the top railing that I almost feared I would damage it. I wasn't in the mood to be analyzed right now and my feelings dissected until there was nothing left. I didn't want to eavesdrop on their conversation but when I heard that I was the subject of their talk, my feet remained rooted to where I was standing and I just got angrier by the minute.

It would be another half hour before Renee joined me in our bedroom. I was drunk. She was quiet when she joined me and remained silent walking into our bathroom. When she finally did emerge, she was dressed for bed and her face was clean of make-up.

I was sitting in the oversized chair with my feet up on the matching ottoman. She removed the tumbler from my hand and crawled up and straddled my body with leaning forward and placing her head on my chest. Instinctively, I wrapped my arms around her back and breathed her in. She sighed deeply and then kissed my chest where my skin was exposed to my open shirt.

"Talk to me, Lawson, please." I shifted my body to move and then I cupped her face in my hands and just stared at my wife.

"Life just snuck up on us, didn't it? I mean, at twenty-five we had the whole fucking world at our feet and free to do anything we wanted. And now I'm fifty fucking years old and I just feel lost."

"Lawson, where is this coming from? Look, I know I went against your wishes and a little overboard with your birthday party, but with all due respect, I had the best intentions for you. I did this because I love you, and your children love you and wanted to do something special for you."

"Come on, Renee, don't use the kids."

"I'm not and never would."

"Oh, please, they have been your secret weapon against me for more years than I can count. Every time you and I disagreed about anything, you would throw the kids into the middle of it and then I would end up feeling bad about it and just concede. I'm over it!"

She was now off my lap and pacing our bedroom. "You're over it? And what pray tell does that mean? Lawson, I just don't understand you and where all this anger is stemming from. I'm not sure if you have noticed but you've been so stressed lately and I and your kids wanted to bring everyone together to make you smile."

"And you did for about a minute. Once the moment was gone, the very reason why I never wanted a stupid celebration to begin with came flooding back."

She sighed again with her voice shaking a bit. "And? What was your conclusion?"

I was now up on my feet and circled my wife standing there in the middle of our room with her hands crossed over her chest. I ran my fingers through my hair and pulled at the ends in frustration letting out an angered growl. I sounded wounded.

I finally said it knowing that anything that would come from my mouth would hurt my wife. I didn't want to and would do just about anything to avoid this conversation but Renee would not give up until I broke.

"I'm not happy. And I haven't been for a long time now. It feels as if I'm standing in quicksand and I'm sinking."

Biting her lip and now her hands on her hips she kept looking at me with a cold stare. "Well, that was certainly blunt. Good for you honey. With just a few words you have shattered the life I never believed we had. An unhappy one you say? You see, unlike you, I don't obsess about the one happy emotion you seem to want to shove down all of our throats. Yes, that was the goal for tonight's celebration because maybe deep down I knew you weren't and it was my way of turning your bad mood to a good one, but clearly, my plan backfired."

"You wanted to know, I'm sorry."

"Sorry? I think I'm going to need a lot more before that word is said again. Let's go back to the part when you said you're not happy or the sinking in quicksand. I can't decipher which point I should begin with. You see, I focus on all emotions and not just one because there is no fucking rule that says you can't be more than happy."

"Jesus Christ! Do you always have to play the fucking martyr! This is a problem. It's always been a problem."

"And? Are you telling me this now? Just what in the hell are you talking about, Lawson? I don't listen? I don't understand your feelings? Because I do more than you give me credit for. Yes, we're not twenty-five anymore. Our kids are grown and living their fantastic lives out in the big world that as you say, we once took by storm. I know this house must seem so big without them in it, but that's how it's supposed to be. This is the next act starring you and me. What's wrong with that?"

"Nothing." I sounded defeated.

She brought her hands to a prayer position and let out her exasperated breath. I felt sick and couldn't look at her. I turned away and held onto the tallboy dresser. She stood behind me and put her hands on my hips. I couldn't move. I felt paralyzed.

"Lawson, I love you. It's what you dared me to do when I was just sixteen and my father was screaming at you to get off our porch and forget about me. But you just ignored him and kept coming back for me. And then the day before you left for your deployment, you handed me a calendar asking me to choose the date for our wedding. I doubted and I was scared but you promised that you would come back to me."

"And I did," I shouted as I pulled away from her.

"You regret it now?"

"No. If I said yes then it would mean our life together hasn't been my reason for waking up every single day. You have given me a wonderful life. Beautiful and smart kids who I adore more than words can say, and an incredible home to come home to for the past twenty-five years."

"And now? What are you not saying to me? Come on, Lawson, I see the indecision in your eyes. Just say it! Damn you, Lawson Douglas! Fucking say it." She completely came undone before my eyes with tears falling from them. She moved closer and then began to pound her small fists against my chest. She cried demanding answers from me. I hated myself for even thinking the words that I knew would devastate her. *What the hell is wrong with me?*

"Lawson, I will not ask you again. You started this conversation and hit me with more truths than I was prepared for, so fire the last shot while I can still stand to hear it. Stop staring at me with blank eyes and just say the fucking words."

"I want a divorce." Once the words passed over my lips, I wanted to take them back.

CHAPTER
Seven

PRESENT...

Renee

Did he just say those words to me? I felt the bile rising slowly up my throat from the bottomless pit of my stomach. I tampered down my emotions because there was no way I was going to break down in front of him.

"Please, say something," he asked. I blinked my eyes open but no words were said. I simply walked out of our bedroom and gave Lawson the very thing he wanted tonight for his birthday—to be alone.

Where could I go? Our kids are home with us this weekend and just across the yard in the guesthouse. Surely they would hear my car roar to life as I peeled out of our driveway and down the path to the main road. No, I didn't do that even though I was well within my rights to be angry and do something reckless.

I've always been the fixer in our relationship and no matter the circumstances. I've been this way since Lawson dared me to be strong in the wake of his sudden deployment. He was nearly finished with his service and then he was given his orders and we were running out of time. It broke my heart to be separated from him but it was what he did on the day that he said goodbye that tied us to one another forever. He promised to come back.

I grabbed a throw blanket and sat outside on our porch watching the stars twinkle in the night sky. It was a cool night and it felt nice on my heated skin. What am I going to do now? My husband of twenty-five years just told me that he wants a divorce. And what scares me is that he said it so calmly like he was telling me he was going to the store because we ran out of milk. Was he out of his mind? What is this? A midlife man crisis?

"Renee?" he softly called out from the doorway. I loved his voice. It could go from commanding a room to attention to mind drugging me into a sexual daze. My husband was beautiful and sexy and oh yeah, he wants a divorce. "Renee!" from soft to hard, he called out again.

"What!" I wasn't so nice with my response.

"It's getting cold out here and it's late. I don't want you to get sick."

"Really? How kind of you to be so concerned with my health and well-being." I snapped back and then pushed myself past him and made a run for the stairs. I wasn't sure if he would follow but then he did but I made it to our room first and successfully locking him out. He slammed his fist on the door and shouted out.

"Dammit, Renee! Open the door. Nothing is going to get resolved this way."

"I agree but I need some time to process our last conversation before we begin a new one. When I'm ready, we will revisit and continue it."

"I'm not one of your patients, Renee, I'm your husband."

"Yes, you are and that's not going to change. You made a promise to me, Lawson Douglas, and there is no fucking way you are going to ask me for a divorce without me reminding you of those promises of forever you made me believe in." My anger had reached the boiling point as he continued to pound on our door. I forcibly opened it and gave him the hardest shove I could manage to do. Lawson didn't fall but he was caught off guard with my attempt to get his attention.

"You asked me for a divorce on the night I hosted your 50th birthday here in our home and surrounded by our family and friends. The same night your son presented you with his master's degree you pushed him to work so hard for. Your daughter, our beautiful Emily has stars dancing in her eyes every time she looks at you. You are her hero and she is counting the days until you walk her down the aisle at her wedding. You don't get to ask me for a divorce when I have been nothing but a good wife to you. I've been with you every second of every day loving and supporting you, and this is what I get? I get four words that make our entire life a lie."

"Renee—"

"I'm not finished. You think I haven't noticed there's been a change in you? This is so much more than losing your mom. Whatever this is, runs deeper and for some reason, you have chosen to shut me out and make a decision such as a divorce without ever talking to me about it. Lawson, this is life changing and will impact every area of your life. You don't get to just say those words and not think I won't fight back and try to help you."

"Look at me. Not on the floor or around the room. You look at me. I see you Lawson Douglas, the real you that is buried under a mountain of burdens that you have been keeping from me and your children. You are not a man who just walks away from his family. You are the man that runs into burning buildings to rescue the family cat. You are the coach of your son's multiple sports teams because your son told you he couldn't play without you cheering him on. You were there, Lawson, always there. You are the man that turned on the sprinkler on the first boy who broke Emily's heart. You told her that first loves were hard to get over and when she was ready to talk that you would be there to listen. She opened the door with her tear stained face and you handed her the box of Kleenex, and just waited by her closed door for hours just to make sure she was okay."

"I see you. Who I just described is not the same man who earlier asked me for a divorce. That man would never hurt me or his family. What I am looking at right now is someone else, a stranger I do not recognize and I want him to leave."

"Renee—" I stopped him again.

"No! You need to pack a bag and leave before the kids wake up. I don't care where you go, it just can't be here. I can barely look at you right now and I'm holding on with the last vestiges of my strength. I need some time to figure all this out and clearly, you need to do the same. Leave me a number where you will be and when I'm ready, I will call you."

"So, that's it? This is the way we're leaving it?"

"What did you expect? Did you believe I would just roll over and allow you to implode my life without having a say in it? Ugh! Maybe you did because men can be so fucking arrogant, can't they? A big powerful man like yourself just declares an order and I have to be what? The understanding wife that is mute and has no voice in the marriage to fight back? You know me better than that and shame on you if you thought otherwise. No, this is me giving you time to peddle back on your emotions and really think about what you asked of me. Because I promise you, Lawson, if divorce is what you want then I will grant your wish, and there will be no turning back."

"I gave you every part of me since I was sixteen years old, and before you remind me, I know exactly how old I am but the only difference is I am not that lovesick teenager that fell at your feet. I'm strong, and to lose you will hurt me, but it will not break me. You remember that."

I said nothing more and moved aside so he could walk into our bedroom and pack his things. It only took him a little over an hour to change and dress in fresh clothes, pack his bag, and walk out the door. I watched from the window as he drove down the driveway not really believing he would actually do it. I thought he would stay and fight with me no matter what I said to him. He actually left. Who knows? Maybe it was forever. I picked up his empty glass and continued what he started numbing all the pain I was feeling.

"Mom! I know it's a Saturday, but seriously sleeping to noon is just crazy. Mom, are you okay?" I rolled over from the mounds of pillows I was buried under. I tried to hide the crumpled tissues scattered all around but Emily found them and there was no way to hide my swollen eyes.

"Mom, talk to me. What's wrong with you?" she asked and then climbed into bed with me like she used to do when she was little.

"I'm fine and I don't want you to worry about me."

"Yeah, like that's going to happen. Where's Daddy?"

"He left."

"To go where? When is he coming back?"

"I don't know, maybe not ever." I could hear the panic in her voice and this is not the way I wanted to tell her but the words were out of my mouth before my brain had time to catch up. "Listen, Emily, last night was an emotional one for your father and for me. What I believed would be a simple conversation shifted to a more serious one. I was completely thrown and he left. I've been here since then and I guess I finally crashed until you woke me up."

"I guess it's my turn to be thrown here. Mom, he just left with no promise of return? What the hell is going on here? We come home for the weekend to celebrate our father's birthday and he leaves in the middle of the night?"

"Hey, what's going on?" Rogan asked as he entered my room with a cup of coffee in hand.

"Mom? Are you going to tell him, or shall I?"

"Emily, that's enough."

"No, I think we are just getting started here."

"Will someone please tell me what in the hell is going on here?"

"Dad left mom."

"What the fuck!" Rogan shouted out.

My head felt like it was about to split wide open and the funny part of it all, I didn't have no more than one glass of champagne last night at the party. No, that's not right, and then my memory was coming back to me. I finished off the bourbon. Ugh! I feel sick and that's not even from the amount of alcohol I consumed after my husband walked out on me. This is not your a-typical reaction to drinking excessively. This is so much worse. This is a marriage hangover.

"I know you two must have a lot of questions, but as of right now I do not have any answers for you. Dad leaving last night was because I asked him to, but not before he asked me for a divorce."

"No! I can't believe this is happening," Emily began to cry with her big brother already comforting her. "I need to call him mom, he's got to be freaking out or something. This is just crazy."

"Yeah, I agree with you there but I don't know where he is at the moment and to be honest, I really don't care. I know you two are already playing it out on how this is going to go but you don't need to."

I kicked the covers off and got out of our bed. Although I hated to, somehow, I found myself sleeping on his side of the bed. He should be here with me. As angry as I am with him, I fucking hate that he actually did leave. Where was the Lawson that would never go to bed angry or dare to even sleep on the couch? He never gave me my space, not one inch to breathe. We promised to always talk it out and resolve any issue we might have had. I tried to do that last night but he accused me of head shrinking him. I believed I had enough justification for my reaction since he totally blindsided me with his divorce declaration.

"Is he having an affair?" Rogan asked. *Oh, my god! The thought of Lawson cheating on me never once crossed my mind. No, he would never do that to me.*

"I don't know. I need a shower. Let me get ready and we will go to brunch."

My children must think I am totally out of my mind to suggest something as simple as brunch, but I have to eat, right? And a few mimosas sound great right now. I sat down and in front of my vanity mirror and wondered about the woman staring back at me. Have I changed so much that I've turned a blind eye to my husband's needs? I know I'm career driven and focused on too many things that pull my attention away from him, but divorce? That's not the solution.

"You love Lawson. I love Lawson. And I know he loves me too." I can't give up on him. Last night was me going into survival mode to protect my heart. I was the same way when he left for his deployment. I prepared myself for the worse just in case he didn't come home. When he did and walked off the plane and right into my arms, all those fears washed away in an instant.

I was wrapped up in the protection of his loving arms, the ones I wanted to hold me right now and tell me everything is going to be okay.

My phone beeped with an incoming text. It was from Lawson telling me he was in the city staying at our apartment we kept there. It was more of an investment property we just held onto all these years, and now it's his escape. I texted him back with a simple reply and then went in search of our kids. This was all that I was capable of right now.

CHAPTER
Eight

PAST...

Lawson

"A re we really doing this? Getting married on Halloween?"

"That was our deal, Lawson. When you got word to me that you were coming home earlier than expected, I knew it was a sign of awesomeness and we had to go all out on Halloween. I love Elvis and all but we can save him for a special anniversary."

"Okay, Renee, Halloween it is. Have you told your parents yet?"

"Yup! And surprisingly my father gave me a hug and told me that he's been expecting our news for a while now and he's happy for us."

"No shit? You're not kidding?"

"I wouldn't do that to you. I can't wait to marry you, Lawson Douglas. So the big question is, what are you going to wear?"

I pulled my girl on top of my lap and hugged her with everything I had. She kissed me all over. "Renee, I love you so much. I can't believe we are free to get married and begin our life together. I'm sorry I missed your graduation but thank you for the photos. They kept me warm at night until I was able to come home. Renee, the day my sergeant told me my unit was being sent home early was the greatest day of my life next to you telling me you loved me. I got word to my parents and then to you. After that, it was just a blur until I could leave. It didn't take long to pack up my gear and then in the weeks that followed I was just in robotic mode until I boarded the plane."

"You were so excited when you picked me up. I thought you were going to plow through the crowd to get to me."

"I almost did. Thank you for keeping your promise, Lawson."

"Thank you for keeping yours."

"Mine?"

"Yeah, your promise. A promise to wait for me until I came home to make you mine. Baby, that day is here and now. Will you come home with me?"

"Yes, I will. You are my home, Lawson, and I don't want to spend one more night without you beside me."

PRESENT...

Two days later and radio silence from Renee, or the kids. Emily has to be an emotional mess with me leaving so unexpectedly. She's always been my baby girl but I guess if she had to choose sides, she would console her mother before me. What I am surprised about is Rogan, I would have thought he would have at least called me.

"Happy Monday, yes, I know you are not a fan of it but we need to go over this week's schedule. Ty and Paul are back from surveying the land and with all the paperwork now filed and approved, we should expect the deeds to come in by the end of the week. Sir, are you listening to me?" *No, I wasn't. I just needed some peace and quiet so I could think for a damn minute.*

"Will you please get out of my office? Hold my calls and close the door behind you."

"Yes, sir." She practically ran for the door.

Any other day I could handle Alison and her energetic pace but not today. I don't know why I even came in today. I half expected my father to bust down my door at any minute but even he was silent. I held my face in my hands and deeply sighed. I was about to call my assistant when my line buzzed.

"I thought I told you to hold my calls!" I shouted back in anger. Fuck! This is not her fault.

"Sir, your wife is on line two." I didn't even respond in return. I just hit the line to speak with my wife.

"Renee," I could barely get out.

"I need to see you. Will you come by my office, say at 7?"

"I can be there."

"See you then."

It felt as if my stomach dropped and I was going to be sick. She sounded calm and direct while I was the one here falling apart. I canceled the rest of my day and told Alison to reschedule any meetings for tomorrow. Sitting here in my office all day would do me no good. My mind was focused elsewhere.

As I closed my office door, my assistant popped her head up from behind her desktop. Wide-eyed, I think she was surprised that I was leaving. "Alison, I'm leaving now. Here are my notes for Ty, and everything else is uploaded to the drive."

"Um, okay, will you be returning back to the office tonight?"

"No. Anything else you need to know on my personal life?" I snapped at her.

She gasped in surprise and simply nodded in silence. I walked off in a huff and hit the elevator button. When the doors opened and I stepped inside the elevator car, I hit the ground level button and looked up to see Alison had her head carefully hidden behind her large screen monitor. *Yeah, I'm a dick and took out my shitty mood out on her.* I silently thought. I had so much anger thrumming through my veins I knew I needed to do something to burn it off before seeing Renee. I went back to the apartment and changed into running clothes. I ran all throughout the city until my legs tired and I needed a break. I gave my body a deep stretch along the runner's trail I had stopped on.

What the hell am I going to say to Renee? I don't have a fucking clue but I better get myself back home to get ready.

I parked my car and made my way through the main entrance of the building that was home to Renee's wellness center. It was seven o'clock and I was right on time to meet my wife. I was nervous to the point of my hands were sweating. I'm never nervous and it's rare to show my hand but this was Renee, so all bets were off.

Renee, my wife, my best friend, mother to my children, and the one I have loved since I was eighteen years old. So why did I ask her for a divorce? Monumental mistake on my part and one that I know hurt her deeply. I don't know if she will forgive me? If the roles were reversed I don't know what I would have done. I probably would have punched a wall and ask questions later. She was mine even before I made her mine. From the moment I saw her, I knew she was the one.

I've been driving myself insane since Renee asked me to leave. We always shared a bed. To be without her for the last few nights has made me restless and cold, no warmth around me. I feel sick. I should have never said those words to her. I wasn't thinking clearly and I felt backed into a corner when she pressed me for answers. No matter what the circumstance, I should have never gone to that extreme. And now we are in an unfamiliar place and I have no clue to what she will say to me.

I approached the front desk and the security officer recognized me immediately and greeted me warmly.

"Mr. Douglas, how nice to see you again. It's been a while."

"Hi Joe, yeah, I guess it has. How have you been? Family good?"

"Thank you for asking. Everyone is well and happy, and I have no reason to complain."

At least someone is. I sighed and kept my thoughts to myself. "Nice seeing you," I said not wanting to offer anything more.

"Take care, sir," he said to my back as I decided to take the stairs instead of the elevator. My run has already been forgotten because my nerves are back. Once I reached her double doors, I didn't know what to do. Should I knock and walk in? Or should I call her to let her know I'm here? She probably knows because I'm sure Joe has already called up to her. Before I could stress another minute, the door opened and Renee was standing on the other side of it. She looked beautiful today and certainly didn't look as if she's been pining away for me.

"Thank you for being on time, please come in." She opened the door wide enough for me to enter her office and once I was far enough in, she closed the door behind her with not a slam but loud enough to catch my attention.

"Have a seat," said Renee, as she pointed to her sofa. I shrugged my jacket off and placed it off to the side. She offered me a drink that I declined and she took her seat in front of me. This is where she switched roles from my wife to therapist. I hated this role and the anxiety I felt earlier has now faded away and it slowly morphed into anger again. I wanted to talk to my wife, and not a therapist whose job was to analyze the fuck out of me and get to the root of my problem. Maybe this was the problem and being here with Renee in this office has just made me realize why I said the words I did.

CHAPTER
Nine

PRESENT...

Renee

By the time the shock wore off from telling the kids about Lawson, our scheduled brunch was now an early dinner. I didn't care as long as I could order a drink, and not just one. I think I needed something stronger than a mimosa. As I finished off my second Cosmo, I looked over to Rogan who was uncharacteristically quiet.

"You know you can talk to me, right?" I said tapping on the glass with my silverware to get his attention. Emily was doing no better but at least she was trying.

"What do you want me to say here, mom? My father has left you and I'm just, no we are supposed to just be okay with it and roll with the punches? Fuck that! He owes us an explanation and instead of sitting here playing happy family, we should find him and drag his ass back home. It's where he belongs." I let out an exasperated breath before addressing the issue with Rogan and Emily.

I linked my hands together and leaned on my elbows as I took a deep breath and addressed our son's anger and hostility. "Rogan, first of all, he was my husband long before he was your father. I know him better than anyone. Before you go conjuring up theories about why he left, just ask me and I will tell you."

"You already told us that it's not another woman? So, what is it? Midlife crisis? Um, he's fifty, get over it."

"Rogan!" Emily shrieked causing the fellow patrons to look in our direction.

"What? Am I wrong? Come on sis, you're not a little kid anymore and neither am I. This is not something dad has just thought of. He must have been going through something for a while now and hiding it from his family when he should have been talking to us. Isn't that what you taught us, mom? You have stressed over and over how important communication is in a family."

"True, but parents like to use that to our benefit. In our case, we've been lucky to have the relationships we have with both of you and please do not rush to judgment and jeopardize what you share with your father until I speak with him. Your father loves you with everything he has in him and although you are angry, this is really between your father and me."

"Mom?"

"Yes, baby girl."

"Will you call him? I hate that he's not home."

"I will call but not today. I want today for us. Tomorrow will be for your father."

Rogan and Emily both left their seats at the table and hugged me protectively already drawing lines in the sand on the side they were on. I didn't want them to do that but I said nothing and just returned the love while promising myself that whatever was going on with Lawson, would not destroy the family we built.

It was Monday, and you know what they say about Monday's right? It's probably voted the most hated day out of the week and most of us wish we could have just stayed home in our warm beds and not face the new week, especially me. I know I wish I could have been anywhere but here but I'm not about hiding and living in denial of my problems. After I phoned Lawson and asked him to meet me here tonight once my workday was done, I knew there would be no turning back. I was sullen and to the point. I didn't want to be but after the kids had left to return to their exciting and happy lives, I was left alone in our big house with no one to talk to.

I caught up on some work and did more dictation for Jeanie to transcribe than I have done in the last six months. What could I say? I had a lot of time on my hands. Our home always filled with light and laughter was now dark and quiet. Roman had called to check up on me but I assured him I was fine and would catch up with him soon. My relationship with his son is mine and although he is a wonderful father in law, he tends to be on my side more than his son's and I never agreed with his tough approach. It only angered Lawson and pushed him away which was not fair to him.

Lawson loves his father. They disagree on a lot of subjects but at the end of the day they are father and son and whatever happens between us, I don't want any of our relationships affected by it. Yeah, says the therapist that would undoubtedly argue my naïve way of thinking but this is not about one of my patients. This is my life with my husband and I have to follow my heart no matter how many times the boss bitch of my natural instinct is telling me otherwise. Again, protective mode. This is why I asked him to leave. I was hurt so deeply when he said those words to me.

I've taken the time to think about all that happened at the party and what was said thereafter. When he gets here, I'm going to just sit him down and ask him straight up what in the hell is going on with him? I may not like the answers but knowing that will not dissuade me from my questions.

"Renee, Joe just sent Lawson up. He should be here any minute."

"Yes, I know. He texted me that he had arrived. Thanks, Jeanie, you can go home."

"Are you going to be alright? I can stay and just do work."

"No, that won't be necessary. I asked Lawson to join me here because I felt this was my safe zone to keep myself in check. There are things to say and it has to be in private."

"I understand. You know I'm talking to you as my friend and not my employer."

"Yes, I know the difference and I appreciate it." The sound of the bell alerted us that Lawson was out in reception. "Will you please get him settled and I will be right out."

"Sure thing. Call me if you need anything, okay?"

"I will," I said knowing I wouldn't. Her heart is in the right place but this is on me and whatever happens, after he walks through my door.

I walked into my private en-suite and fixed my hair while touching up my makeup. I never wore too much but today I want my look to be killer and my five-inch stilettos helped my bruised ego a great deal. After I was satisfied with my smoky eye and perfect lip liner application, I gave myself another pep talk.

"Stay strong. Don't cry. Listen and don't interrupt him. Renee, you need to allow him to have his voice in your marriage."

Okay, I was polished enough and walked out to greet Lawson. When I opened the door, he looked apprehensive and maybe a little regretful. His eyes found mine but not before taking in my appearance. Yes, he knew I cleaned up nicely when I went for something better than yoga pants, but the way he was looking at me now made me angry for some reason. Why couldn't he have looked at me this way on the night of his party? And I had a spa day getting primped and plucked for half the day just to please him and holy hell! I went to bed without a damn orgasm.

"Have a seat," I said gesturing over to the sofa while I took the chair placed in front of it. He didn't look happy with my cold greeting and shrugged his jacket off and took his seat. He loosened his tie and looked so restless I thought he was ready to spit nails.

"Care for a drink?"

"No, thank you."

"Thank you for coming," I said.

"Thank you for calling," he politely replied.

"Tell me something, Renee, is there a reason why you are dressed like that?" he pointed at me with his index finger and once again staring at me from the top of my head down to my shoes.

I looked myself over and found nothing wrong with my chosen attire. And then a smile crept over my lips knowing what Lawson was probably thinking. I was dressed up because I was proving a point because of what I said to him on the night he left. I would be fine and no matter what happens between us, I will not break. Yeah, again, boss bitch protective mode. Who was I kidding? Because I certainly was not fooling myself. If Lawson divorced me and left our marriage, I know there would be a part of me that would have to move forward because it wouldn't be an option to fall apart. The other truth is I would be shattered because the man whom I have loved since I was sixteen years old has just moved on without me and broke every promise he ever made to me.

Yes, this is why I've retreated back to protective mode. He's not making it easy on account of how he is looking at me right now. If I didn't know any better, Lawson almost looked aroused which made me secretly happy inside. I wasn't going to give him the satisfaction of feeling uncomfortable around him. No way in hell. This is the first time I have actually felt better since he left. *I loved when he got this way which usually led to great sex. Keep on looking. Maybe you should have appreciated what you had before you so easily let it go.*

PAST...

After our parents collectively picked up their jaws from the floor, we all laughed and began planning our Halloween themed wedding. Lawson didn't want to wait one more day than he had to. It was a long deployment and even a longer time to officially process out and begin the next chapter of our lives.

We married on the Douglas property. They had a massively sized barn that was transformed into a castle fit for a queen and a king. The inside was designed into a fairy tale theme wonderland. And why not a wedding with a magical theme? After all, I was marrying my prince, so it just made sense to be a Cinderella bride with the matching diamond tiara to complete my look. Our families were great and my father was in seventh heaven because at the end of the day, he just wanted me happy and I was. I was marrying Lawson Douglas and I couldn't wait to be his wife.

PRESENT...

"Renee, did you hear me? I asked you a question."

"What?" I responded.

"Why do you look the way you do?"

"And how do I look, Lawson?" I said as I straightened my posture and looked directly at him.

"You look beautiful but that's not the point. Tonight, you look as if you tried extra hard to make me notice you which pisses me the fuck off."

"Why is that? You are unbelievable, Lawson Douglas!" I shouted and now up on my feet.

"No, you are! I get it, Renee, you are equally mad at me and this is your way of telling me to fuck off, right? I have news for you sweetheart, you never have to try because I see you every single day and I never asked you to play a role for me. I just wanted you."

"What does that even mean? I don't understand you at all. Just because I don't look like a damn train wreck doesn't mean I don't feel like one. You hurt me, Lawson, probably more than you ever have in your life. You asked me for a divorce without any warning whatsoever. You're angry because of my choice of clothing? A weapon of choice I am using to get back at you? Oh, that's rich but please don't flatter yourself. Once upon a time and long before you said those words to me, yes, I would have worn this for you. To make your heart race a little faster, or your dick tent a little tighter against your zipper. I know I'm not a supermodel by any means and we can't turn back time, but as hard as I work to keep up with you, I deserve to wear whatever the fuck I want."

"To keep up with me?"

"Yes, you! Have you seen yourself lately? Do you ever age at all? This right here?" I gestured to my ensemble and then to my hair. "Takes work but I don't care because I love the end result."

"As do I," he whispered.

"Hmmm, well it's a little too late now, isn't it, Lawson?"

"It doesn't have to be, Renee. I know I'm doing this all wrong and that's on me, but please let's talk."

"Change your mind on that drink?"

"Yeah, I think I'll take it now."

"Coming right up." I filled two crystal tumblers with scotch for Lawson and a double Bourbon for me. Screw it! These shots of liquid courage will hopefully help me get through this conversation. "Here you go," I handed over his glass and he simply nodded.

I got comfortable on the couch opting not to resume my place in the chair. Why the hell not? This couch is awesome and I would never tell Lawson but I'm about a minute away from chucking my shoes and demanding a foot rub from my confused husband.

"Renee, I'm sorry for hurting you. I know I hurt you deeply and I will regret my actions for the rest of my life. I know you want answers and you deserve to hear them but baby, I don't know myself. The man I know I am would have never ever said those words to you the other night, least of all think them. I felt as if I was—"

"You don't recall? Let me refresh your memory. You said that you felt as if you were standing in quicksand and you were slowly sinking. Is that how you feel about our marriage, Lawson? It's an invisible weight tied around your ankles and you feel stuck so instead of fighting you decide to just give up and sink until you are so far under the surface that no matter what I say or do, I can't bring you back. Am I close?"

"Baby, please"

"Don't call me baby! You lost that right on that night you asked me for a divorce." My hands began to shake and my tears were unstoppable now. I placed the glass on the table and got up from the couch and away from my husband. I couldn't concentrate while I was so close to him and a few whiffs of his cologne and I was forgetting why I was so angry. He was by my side in a heartbeat with his hands on my hips and his warm breath on my neck.

"I'm sorry. I'm so sorry, baby." He began kissing me on my neck and I leaned into him like I've done thousands of times before. Lawson's touch on my body made me come alive and feel so desired and wanted. I know I should be pulling away but I want him and I know he wants me. I don't understand him, and I'm too emotionally drained to figure it out. He turned me around and kissed me hard on my mouth begging for entrance to claim even the smallest piece of me.

CHAPTER
Ten

PRESENT...

Lawson

This was sheer madness what I was doing here right now with Renee. Knowing her as much as I do, she's got to be spinning out of control with all the mixed signals I've been giving her but I don't care. I have to have her and I will take my wife anyway I can get her.

Renee is everything. She's so compassionate with her patients and devotes all her energy to helping them. This is one of the many reasons why our daughter followed in her footsteps and chose the same career to help people find their way. I was the one that was lost and I never allowed her to help me, and I've hurt her over and over again with my silence and now because I'm a selfish asshole, I'll do it again by taking her body.

When I pulled away from her mouth, I turned her again and shoved her down over her plush chair. Her face was pressed into the leather with her long legs spread and positioned high on the sexy as fuck shoes. She began to move against my body with my hard erection pressing into her backside. I've taken her there in the past and although it wasn't often, it was the most erotic sensation we ever felt together making love and experiencing the high it brought to the both of us. I wouldn't do that tonight and if I was a better man, I should walk away right now and ice my balls because it's what I deserve for hurting her.

"Lawson, what are you doing?" she rasped out in frustration. I didn't answer her, and I wasn't gentle about what I did next. I pulled her tight pencil skirt up and ripped her thong that was practically dental floss. Why bother with such a skimpy scrap of material? I ran my hands up her legs feeling the silk under my fingertips. She bucked against me again and I think I heard her curse under her breath to get inside of her. *Sassy little thing*, I thought and before I could question it, I did just that. I thrust my hard dick inside of her making her jump before my entire body was cloaking hers and holding her hands down.

"This is going to be rough baby, tell me to stop if it becomes too much."

"Fuck you, Lawson!" she cried out as I entered her again and again.

"Oh, fuck, Renee, give it to me," I shouted the fucking walls down and came harder than I ever did in my life. Renee was clawing the hell out of her Italian leather and joined me in the best fucking orgasm of my life.

"Lawson," she mumbled into the chair. "You need to get off."

"I just did sweetheart. Give me a few minutes and I'll be ready to go again." I stumbled back on my feet just a little to regain the strength in my legs. Fuck! That was hot. Renee slowly got up from the chair and made her way into her private bath to clean up. I saw my release slide down her sexy thighs and it took everything I had not to pounce on her again.

I grabbed a towel off the bar and cleaned up the best I could without showering. Once I was put back together, I grabbed my glass and refilled it with a double serving of scotch. I paced her office and waited for her to come out. After a few minutes of silence, I tapped my knuckles against the door calling out for her. When she didn't answer, I turned the knob to find Renee curled into a ball on the floor silently crying into a towel.

"Oh, baby, I'm sorry. What are you doing?"

"You say that a lot, don't you?"

"What?" I said as I pulled her off the floor and into my arms. She fought my hold and tried to get up.

"Stop this and talk to me?"

"No, I think the time for talking has long passed, don't you think? I was crying because I feel like I am mourning a life that has been ripped out from under me and I don't know how to get it back. You hurt me in a way I never believed a single person could. Lawson, all these years I have placed you on this high pedestal, a pillar of perfection if you want to call it that. You have been larger than life for so many years, I had no idea that you were knocked down a few pegs. I blame myself for not seeing it sooner."

"Renee, I'm not perfect and I never claimed to be."

"You didn't have to, I did it for you."

"Look, we did this all wrong tonight. Let me take you to dinner and we can talk."

"No, I don't think so. I need to get home and be by myself for a while. And you, well, I don't know what's next for you and I can't be the one to help you. Lawson, you have taken the first steps to the next path in your life and I don't know if there's room for me or your children."

"That's not true, Renee, and everything you are saying here right now is just you flipping the switch into what? Protective mode? Survival? Because you don't want me to break you? I have news for you sweetheart, I'm already there because I fucked up monumentally with you the other night and I have no idea how to fix my mistake. I'm not deluded into thinking all our problems will get resolved tonight. If you believe that was my intention when I came here tonight, then you are wrong. I just wanted to be able to talk and try to explain even in the smallest measures of the colossal error in judgment I made."

"Monumental, colossal, two words that mean the same but best describes us right now down to the very core of our marriage. The point of it is, is that you said four words to me that changed my entire life once I heard them. You are a completely different person to me now and I don't know how I feel about that and I have no time frame when I will."

"Renee, what we just shared, I"

"Don't do that. You don't get to use my actions against me. While I still hold the title as your wife, I exercised my right and fucked my husband. Don't make it anything else than what it really was."

"Don't sugarcoat it, sweetheart, tell me how you really feel."

"I just did, and now I want you to leave."

"Renee, please, we haven't settled anything between us."

"No, we haven't and we are not going to either. You need to call your children and talk to them. They are hurt and confused by their father's actions and I can't play the mediator here, it's your turn to figure it out."

"Fuck!" I shouted and then took my glass and shattered it against her office wall. My girl was tough and wasn't even fazed by it, maybe she expected it. "Why are you doing this to me? Please don't let me walk out of here feeling more lost than ever. I need you."

"Hmmm, now my skills are needed? You hate when I head shrink you. Isn't that what you always accuse me of doing? You told me so on the night of your birthday. Hell, if I could read your mind, you probably thought that's how this night was going to go. Sorry to burst your bubble but I have no fucking clue on how to fix us. Now get the hell out of my office and leave me alone."

"This is not over."

"Are you sure about that?"

"Yeah, it's the one thing I do fucking know." I rushed over to her and held her face in my hands crushing my mouth down to hers, making her feel something.

"Fuck what I said. We will never be over." I kissed her again and again and then held the sides of her head to make her look at me. She held on to her convictions and made no moves of softening her anger. I get it and totally deserve it. I placed one more kiss on her forehead and then grabbed my coat and left her office.

After leaving Renee at her office and alone, I went back to our city apartment and drank until I passed out. I wanted to feel nothing but only remember how she felt beneath me as I fucked her hard. Damn, it was hot but now I feel like shit because I never used her like that. We always had a hot sex life but it was a mutual give and take. I feel that I took tonight and she just had to take it even though she didn't word it that way to me. She was bold and sassy and right in my face. Fuck! I loved that side of her. It's been a long time since she challenged me like that and if I was being honest, I loved it and wanted more of it but that wasn't going to happen again until we talk for real.

When I woke up the next morning, I had the hangover from hell and called my assistant to send the necessary rations I would need to recover from last night's drinking session. I'm too old to punish my liver like that and drinking gets you nowhere but a fucking headache and emptiness in the pit of your stomach. The messenger delivered a bag of food and a bottle of hair of the dog. I downed the disgusting elixir and dragged my tired ass in the shower where my dick was standing attention and needed a release. It didn't take long to accomplish that and after I came, the pounding just increased in my head for all the distress I had created.

The loud pounding continued and once I shut the water off, I realized it wasn't just my head. Someone was at the door and not going away. For a moment, I believed it might be Renee, but she would never knock, not when she had a key. I grabbed a towel off the warming rack and wrapped it around my waist.

"I'm coming, hold on," I shouted and then opened the door to find Rogan on the other side of it. I stepped aside and let him in. Both of us not knowing what to say to the other. I stood there for a minute and then closed the door. "I was going to call you today, but as you can see I kind of had a late night." He looked around to the mess that was scattered on the table and he didn't miss the empty bottle of scotch. He picked up the bottle and studied it for a minute before tossing it into the trash can.

"Are we alone?"

"Yeah, who do you think would be here?"

"I don't know, dad. I know the one person who should be here but she's licking her wounds back at home where you're supposed to be."

"Let me get dressed and then we will talk." I left him there while I walked into the bedroom to grab a pair of jeans and a t-shirt. It was too late to go to work and the way I was feeling, I would be no good to anyone.

"Rogan, I know you have a lot of questions and I will try my best to answer them."

"Dad, what can you say that will make me understand your behavior. You hurt mom and by hurting mom, you've hurt me and Emily. We feel lost and we don't know what to do. This is supposed to be the best time of our lives right now. I just finished school and I want to begin working with you again. Emily has stopped planning her wedding to Gus because she can't be happy for herself when mom is so upset."

"Is there someone else? Are you leaving mom for another woman?"

"Don't ever say those words to me again. I would never betray your mother like that."

"I'm sorry, but you haven't said much so what do you expect me to think?"

"Not those words!" I shouted back. "Look, I fucked up the other night with your mother and hurt her deeply. I wasn't thinking at all and asked her for a divorce."

"What the fuck!" He shouted back at me with his fists balled at his sides. "How could you do it? Why?"

"I don't know. I'm tired, son and have been feeling overwhelmed and maybe even trapped in my own life. I've spent years navigating through all the roles I lead each and every day. Husband, father, son, CEO, the list goes on and I'm just fucking tired. I know this doesn't make sense because this is exactly what I've expected from you. I pushed you hard to get your degree. I expected no less of you. I demanded excellence and you gave it to me without question."

"What the hell does it matter now? It's over. I now have it and I am ready to take my rightful place where I belong."

"No! It's not what I want for you."

"It's a little late now, don't you think? So, now that you are having this big past mid-life crisis, you are having what? An epiphany? A pretty big change that will affect my life and leave me hanging out in the wind with nothing to fall back on."

"It's not what I mean. Please stop reacting until I get out what I want to say. Nothing would please me more for you to officially come on board at Douglas ECO, but having said that, I want you to consider every opportunity you are given. You have your entire life ahead of you and although you tell me you want to be out there being this world-changing environmentalist, you will also find yourself sitting behind my desk one day and making life-changing decisions that will not only affect our company but you as a person. So, my son, that's where I am right now. I had those same dreams and most of them came true when I was just your age. My eyes were alive with excitement and possibility. Then one day, your grandfather sought me out while I was surveying a patch of land, and told me to take a break. I dusted my dirty hands off and hopped on to the back of my flatbed."

"What did Grandpa Roman say?"

"It wasn't what he said exactly, it was the way he said it. He asked me where I saw myself in the next five years and I told him that I would have the best of both worlds. He wanted to know what I meant and then I realized him stopping by was not just a social call. My father was testing the waters to see if I was ready and what I said next confirmed it."

"And? What happened?"

"I said I would have it all. I would run Douglas ECO and get to be out here as much as I wanted to be. I already got the girl who was pregnant with you, and the rest would happen as I made them too. He shrugged and patted my back. I thought I was going to hear this big pep talk he was famous for giving but all he said was, okay, it's yours. Come to the office in the morning and Douglas ECO will have a new man in charge and you son are that man."

"Dad, I don't see the problem here. Running the company was your dream and you have taken it further than grandpa ever could. It's thriving because of your vision and determination to make the lives of so many better. Our ecological systems have revolutionized the way farmers work their farms. It's amazing, dad, and my eyes are open. I want to follow you and be like you."

"Rogan, have you heard a word I have said. Don't you under-stand? That day grandpa found me working out in the hot sun with my hands buried in dirt, he was giving me an out and I didn't get it until last week standing in the middle of our house while I listened to every-one sing happy birthday to me."

"I want more for my kids. I want you to look at a map and pick a place to visit and then go there. Don't say one day I'd like to do this or do that, just do it. Seeing the world is one thing but living in it is some-thing so much more than I ever realized. I want more for you, Rogan. You are going to change the world. I know you will but you have to get out there to do it."

"Okay, let's just say I follow your advice and grab my pack and take off for parts unknown, sending you a postcard from time to time. Where does that leave you? What about mom?"

"I'm going to love Renee Canton Douglas until I take my very last breath, and I intend to fight for her. In the meantime, I'm going to take a trip of my own and find out who the fuck I am. The company will be fine on its own for a few weeks, and when you come back from your trip, you can take your rightful place. I want that for you more than you know."

"I love you, dad. All I ever wanted to do was make you proud of me."

I laughed almost into a fit of hysterics. My son grabbed a beer while I had my moment and I finally began to feel lighter. I needed this cathartic rush.

"You okay over there, dad?"

"I'm good, better than I've been in a long time. I guess what you said made me remember yet another whimsical talk with grandpa. It was right before I left for my deployment. I was struggling to leave my parents and your mother behind. Just as I was getting ready to have my last date with mom, he pulled me aside and began telling me how proud he was of me. I then said it's all I've wanted from him and he laughed, kind of like I just did now but I had more gusto to mine. He said he was and never felt anything else."

"Come here, Rogan." He placed his beer down and walked over to me. I pulled him into a hug and then I grabbed his shoulders and said, "I am so proud of you, Rogan Douglas. You are amazing and I have no doubt in my mind that you will do great things that will better this jaded world. I love you."

"I love you too, dad. When I found out you left the house, I almost wanted to punch you in the mouth but I also know there was so much more to it and I promised myself to hear you out and give you a chance to explain. Despite what mom feels right now, you haven't shattered my world. You are still my hero in all things and I am honored to be your son. I have to go. You'll call Emily?"

"I planned on doing that today."

"See that you do, our girl needs a hug right now and she doesn't want it from anyone else. I'm going to make a few calls and see if I'm still needed in Argentina. I'll keep in touch."

"See that you do. I love you, Rogan."

"Yeah, I know."

CHAPTER
Eleven

PRESENT...

Renee

"Mom, why do you sound out of breath and look all sweaty?" I rolled my eyes because if this was anyone else, I probably would have said that I'm in the middle of a hot and sexy romp with my hot as fuck husband, but I can't say that to Emily. Although our daughter is an adult and about to be married, she is incredibly shy when it comes to talking about sex.

"Em, this is not a good time. I'm on the treadmill and I need to get a couple of more miles in before my next appointment."

"Skyping is always the way to go so I can see your face and make sure you're okay. So, are you?" she asked as I hit the cooldown button.

"Honey I am as good as I'm going to get right now. I'm a big girl in more ways than one and I can handle this."

"Why do you do that?"

"Do what?" I asked as I grabbed a towel to wipe my face.

"Put yourself down. You are a gorgeous woman and most women

would kill to be you including me."

"Damn, I raised you right but the pleasantries are not necessary. Age is not slowing down for any of us but as long as I have my health, I'm good. Now, I have to run. See you at the office." I hit end and let out a deep breath. *Shit! This being strong is tough work. And I hate the treadmill. Damn you, Lawson! I want to nosedive into a jar of peanut butter but I can't because I would regret it for days. Fucker!*

"Renee, I just want to be bold and let loose for once in my life." My client says as I chew on the end of my pen. "When Harry left me for that teeny bopper, I wanted to just hide under my covers and stay there for days but I didn't Renee, and I will never be that weak."

"Have you ever felt weak, Maggie? Because it's okay if you have."

"I want to lie to you and say no, but I can't. Yes, I have felt weak, alone, and so ashamed that I wore blinders for more years than I care to remember. He cheated on me over and over again, and because he dedicated so much time to his whores, I lost myself for a long time. The day I came home from work and saw his suitcases by the front door, it was like an alarm sounding off in my head and I was done. I was so done with just taking it, so when he asked me for a divorce, I said, what took you so long?"

"Maggie, it's been over a year now since that night and your divorce is now finalized. How do you feel right now?"

"Free. I feel free but I also feel like it's time to find me again, and I have learned so much from our sessions, but now I want to take what I have learned and run with it. Your head would spin if I told you how much vacation time I have banked at my company. I don't have kids. I don't even have a pet that needs me. I'm free to do whatever the hell I want and I want to board a jet plane and take off for parts unknown. I need it, Renee, so this will be my last session for a while but I'll send you a postcard."

"Sounds great, Maggie. You've grown so much in this past year and I know you say you have to find yourself again, but I say you're already there and you're doing just fine."

"Thank you for saying that, I appreciate it."

It wasn't her usual style but the new Maggie gave me the biggest hug and shouted, "Bon Voyage Bitches" I laughed and waved her off. She practically skipped all the way to the elevator with Jeanie raising up one of her eyebrows.

"Well, that was fun," Jeanie remarked as I handed her a file. "And, you, boss lady, are finished for the day. Want to lock up and get a drink?"

"Thank you for the offer but I'm going to pass. I have to catch up on some work and then I guess it's take-out for dinner."

"Can I go off the record here?"

"Sure," I said hesitantly.

"I kind of caught the tail end of Maggie's goodbye with the bon voyage bitches and all that. A little vacation doesn't sound like a bad idea. You know you have that conference two weeks from now in New York. You can go before or stay a few extra days and catch some shows, nightlife, it's New York."

"And I would be alone doing all those fun things. The difference between Maggie and I are worlds apart. She will probably pack a box of condoms, a bathing suit, and a pre-paid calling card when she has to be bailed out of jail in a foreign country. I will pack my business attire, make-up bag, and if I can pass it through TSA, my favorite vibrator."

"You know I love you, right? Oh, Renee, you sit here all day and every day with your game face on and dish out the best therapeutic advice you can manage, but what about you?"

"There is no me. I am a professional and this is my job. I help my patients first, and then I will take care of me."

"Sure you will. Right after Lawson, Rogan, Emily, and the list goes on before you get to you."

"Good night, Jeanie."

"Night." and then I had one more person hugging me.

PAST...

"A toast to the new CEO of Douglas ECO Systems," I raised my glass as Roman, my father in law, stood on the stage and began to toast my husband.

I watched Lawson network and schmooze established and new clients while I played the voyeur from the secret corner I was in. This was his night and although he included me in all areas of his life, it was me who decided to be discreet and give him his moment.

"Buy you a drink?" I turned around to see a very tall man standing before me. I smiled before answering.

"Well, it's an open bar and as you can see, I'm all set but thank you."

"Touche. How about I get you a refill on that champagne?" he winked and then grazed his hand over mine.

Before I could say another word, a strong arm was wrapped around my shoulder and I was being pulled in to my husband's equally strong muscled chest. "If you value the use of your hands, I would suggest you not touch my wife and keep your hands to yourself." I inhaled a deep breath reacting to my husband's caveman ways.

"Um, sorry man, I thought she was on her own for the night, my mistake." Lawson eyed him suspiciously with his fingers digging into my hip.

"And you are? And why are you at my party?"

"I'm David Clayton, and I'm a developer over at Statler and Nance."

"Yes, you are from New York and are heading up the new building over on fifth."

"For someone who didn't know me a few minutes ago, you sure do know a lot about me."

"I know every single person in this room and their backgrounds, especially ones who flirt with my wife. Most are smart and know their place. Now I'll just sit back and wait for you to take yours. Darling, it's time to say goodnight. I have plans and they don't include Mr. Clayton."

PRESENT...

"I'm coming, hold on a second." I heard him call out as I banged on his door. When it opened, he looked surprised to see me. I've been successfully avoiding him since the night in my office.

"Hey, it's late. Are you okay? do you want to come in?" he looked concerned.

"I have to ask you a question."

"Okay, what is it?"

"Do you remember the night we celebrated your installation as CEO at Douglas ECO?"

"Yes, of course, I do."

"I know you are going through something that I may not under-stand or even be able to help you through, but it doesn't mean I don't want to try. I love you, Lawson, you know I do but as much as are on this new self-reflection journey of yours, I was thinking I might need one too. It's become evidently clear to me and it hit me all at once to-day when I was with a client. And then my memory brought me back to the night of your party and how you strong-armed me when you felt threatened by that real estate developer guy who was hitting on me."

"I have never been threatened, I just protect what's mine."

"Yeah, well where is that guy? Because he wasn't present when he asked me for a divorce to end our marriage."

"Renee—"

"Don't." I raised my hands up to stop him from talking. "I didn't come here to fight and analyze you. I'm just your wife tonight and I'm here to say that if you want out, then you have it. You see, in my dreams, I fight for you with everything I have. I turn myself inside out for you and then I wake up to an empty bed and a raging headache because I realize that my husband gave up long before I did. You broke my heart with those four words and no matter what I do, I can't seem to unhear them."

"Renee, please come in and we can talk. Do you realize you haven't stepped a foot in our apartment?"

"No, coming inside would be a bad idea. I have to go."

"Renee, I don't want an out, and I don't believe for a second that you want a divorce. I'm sorry, so fucking sorry for hurting you. Please baby, I want to come home and work on us."

Smack! I don't know where the impulse came from but I sure loved seeing the shocked expression on Lawson's face when I did it.

"Where's that guy who was so jealous of a stranger offering to buy me a drink? Where is he? We made love all night long and worshipped each other until we were so high on each other."

"Dammit, Renee, he's still here standing in front of you. I don't know what else to say here. I fucked up and have been apologizing ever since. Men are allowed to make mistakes, even me, Renee."

"No, you're wrong, Lawson. Mistakes are forgetting to pick up the dry cleaning you said you would get on your way home from work. No, I think what you did goes way beyond that. On that day on my parent's porch, you promised me an amazing life with you, and for most of it, it was. I have to go. Will you do me a favor before I do?"

He ran his fingers through his hair and sighed in anger. "What?"

"Will you kiss me goodbye?"

"I can do better than that." And the man who had shattered me on the night of his birthday pulled me into his arms and put me back together again with just one kiss. He didn't stop there and then he led us both into the bedroom where he made love to me. I knew it was futile to stand on my strong principles and be angry when all I was doing was falling deeper and deeper in love with him. How is this possible? I go from raging mad woman to horny, I need an orgasm kind? I was never one of those girls to do the walk of shame but there's always a first time. I wrestled under his heavy arm that was splayed across my chest and managed to get out of bed without waking him.

I gathered my clothes that were on a trail that led to the living room. I knew he would be angry waking up and finding me gone but the hell with it. I have not done one thing rationally since the night of his birthday party. I jotted down a note and left it taped to the fridge for him to find. Who knew if I would be walking through these doors again, but right now I'm leaving and going to try to find my dignity that vanished the minute I allowed Lawson to make love to me.

CHAPTER
Twelve

PRESENT...

Lawson

When I rolled back over to her side of the bed, I found it empty and cold. I let out a breath and to be honest, I wasn't that all surprised. Renee was in a state when she arrived last night and her emotions were all over the place. What I should have done was let her go when she wanted to leave but the temptation was just too great and I had to keep her with me.

My great plan may have worked last night but I'm sure today looks different. She's standing on the precipice, torn between our past and our present. Her scent was all over this bed and in this room. I planted my face in her pillow and just inhaled her flowery scent. I prolonged my shower long enough and knew I had to get into the office. I took the last few days off intending to go somewhere and clear my head, but I never made it out of the apartment. The joke of it is, I am not any closer than I was last week. As I made my way into the kitchen to make coffee, I found her note on the fridge.

My heart ached just looking at her perfectly written script. I took a seat at the breakfast bar and began reading her note.

Dear Lawson,

Newsflash! It takes two to make a marriage work and you're not the only one to blame for our current situation. Are we even now? You hurt me and I hurt you. Just so you know, I didn't mean it and divorcing you is the last thing I want but I can't make you stay either. I'm going into the office today to clear my calendar and then I am off to New York for a conference that I just decided on attending. Can we talk when I get back?

Xo,

Renee

God! I love her. You are an asshole, Lawson Douglas, and if she never takes you back, then you deserve the lifetime of misery you surely will get for fucking up the best thing you have in your life.

"Hail our fearless leader who has returned to his abandoned ship."

"Okay, laugh it up, Alison. If you are finished, please get me a cup of coffee and let's get down to work. We have a lot to catch up on in a short amount of time."

"Something I don't know?"

"I'm working on something and I may need your assistance with but nothing I can say right now, so let's work on what I can control."

"You got it. I'll be back in a few with the coffee."

"Oh, Alison, one more thing."

"Boss?"

"Can you track down my daughter and ask her to stop by today?"

"She's down in the diary for this afternoon."

"How did you know?"

"We don't have time for me to explain to you how awesome I am. She will be here at three, and the rest of your afternoon is cleared."

"Thank you," I called out to her retreating back.

A few hours later and one too many coffees, my eyes were bugging but it was a productive day I can be happy with. "Okay, one more thing before you guys leave," I said to Paul and Ty, my two right hands.

"As you know, Rogan is chomping at the bit to begin work here at Douglas."

"Yeah, we've been waiting for this day. So, when does he start?" asked Paul.

"I'm excited as well, and so is Rogan, but his start date will have to wait a little while longer until he returns from Argentina."

"What's in Argentina," asked Ty.

"An opportunity and a chance to follow his true passion before he takes this seat beside me."

"It sounds great. How long will he be gone for?"

"I'm not sure, Ty, but I'm anticipating a few months. So in the meantime, life will move forward without our amazing Rogan, and we will concentrate on our current projects mainly Creekside Orchards now that Winston Lockhart has been neutralized and enjoying his retirement like one of his cows."

"Damn, that's one way of looking at it." Paul chuckled.

"Hey baby, thank you for seeing me," I said as I hugged my beautiful daughter.

"What can I say? I couldn't stay away."

"Just my luck. Let's have a seat and talk. Alison made us dinner reservations down at Harbor View if you want to stay."

"Mom's favorite restaurant."

"Old habits are hard to break. So, I know you must be incredibly disappointed in me and for that, I am so sorry and will always regret hurting all of you."

"Daddy, I'm a grown ass woman and it seems every time I am around you, I retreat back to the age of 7 when you twirled me around the living room and played tea party with me. I'm not disappointed in you but I was mad at you for leaving. You know you are Superman to me, right? The hero in all things that keep the bad stuff away."

"I love that you and Rogan still believe in me and in that way, but baby girl, I'm just a man who has made his fair share of mistakes. Some I regret and some I can't ever change, but I promise I will try."

"Mom?"

"Yes, starting with her."

"Can you tell me why you asked mom for a divorce."

"I really don't know."

"How could you not know? Wasn't you who always taught us to think before we speak?"

"I believe that was your mother and it's beside the point. I made a mistake."

"Yeah, a pretty big one but that's beside the point. Look, I'm not going to sit here and chastise you anymore. What I want to know is how you are going to fix it? Win mom back and make her feel like the most special woman in the world. You can make it my wedding present, I don't care, just fix it."

"Baby, I promise to try. What I have with your mother is not lost, it's just kind of confusing right now. I've been in love with your mom for over 30 years, that's a long time loving someone and I do with all my heart. What I said was selfish and in the heat of the moment in an argument that was so stupid. Your mom is kind and loving and she just needs her time to process the last few weeks that we've been apart. It's temporary, I swear."

"I believe you. I love you, daddy."

"I love you more."

I can't remember the last time I had such a delightful evening with my daughter. We ended up closing Harbor View with many rounds of drinks between us. Gus, Emily's soon to be husband joined us for dessert and we caught up with the wedding plans and all their ideas for when they join Renee's wellness practice.

I definitely left my daughter in good spirits and I was feeling a hell of a lot better about everything. I can't wait to walk her down the aisle and celebrate her marriage to Gus, who is a great guy and I have no doubt will make a great husband. Emily is so much like her mother. They walk around with dreams in their eyes and I saw that tonight when she looked at Gus. I had that with Renee, a long time ago and I will have it again no matter what I have to do to win her back. I would have liked to stop by the house to check in with her, but I opted not to do that in the name of giving her space and texted instead. I won't tell her that I wrote and deleted about ten messages before I simply just asked her if she had a few minutes to talk.

Renee: *Hi, it's not a good time for me right now. I'm catching up on work and getting ready for my trip.*

Lawson: *Yeah, no problem. Just wanted to tell you that I met with Emily, and then Gus. All is well.*

Renee: *Yes, I know. I'm happy for you.*

Lawson: *Okay, that's all I wanted to say. Have a good trip. Talk soon.*

Renee: *Thanks, I will.*

"Yup, asshole, your circle of hell is complete," I said while I tapped my cell phone against my forehead. I was just about to go to bed and as I clicked off the last light, my doorbell rang. "Shit! It's after midnight," I said aloud. *Who could be here at this hour?* I opened the door to find my father standing on the other side. *I take it back. This is my circle of hell. So not in the mood for the lecture I'm sure to get.*

"Dad? What are you doing here? It's late."

"Is that your way of telling me I'm not welcomed?"

"Stop it old man and get your ass in here. Can I get you something to drink?"

"We can skip the pleasantries and get down to it. I want to apologize for the things I said to you a few weeks back. Your life and how you live it is your business. I'm sorry I overstepped."

"Dad, you are the one and only who gets a free pass. Feel free to call me out anytime you want."

"I was hoping you would say that because I have something else to say and I want you to hear me out."

"Okay, what's up?"

"I spoke to Rogan, and we took the day to go out and survey the orchards at Creekside. It's going to take a lot of work to restore it before we even think about laying the lines for the systems."

"Yes, I know this already. I am the CEO after all. As for Rogan, he was supposed to be on a plane to Argentina."

"Yeah, he changed his mind. I know it's not what you want to hear but he came to me."

"And? Did you feel the need to encourage him to stay? Dammit, dad, that's not what I wanted for him. He is an eco-engineer and is needed elsewhere to do some good. I'm not saying we're not in it for the same reason but we make a lot of money doing what we do. My son is special, dad. He has so much passion for community and the good for others. You should have told him that instead of the latter."

"Lawson, I know who Rogan is and I am so proud of the man he's become. He's not wasting his life or his passion. Don't you get it? He will be living out his passion right here in Georgia, and he's the one who wants this son but won't do it if he doesn't have your approval."

"So, use you for what? A buffer?"

"It's worked before and he's hoping it works now. And if I may run one more thing by you."

"Yes?"

"I would like to assist him in any way I can. He needs my expertise out there and I want to help."

"Dad, are you ready to take on such a project like that? Look where we live. It's Georgia and you being out there under the blazing sun trying to keep up with your 25-year-old grandson does not sit well with me. Have you thought about that?"

"Yes, and I'm fine. You don't have any cause for concern when it comes to me. I know my own limitations and I promise I will not push myself beyond that. Please, Lawson, I've never asked you for anything. I handed over my company to you because I saw what you see in Rogan today."

"Fine. You have my blessing. I will talk to Paul and Ty about the change of plan and I will get back to Rogan."

"Thank you."

"You're welcome. It's late. Do you want to stay?"

"Yeah, I think I will take you up on that and not because I'm old or too tired to drive."

"The thought never crossed my mind."

"Good. Oh, and tomorrow at breakfast, we will talk about Renee. Good night son."

"Oh, goody! I can't wait."

I closed the door to my bedroom and flopped down on my bed, breathing in Renee's faint scent that still lingered on our pillows. I opened my wallet and pulled out one of my favorite pics of Renee. The photo was so old, sometimes I'm afraid to touch it. Renee is blowing me a kiss. It was in one of the first letters I received while I was overseas. She said although she's not with me to give me a kiss in person, this would have to be enough until we could be together again. I tucked it inside of my helmet and kept it there every time I went out on patrol.

I took the photo and kissed it and then I prayed on it. "I love you, Renee. Pleasant dreams, baby."

I woke up to the smell of coffee and bacon. For a minute there, I thought I was back home with my wife. My father was busying himself in my kitchen and looking right at home. I took my place at the counter and he handed me an overloaded plate of pancakes, bacon, sausage, and fruit.

"Morning, this is quite the spread you cooked up."

"Morning, son, what can I say? I was hungry and I have to imagine you're not eating as well as you did when you were under the same roof with your wife. Eat up before it gets cold."

"I'd rather have my coffee first, thanks. And I'm eating just fine. Dad, just say what you have to say and then you can be on your way to mentor my son."

"You don't have to be so snide, I was just simply pointing out the obvious. You need to go home and fix your marriage before this separation gets out of hand. I miss my girl and I need you home."

"You don't need me around to visit with Renee, she loves you and you have a great relationship. As for mine, I have apologized a thousand times and I will continue to do so until I am back home with my wife because that's exactly where I want to be. She's taking a trip to New York for a conference but also taking a few days alone to relax and have some fun. She doesn't know it yet, but I plan on surprising her and sweeping her off her feet."

"Damn! I knew I raised you right. Go get your girl."

"I plan to." I smiled and enjoyed the morning with my father.

A few hours later...

"Okay, guys, change of plans. You know what I said yesterday about Rogan, and his big adventure he's taking in Argentina?" Paul and Ty both give me skeptical looks. "Forget my big speech yesterday, because we have a new change of plans, he's decided to stay and bring in my father to assist him working at Creekside."

"No sweat boss, Rogan can do as much or little as he wants until he gets the lay of the land. As for your dad, Roman's expertise and vast knowledge are always welcomed around here."

"Thank you, Paul, but I'm a little worried he may do too much so if you can just keep an eye out, I would appreciate it very much."

"You told us yesterday that we have this and we do. No worries." Ty reiterated and then began showing me new plans for the orchard revitalization we just put in place. Several hours later, I was beyond hungry and regretted not ordering take-out like Ty and Paul. I valued my arteries and didn't want to have a heart attack before I had the chance to make up with Renee.

I was spent and happy to call it a day when Rogan had called and talked my ear off for an hour on his wonderful day with my father. I loved listening to his excitement and maybe this would be a good thing allowing him to steer his own course. My team had left for the day after an entire day holed up in my office. I had no one at home waiting for me back at the apartment, totally my fault, so I'm here. I'll stay and work some more while the rest of the world has a life.

I think this right here and what I'm doing at the office buried under work on Friday night is one of the reasons why I had my meltdown with Renee. I am convinced that I am an exhausted workaholic that has led me here to this moment.

My phone vibrated and not bothering to check, I answered it and was taken by surprise that it was Renee inviting me for a late dinner. I never moved so quickly in my life. I sprinted down the stairs and to the parking garage in a flash. I peeled out of there and thanking the heavens I chose my Maserati Gran Turismo to drive today. Yes, it was totally an impulsive buy that I do not regret and although she will not admit it, Renee secretly loves it.

"Mr. Douglas, welcome back to Harbor View."

"Thank you, Saul, has my wife arrived?"

"She has and has been seated at your table. Follow me, sir." Once we reached the table, Renee rose from the table and walked over and pulled me in for a hug.

"Hey, thanks for calling."

"Thanks for saying yes."

We took our seats beside each other and Renee placed her hand on my thigh and just smiled at me.

"I mean it, Lawson, thank you for saying yes. I felt horrible for my curt responses to your text messages. I was feeling, no scratch that, I don't know what I was feeling and had no idea what to say."

"Your note was pretty clear."

"I imagine it was."

"Are you still going to New York?"

"Yes, tomorrow morning. Emily has my itinerary and she can forward it to you if you want it."

"Sounds good, I'll call her."

"Great. Let's order drinks. I'm in the mood for a very dry martini."

"You only order that drink when you're stressed. Are you stressed?"

"What do you think? I thought I was simply attending the conference but the minute my name was added to the list, Darcy got so excited she asked me to deliver the keynote speech."

"Congratulations," I said and then brought Renee's hand to my lips. Her skin was soft and she was wearing the same perfume from the other night. "Thank you," I said.

"For?"

"I don't know, just being here and talking to me. What happened next?"

"Darcy didn't leave any room for discussion. All I planned on doing was attending the conference as a guest and network with my colleagues, but I didn't get the chance to say that to her. I tried but she probably knew I was going to decline and kept on talking over me. I think the last thing I heard her say was that the liaison for the event would meet me at the hotel and assist me in anything I would need. Again, I tried to ask questions but Darcy disconnected the call before I had a chance."

"Renee, it's a huge honor and I'm proud of you. You are going to be great."

"You don't have to say that,"

"Why? It's the truth."

"You hate what I do," she said quietly.

"No, I don't. You are an amazing doctor and have helped so many of your patients, I just didn't want to be one of them." *There I go again with my honesty? She looked away for a moment and then was quiet.* I didn't want to upset her, especially on the night before her trip. Did you write a speech?"

"Yes, it took me all afternoon with Jeanie's help."

"Hail to amazing assistants," I said in a toast breaking up the obvious discomfort between us.

CHAPTER
Thirteen

PRESENT...

Renee

"I'll drink to that." We both clinked our glasses knowing what gems we had in Alison and Jeanie. Just above the rim of the glass I could see Lawson's eyes solely focused on me and waiting for me to begin talking. I haven't been very nice and I couldn't blame him for being a little guarded with me considering how we left things the last time we were together.

"Anyway, another reason why I asked you to dinner is to really talk the way we should have the first time around. I was angry and wanted to scratch your eyes out. In the time we've been apart, I've done a lot of thinking and trying to find my place where I fit and how much blame I should accept as mine."

"Renee,"

"No, please allow me to finish, this is hard enough. Do you remember when I wanted to quit school just to spite my father?"

"Yes, that was a great day."

"And, you convinced me not to and work hard for my degree. You said it's hard now and it will get worse before it gets better. And when it's all over, I will be walking in an ugly cap and gown with my loving husband shouting at the end of the aisle on how much of a rock star I am. Something like that."

"Exactly like that. I was in awe of you. I was so proud of you then and I'm proud of you now. You're not the only one who has done some soul searching. I've practically ripped mine apart and you are the only one who could put it back together. I love you. Those three words are branded on my heart, inside and out. I'm a fool forever saying the other words I did and you have every right to hate me for it. I'm praying you don't because other than saying them, the knowing part would be so much worse."

"I don't hate you, Lawson. Love is stronger than hate and my heart has no vacancies for anything else."

"Thank you, I needed to hear that. And there is something else you need to know. You see, somewhere along the line, I think I stopped romancing you and making you feel special because I already got the girl, and then came the career, kids, and the grand life we always wanted. I took you for granted and I got lazy. Not wanting a party was my way of punishing myself because I didn't feel I deserved it."

"You are an amazing woman, wife, and mother, and deserve so much in this life. I love you always and forever and that will never change. I need you, Renee, probably more than you need me but I don't mind telling you that. The realization was never clearer on the night I walked out of our home. It was cruel of me to say those words to you, and an act of weakness on my part. I'm ashamed of myself. I should have stayed and talked to you. Be the man you know I really am. I'm so sorry I didn't. I'm sorry I failed you."

I knew he was sorry. His eyes were so telling and could never betray what was in his heart. I couldn't miss the tears that were building but he had his pride and when it's on the line, he would be as strong as he could before he would allow one to fall.

"Renee," his hands tightened in mine. "When you get back from New York, will you allow me to come home? I know I need to work on me to be better for my family and that's going to take time. My wish is that I won't have to do it alone. Please let me come home to you. It's where I belong."

I pulled my hands away and wiped my eyes before my make-up had a chance to run all over my face. I took another sip of my drink and willed my nerves to calm down. What I wanted was to leap across this table and take my man in my arms but we needed this talk. I had to be strong enough to get through it. Of course he sensed my hesitation. He could read me like no other.

"Renee? Are you okay? Can I come home?"

"Oh, Lawson, when you talk like this, I feel it's a rewind of our early days when we were falling in love and were so carefree to do whatever the hell we wanted. It would be so easy to say yes to you and there is a huge part of me that wants to."

"But, you're hesitating?"

"More like being careful, so I don't match you in monumental mistakes. I need some time for myself and if I don't put some distance between us right now, I will never leave and the issues that separated us in the first place will never be resolved. Please give me this chance to do that. I'll go to New York and when I get back, I promise to continue this conversation."

"Whatever you want." He winked and took my hands up to his mouth to kiss them. A relief washed over him and he visibly relaxed.

"I love when you say that."

"Say what?" he asked.

"I can talk for hours and when I'm finished, you give me the simplest of answers which also makes me crazy because it's so hard to figure out what you're thinking."

"I'm thinking I love my wife and I know I've been an asshole who hurt her deeply. What would make me a bigger asshole is to not meet her halfway, go all caveman and come home because it's what I want.

No, I'm smarter than that and I know you need some time and I'm willing to give that to you. Having said that, I can't tell you how patient I'll be, it was never one of my strong suits but I'll try for you. I promise."

"Yes. Lawson you can come home." The words were right there but I couldn't bring myself to say them. He was right. I needed this time and I was going to take it. For once, I choose me and I love him even more for knowing how important that is for me to do at this time.

"Lawson," I practically whispered his name to get his attention. I knew I had it since he hadn't taken his eyes off me.

"Yes," he answered seductively.

"I'm hungry and I want crab cakes."

I watched his gorgeous lips quirk up into the perfect smile. He raised his hand up to signal Saul, who immediately sent over our waiter. We had a lovely evening talking and reconnecting over crab cakes, martini's, and because I wouldn't share, two servings of Crème Brulee.

I needed this night more than I would ever admit to Lawson. I've been petty and so lost in my anger. I should have accepted his apology the first time he offered it and asked him to come home to me but I was stubborn and wanted him to suffer and to feel the consequences from the words he said to me. They hurt to hear and as much as I missed him the second he left, I also needed to feel them as well and what it would mean if we did divorce. In a million years I never believed a word like divorce would ever cross into our life but it did and now here we are.

Two people who truly love each other but will it be enough? I'm not going to know that answer until I do some self-reflection on my own misgivings. The joke is on me because I'm probably more dysfunctional than Lawson, but since I'm the professional, I just hide it better.

As we waited for the valet to bring our cars around, Lawson reached for my hand to hold and I passed it as easy as gravy. His touch and warmth against my skin felt right, kind of like home. I want him to make love to me all night long. It would be so easy to fall back into that pattern with him. We stood there in happy silence and just when I was about to break it, my car arrived.

"This is me,"

"Yeah, it is. The parking attendant has terrible timing." His hand moved lower and he adjusted himself. He didn't even try to hide it. I bit my lip so I wouldn't laugh. I loved knowing we were thinking about the same thing.

"That he does, but it's been a great night and why spoil it?"

"Come here," he said opening his arms for me to walk into. Thank god he was close or I would have lost my nerve. When he wrapped his arms around me, every single question in my mind about our life had been eradicated with Lawson being the man I have always known him to be. "I love you, Renee. I had a wonderful evening with you and I don't need an answer right now. I want you to go to New York and be amazing at that conference. I say this not to build you up. I say this because it's true. You are a rock star. Mine."

"Will you kiss me?"

"You never have to ask." I closed my eyes and waited for Lawson to give me an epic kiss but he went the gentler route and kissed my forehead, my nose, and then my lips before pulling away. I wanted more. I wanted my husband always. He smiled and then said, "Inside you go," he opened the door and practically placed me in my seat. "Have a great trip and don't go charming any strange men in New York with your southern accent."

I silently giggled inside. "There's only one man I want to charm. Night, Lawson."

Arriving in New York the following day was easier than I originally thought. I usually hate to fly anywhere and without Lawson, it's even harder to do. However, I'm an independent woman who can easily handle a business trip on her own. I actually enjoyed dinner with Lawson and had my first good night's sleep in a long while.

The first couple of days spent in the city were for me. At first I thought it might feel weird to dine alone and do sightseeing on my own, but the more I made my way around the city, I felt at ease. I was enjoying myself and happy I didn't come up with an excuse to change my mind. Now, it was time to work. I made my way through the hotel when an unknown woman was running straight for me.

"Dr. Douglas, can I just say what an honor it is to have you with us this week?"

"It's my pleasure and please, call me Renee."

"I will try but with your stellar background, it may be hard to just be so casual."

"Why don't we begin with telling me your name."

"Oh, my goodness, I'm Jacque Gillespie. Would you like to get settled in your room before we meet the others heading up the panels?"

"Yes, I'd like to unwind a bit and then according to the schedule, I have a few hours before the reception meet and greet this evening in the Colonnade Room."

"I see you have gone over your itinerary which saves me time that I never seem to have at these things."

"Well, time is precious and I would like to take some for myself. It was a pleasure meeting you and I will see you this evening." I made my fast getaway to the nearest elevator with the bellhop following close behind. New York City hotels did not disappoint and neither did the huge tub I soaked myself in until my skin pruned. It felt so good to relax and soak my sore muscles and allow my mind to dream of Lawson.

PAST...

"Renee, I want to go away with you, anywhere I don't care. Let's get in the car, book a flight, I don't care as long as you are with me. Please babe, say yes."

"I love how you think Lawson, but how? We have so much on our plate right now and the kids? I just can't up and leave them."

"How about a long weekend? Our kids are teenagers and it's not like we will just leave them unsupervised. We have our folks nearby to check on them. Come on, we need this."

"I'm sorry but I just can't clear my schedule right now. There will be other trips. Okay, I have to run. My next appointment is here. Love you."

"Dammit! Rogan, you don't get to pick and choose what works for you. We had an agreement and I expect you to follow through with your commitment."

"Mom, will you please talk to him? I just want to take a semester off to clear my head. What is so wrong with that? Graduate school is not going anywhere. Come on, give me a break."

"Lawson, why don't we table this conversation for now and I will speak with Rogan when he's a little calmer to understand all the valued points you just presented."

"Renee, I'm not one of your patients and neither is our son. There will be no calming down to process. You are not taking any time off and will stay in school. And that Dr. Douglas is my final word on this subject." I watched him slam his hand down on the table and then Rogan storm off to his room. Once it was just the two of us, I tried to talk to him.

"Lawson, why are you so angry with me?"

"You don't know, do you?"

"Enlighten me then?"

"Why? You never listen unless it's me on that damn couch of yours and you sitting in front of me with your notebook and pen. I'm so fucking tired of being your patient rather than your husband. You need to stop undermining me when it comes to Rogan. We had a plan and he agreed to it. I know he wants to take a break but that is the last thing he needs right now. Believe me, he will thank me for this one day."

"You're right, I'm sorry. I should have backed you in there. I will talk to our son and tell him that I agree with you."

"Thank you, but if you would have just said that in the first place, we wouldn't have had this fight. It doesn't always have to be so hard, Renee. I can manage this family just as well as you can."

"Why don't you want a party? I just don't understand you."

"Renee, we have been over this and I don't want to discuss it again."

"Well, you have to because I don't understand you at all. It's a party in your honor for your 50th birthday. We love you and want to celebrate you. What is the problem?"

"The problem is, you never listen. I mean, seriously, Renee? This is what you do for a living. You listen to other people's problems every day and all day long but when it comes to the problems in our marriage, it's like you've gone silent on me. You continue to do what you want. You continue to make decisions that best suit you and your needs, but what about me? I thought two people were supposed to be in a marriage."

"It is, how can you believe otherwise?"

"It's easy, you don't listen to me. All I wanted and have been wanting is a break which is just a joke by now because I never seem to get one. Every year we talk about going on vacation and every year you come up with a million reasons as to why we can't. I'm done, Renee. No to the party."

PRESENT…

I couldn't help my tears that were falling. He was so right. I don't listen to him. He wasn't asking for much. He just wanted one weekend alone with me. He wanted time with his wife and I always said no and listed a thousand reasons why it wasn't the right time.

God! I feel like such a bitch. It's no wonder why my husband asked for an out because I have to control every single situation in our life and I never give him any room to breathe.

"Because I suffocate him. There you have it, Renee. You are sitting in a luxury New York Hotel bathtub and your life just got all summed up in one big in your face realization." I slapped the water with my hand make a huge splash. "Damn, I hate me sometimes."

I did the once over in the floor length mirror and deeply sighed. I was in no mood to entertain my fellow peers in my field but this conference is a good thing and the perfect reason to get my mind off Lawson. The moment I stepped off the elevator, my eager host was right there to greet me.

"This is the topic for the keynote speaker?" I asked in complete surprise reading over the sheet Jacque just handed me.

"Yes, it is. It's perfect right?"

"That's one way of putting it. Um, Jacque, I thought the topic was today's family competing with time and social media?"

"It was supposed to be and then once we heard you confirmed, the board changed the complete direction and focused on communication, the heart of today's married life. Dr. Douglas, you have literally changed my life when it comes to having a successful marriage. Your webinars on communication, marriage, the family aspect is amazing, award-winning in fact. This is your moment, let's run with it."

I needed to get out of here. I couldn't breathe. "Will you excuse me?"

"Are you okay, Dr. Douglas?"

"It's Renee, and I'm fine. It's been a very exciting and eye-opening experience so far but having said that, I need to take a break and make a call."

"Anything you need, it's yours." I found a quiet room away from the conference goers and called Emily.

"Mom! I didn't expect to hear from you? How are you? How's New York?"

"Honey, this isn't a social call. I need a favor and I need it like an hour ago."

"Okay, what is it?"

"Are you in the office?"

"I am. You're lucky you caught me, I was just on my way out. How can I help?"

"I need you to email all my recent webinar files that were on communication and marriage. Without my knowledge, they changed the closing topic of discussion to that exact topic and now I have to re-write my entire speech."

"I'm on it, mom, and you should have it right now."

My iPad pinged and everything I needed was in my inbox. "Oh, Emily, thank you for saving my ass. I wish I could just hop on a plane and come home."

"Why? I thought you were having fun up there?"

"New York is fine, that's not the problem. I've seen a play and ate lunch today at Bryant Park, but…"

"But?" *I hate this part.* "What's going on, Mom?"

"I'm here, and I'm alone. It wasn't so bad at first but now the silence is killing me. Emily, I miss your father and I want him to come home. I just want to put these last weeks behind us and never think of them again. What the hell am I doing?"

"You are living your life. Stop beating yourself up about it. If it makes you feel better, he wants nothing more than to be home with you. Have you talked with him since you've been gone?"

"No, not since I left for New York." *Although our last dinner to-gether ended on good terms, I was still upset with myself for my previous behavior. I couldn't bring myself to tell her the truth about how I lashed out in a fit of anger and then to make matters more confusing, I made love to her father not knowing if it was really over between us. I felt ashamed for my actions. So, I pretended to not know and ask Emily about Lawson.*

"Have you talked to him recently? Is he okay?" I could hear the desperation in my voice. Who was I kidding? I missed him.

"He's fine, better than ever." She happily replied.

Better than ever? What does that mean? "Well, good. I have to run honey. Thanks for the files." *I had to get off the phone before I cry.*

"Mom, it's going to be alright. You and daddy are going to make it. This has just been a bump in the road. Now go rock the rest of the conference so you can come home to us. Gus misses you. He said he needs his partner in crime for the rest of the wedding plans to be final-ized."

"Sounds good. Give him my love, and Rogan too. I'll be home soon."

"Any messages for daddy?"

"No, I think I will wait until I see him in person to tell him what I have to say."

I was about to get back to working on my speech but all my thoughts went to Lawson. What if I call him and ask him to meet me here in New York? Or I could call Alison and ask for his schedule, maybe I could plan a surprise for him? In any case, he's been doing wonderful things for me all these years. I'll think about it once tonight is over and I can have a minute to think. I know it's crazy in a city that never sleeps but for some reason, I can relax here. After revising my speech, no, totally re-writing it, I was way past the point of starving. I had called ahead for room service and as I approached my room, I saw a waiter exiting with an empty cart.

"Hi, Dr. Douglas, everything has been set up on the dining room table. If you need anything else, just call down."

"Thank you, I will."

"Wow, Dr. Douglas, you look amazing. I love your suit, Chanel, right?"

"Yes, Jacque, it is."

"I knew it, I know my power suits."

"Jacque, may I say something to you?"

"Um, yeah, anything."

"In my time I've been here, you have been most accommodating. You have gone way beyond the job description of host and I just wanted to say thank you. The foundation should be honored to have you on staff."

"Oh, thank you, Dr. Douglas, you just made my night."

"Okay, let's go mingle and then I have a speech to give." Ninety minutes later of a lot of talks, it was time to deliver my speech. I glanced down at my phone and saw no messages, at least none I wanted. I stepped aside to a quiet corner and called Lawson. His phone must be off, so I left a message.

"Hi, it's me. I'm still in New York and it's the last night of the conference. I'm actually getting ready to deliver my speech and you'll never guess what they've asked me to talk about. I'll keep you guessing until I can tell you in person. Um, Lawson, do you remember the question you asked me before I left for my trip? Well, my answer is yes. I have to go, they're calling my name."

"Please welcome, Dr. Renee Douglas, your keynote speaker." I made my way up to the podium and waited for the applause to stop but I guess a lot of people were interested in what I had to say because I received a standing ovation.

"Thank you. Thank you. I truly appreciate your warm welcome. I'd like to also extend my gratitude to The Elliman Wellness Foundation for inviting me to join all of you here this evening. I have to say I was surprised to hear what topic I would be addressing this evening.

So, let's talk about communication."

"That is one subject that I don't believe not one person in this room has mastered, including myself. I may have many degrees that line the walls of my office that prove I know what I'm talking about most of the time, but I have to be honest here and admit to you that I wish some days could just be silent. I can be silent and just listen. Yes, communication is key to any successful relationship we have in our lives. From marriage to friendships, it's a key component and one we can't live without unless you want to spend your life in a world of silence. I've recently learned a valuable lesson on this very subject. You see, I've been married for 25 years and so much in love since I was sixteen years old. Along the way of getting everything we ever wanted, some things in our lives were so loud that we actually went silent." *I paused for a brief moment to look out to the audience who were attentive and waiting for me to continue. This wasn't the usual speech I was used to giving. This was my truth. The truth Lawson has wanted me to admit for so long now but I never could until he walked out the door and left me all alone in my—silence.*

"It took a major wake-up call in my life to realize that I was too busy and wrapped up in my career and putting the needs of my patients first, then my children, and lastly, my husband. It's very easy to exert power and control over others when you're the one at the top of the food chain. The truth of the matter is, I stopped listening. I never knew how much my avoidance of certain things in our lives was costing my family, especially my husband. But I certainly did know on the night he finally had enough and reached his breaking point with me. Of course, I was totally taken off guard and played the victim and blamed him for everything."

"Why did I do that? It's a question I've been asking myself for weeks now and have come up with this answer. I got used to my own rules and totally disregarded the ones I had promised to my husband. I stopped listening. As I look around this room, I see the shock registering on your faces because I'm sure you were not expecting to hear this kind of speech from me. I guess I surprised myself too because I've never found myself in a situation that I couldn't control. A problem that I couldn't solve. Yes, all new territory for me, so this is not my usual speech that I give at conferences to a room filled with my peers. Right here and now is my confession. I'm not perfect." I paused for a moment and then I laughed so loud that I had to hold my stomach and then the room laughed along with me. "Wow! The world didn't stop with those words, did it? No, I'm not perfect, far from it and it feels damn good to finally admit it."

"You can open any medical textbook and look up the definition of communication and you will find many answers to this very complex subject. Look, let's be honest, it's not pretty. We make our living using our fine communication skills to help others but I am here to say, the real work begins at home. We can only be our best self when we acknowledge our faults first, and I intend to work on mine the minute I can board a plane and have a real conversation with my husband. One where I will listen and allow someone else the chance to speak because I now know I can't always take the lead."

"I'll leave you with this. You ever hear the reference a good paint-er is only as good as his paintbrush?" *Again I paused in my speech. I heard some laughter and then I saw some confused faces.* "Yes, I know, I shuttered the first time I heard it too, but it has merit. A good communicator is only as good as their last conversation. Think about it and give yourself time to really believe how it will apply to you, your patients, and your life. And while you're doing that I will say, "Thank you for your time." And when I thought I was going to be pelted with rotten tomatoes, I received a standing ovation with Jacque leading the applause. I stepped down and was flanked by a colleague and then more approached and asked all sorts of questions and wanting meet-ings to further our discussion.

"You were amazing!" Jacque said as she wrapped her arms around me in glee.

"You are being kind but thank you."

"No, I'm not. Renee, I'm being honest and what you said really moved me. It was real and human, and exactly what we needed to hear. I know you must be exhausted, so I won't keep you. Thank you, for this week. And I hope you get to have that conversation with your husband, he needs to know you're ready to listen."

"I hope so. See you next year?"

"I already have you down for running a panel."

"Bye, Jacque. If you're ever in Savannah, look me up."

I looked down at my shoes and was regretting not changing into something more comfortable, but the city was waiting for me and I didn't want to miss another minute of it. I stepped outside of the hotel and just smiled as I looked all around. I felt lighter as if a weight had been lifted off my shoulder. I didn't hear him at first and then I felt a gentle tap on my shoulder. I turned around to see one of the many doormen the Plaza had employed.

"May I get you a taxi?"

"Excuse me, what?"

"I'm sorry, I asked you if you needed a taxi. Can I assist you in any way?"

"No, thank you, I think I'm going to take a walk."

"No disrespect ma'am, but this is a big city and I don't think it's safe for you to be on your own."

"Thank you for your concern but I'm only going across the street to that Starbucks," I pointed to the building on the other side.

"Okay, fair enough."

Who knew New Yorkers had chivalry? I was still high from the conference and all the accolades I had received from my peers. It was a wonderful conference and in the end, I was happy I went. The night air felt great as it breezed against my skin. I just wanted to take a walk and for the first time not to clear my head.

I felt better and more secure about my life and the one I intend to continue having with my husband. I waved to the doorman and smiled back as I waited for the light to change to green. I was standing there on the curb just thinking about Lawson when I heard his voice call out my name. Seriously? How can that be?

I looked around the busy area surrounded by New Yorkers coming and going and then I heard his voice again. Lawson was here and standing on the other side. He had a duffle over his shoulder and was waving to me. He began crossing the busy intersection and it was my turn to go. I stepped off the sidewalk and into the street when suddenly the heel of my shoe snapped sending me careening out into the busy crowd. As I rose to my feet, a taxi ran the light and it was too late to run to safety. It happened so fast. Three tons of steel crashing into me. My body was launched off the ground and it felt as if I was soaring through the sky. I heard him screaming my name in pain.

"Renee!" was the one thing I heard until he was kneeling beside me and over my body. "Baby, you hold on. Help is on the way. Renee, I'm here. Don't you dare leave me."

"I love you, Lawson..." I didn't have the ability to speak but I hoped he knew as all that was light in my world a moment ago has now turned to darkness.

CHAPTER
Fourteen

Lawson

"**O**h, daddy, mom is going to flip when she sees you."

"Yeah, dad, who knew you were such a romantic."

"Thanks, Rogan, but I've been known to wine and dine your mother on many occasions. Okay, listen to me. I don't want you to worry one bit. Mom and I are meant for forever and my stupid lapse is not going to end us. I believe she's over the initial shock of my error in judgment and she wants to forgive me."

"You have our support."

"Thank you, Emily. What about you? You're quiet, Rogan."

"I'm sorry dad, I was reading a report."

"Spoken like a true workaholic."

"Says my baby sister who works what? 12-hour work days while planning her nuptials."

"Okay, you two, that's enough. I love you very much and it's going to be great. Listen Em, I still have to go home and pack and tie up a few things here with Rogan before I leave for the airport."

"Is that your subtle way of asking me to leave?"

"Yeah, genius."

"Shut-up, Rogan."

"Enough. Can we pick this up when I get back?"

"Absolutely, I will see you and mom."

"You definitely will. I love you," I said as I took my daughter in my arms.

"Now, let's talk about you. I believe the last time we had spoken, I asked you to take some time to think about the next chapter in your life."

"And I did."

"Oh, yeah, what? A day? If your grandfather hadn't shown up on my doorstep, when were you going to tell me? because I thought you were on a plane to Argentina."

"Dad, I'm you, and I'm not sorry for it. Everything I have learned about life comes from you, and I'll be damned if I take a fucking vacation when all I want to do is work hard and make my own mark on Douglas ECO. I know you worry about me but I'm okay. I promise you I won't allow the work to become bigger than me."

"I know you feel as if it has swallowed you up and has left no room for anything else in your life, but you're wrong, dad. You have so much, probably more than most. I intend to have a family of my own someday and I can only hope for a marriage like yours with mom. I just want the work now. It makes me so happy and complete, I really can't think of anything else."

"Wow! You sure know how to build up a father's ego. Thank you, son. I am a very lucky man to have the life I have but I didn't do it all on my own. I had your mother. Your mom was always there for me, and never missed a day when it counted most. She's had to put up with a lot from me over the years and never once complained. I was selfish that night and cruel. I had been feeling unsettled and not fulfilled with work, life, you name it. I took it out on your mom knowing she didn't deserve it. I swear I will do everything in my power to make things right between your mother and me, and that begins today with my trip to New York."

"So, in my absence, you are in charge."

"Really?"

"Yes. I have complete faith in you. Ty and Paul will be here along with your grandfather. It's always been a team effort, and you must always remember that."

"Always. I won't let you down, dad."

"I know. I have complete confidence in you. Now, I have a plane to catch."

Bless my daughter. I don't know how she managed to do it. I took the elevator down to the ground floor and there was Emily standing there with my bag in hand.

"How?" I said.

"Oh, please! Mom taught me well. Here's everything you need. Now go get your girl and bring her home."

"That's exactly what I intend to do," I practically lifted my daughter off the ground in a big hug. "Thank you, Emily."

I made it to the airport and boarded my flight with a few minutes to spare. I knew I was cutting it close even with Emily's help. The flight attendant took my jacket and bag and I sat in my first class seat. I finally had a moment to breathe and think about what I wanted to say to Renee when I finally get to hold her in my arms again. I don't know how I missed her call but I had a new voicemail.

"Hi, it's me. I'm still in New York and it's the last night of the conference. I'm actually getting ready to deliver my speech and you'll never guess what they've asked me to talk about. I'll keep you guessing until I can tell you in person. Um, Lawson, do you remember the question you asked me before I left for my trip? Well, my answer is yes. I have to go, they're calling my name."

Listening to her voice, I had this incredible overwhelming feeling that just washed over me and I wished I was Superman so I could get to her at the speed of light. My woman needed me, I could sense it in her tone. I should have put my plan in place earlier but no matter, I'm on my way and she will be back in my arms soon.

Once I landed in New York, I practically sprinted through the airport to the car service. All I wanted to do is see Renee. I looked down at my watch and she was probably still at the conference. If I hurry, I could probably be there just as it's ending. I wanted to call ahead and arrange champagne to be waiting for her in her room but we can order that together once we are reunited.

"Damn, this traffic. Does it ever end in this city?" I said aloud as I took in the path of red stopped lights.

"Let me guess, you're not from here?"

"No, I'm not. What gave me away?" I mocked.

"It wasn't your sparkling personality."

"You got me there. Sorry, man, I just need to get somewhere and I'm in a hurry."

"Well, maybe you have a little New York in you but sorry pal, we are at a standstill."

"How far is The Plaza from here?" I asked the driver.

"About twenty city blocks pal, it's a hike."

"Yeah, well thank goodness I'm in shape to run it. I'll get out here."

When I finally reached Fifth Avenue, I was feeling the burn in my chest and legs but it was so worth it because I was that much closer to Renee.

I was standing on the corner and right across from the hotel. It was like the stars aligned because there she was. Renee looked beautiful and her smile had the ability to stop my heart from beating. My wife was just within arm's reach.

Who knew if she could hear me over the city noise and traffic, but I called out to her anyway. I was waving like a lovesick fool but I didn't care. "Renee!" I shouted in my cupped hands and then she looked up and everything in my world was righted. Would it be cliché to say we looked like two star-crossed lovers? It certainly felt like that. I began to make my way to Renee, and she to me. I was almost there and then I watched in horror my wife get struck by a fucking taxi.

"Renee! Renee!" By the time I reached her, she was nearly unconscious. I begged her to stay with me.

I held her broken body in my arms and wept over her begging her not to die. Her eyes were closed but she still had a pulse which was my lifeline right now. The ambulance arrived and loaded her inside within seconds of evaluating her injuries. They said I couldn't ride with them with the two EMTs in the back with her.

"I want you to take her to New York-Presbyterian Hospital." They looked at me like I was crazy which enraged me more.

"Hey, don't let my southern accent confuse you for being stupid. I want the best for my wife, and you will take her there," I shouted.

"Yes, sir."

There was no time to argue, every minute counted on saving Renee's life. After they pulled away, I just stood there for a second trying to take in what just happened. My wife was just struck by a car right in front of me. The sounds of blaring horns made me move onto the sidewalk and that's when I saw the taxi driver being handcuffed and placed into the back of a police car. His entire front end was smashed in. Holy shit! That's the impact of hitting my wife.

Rage flooded my senses and all I wanted was to kill the motherfucking driver. "Hey! You!" I called out as I rushed the police cruiser. I was thrown back by two NYPD officers. "Let me go," I shouted and struggled to be free. "That bastard hit my wife. She's fighting for her life because of him."

"We know, sir, and you going to jail tonight for assault is not going to help her. You need to get to the hospital. I swear to you that this asshole will get what's coming to him."

"Please, five minutes with him, it's all I need." I cried out.

"Sir, he isn't going anywhere, I promise."

"You hit my wife! What in the hell is wrong with you!?" I shouted. I stepped back and raised my hands up showing the police I would not lunge again. I tried to take a few calming breaths but it felt hard to breathe not knowing what was happening with Renee. I was offered a ride to the hospital as I watched the drunk driver be pushed into the back seat of the other police cruiser. I had to get to my wife, that's all that mattered right now. I sat in silence and prayed for my wife to survive.

"Please drive faster."

"Sir, don't worry, I'll get you there."

"Please god, don't take her from me or our kids. We love and need her. I can't lose her." I gripped the sides of my head in frustration. How the hell did this just happen? All I wanted to do was to reunite with Renee by surprising her in New York.

She always loved my over-the-top romantic gestures and all I wanted was to re-create something special for her. My birthday party was an epic letdown which was totally my fault and I've been trying to make it up to her ever since. From our kids, my father, and too many hours of soul searching, my head is on straight now and I will never fuck up again with my wife. She has to be okay so I can spend the rest of my life making her happy.

The cop escorted me inside to the entrance of the emergency room and brought me right through so I could get information on Renee. A staff member must have recognized the cop with me as she greeted him warmly and then said hello to me.

"Hi, Mr. Douglas, I'm Raj. I work closely with Dr. Amsterdam."

"How's my wife? I'm going crazy."

"She was just taken into surgery. She has a broken leg and several broken ribs with one puncturing her lung."

"What about head injuries?"

"We will know more after we get the MRI results. Her leg was in need of emergency care."

"What are you saying? Is she going to lose it?"

"We don't know yet. Dr. Amsterdam and her team are the best. I'll keep you posted with every update I get down here. Is there anyone I can call for you?"

"No, thank you. We don't live here in the city. Is there a waiting area I can go to?"

"Yes, I can take you up there." We rode in silence as the elevator reached the floor. We stepped out and Raj directed me to the waiting room just off the OR doors. I thanked her and took a seat by the window looking down to the busy city below.

I slid my finger across my phone screen to open up my contacts. It was so late and I knew I should call our kids but I couldn't bring myself to even say the words. I shoved my phone back into my pocket and just waited. It had been a few hours and I was just about to lose my mind when a tall woman in scrubs walked through the door.

"Mr. Douglas?"

"Yeah, that's me. How's my wife?"

"She's stable and in recovery. Why don't we have a seat and I can go over the surgery with you. Due to the impact, her femur was shattered resulting in me reconstructing the Femoral shaft. She's kind of like the bionic woman and will need at least six months of recovery time."

"So, my wife is like Humpty Dumpty? The accident shattered her and you what? Put her back together?" *WTF? How am I even saying these words? The doctor just stood there and patiently listened as I ranted off complete nonsense. Does she hear this often from worried family members?* "I'm sorry, that was rude. I'm just running on empty and in need of coffee."

"Actually, that wasn't so bad considering what I'm used to hearing doing this job. Mr. Douglas, you have a right to be upset. Your wife has been through a great ordeal tonight. As for Humpty Dumpty, only her leg. She will probably set off the airport security alarms anytime she travels, but she still has her leg and although the recovery will be difficult, the thing to remember is she will recover and be able to walk again."

"Thank god, and what about the rest of her injuries?"

"She has three broken ribs, one that got really close to her lungs but thankfully the scan was wrong and they were not punctured like you were initially told. She has no cranial damage which is a miracle but she does have a bump on her head. Her vitals are strong and we want to keep them that way. I am going to keep her sleeping for the next 24-to-48 hours to rest. This was a horrific trauma that could have killed her. My best advice is to get some rest tonight and we can talk again in the morning."

"I'd rather stay. Please, can I see my wife?"

"I know you're anxious to see her, Mr. Douglas, but like I said, she's sedated and no visitors are allowed up in the ICU recovery room. Please, do yourself some good and get some rest. The next few days is going to be hard and you will need your strength to get through them. If you have anyone to lean on for support, I encourage you to call them. I will have Raj call you after I access her condition in the morning."

"It is morning, doc."

"How about nine? You can see her then."

"Fine. I'll be back."

CHAPTER
Fifteen

PRESENT...

Lawson

By the time I got back to the Plaza, it was nearly four in the morning. The concierge expressed his sympathies for my wife and handed me a stack of messages from I imagine her colleagues from the conference. He escorted me personally up to her suite and even had some food ordered up for me. The accident happened right in front of the hotel and some of the staff who had interacted with Renee were upset.

I was grateful for all their kindness. All I wanted to do was get some rest and get back to the hospital. The minute I stepped inside of her hotel room, the smell of her perfume hit my nostrils. She was here with me in some kind of way. I closed the door and slid down to the floor in a heap of tears. I remained there until I heard a knock at the door. It was room service delivering whatever the concierge ordered for me.

I took a hot shower after letting them in, and when I came out of the bathroom, the dining table was elegantly set. Under the silver dome covers were filet mignon, roasted red potatoes, and asparagus tips. Wow, and here I was expecting a burger and fries. Not remembering the last time I ate, I just devoured the delicious meal and then caught a few hours of sleep before returning to the hospital.

I was exhausted and my legs felt heavy with every step I took. I wanted to see Renee so badly but I was scared at the same time for fear of what the doctor will tell me. Once I reached the nurse's desk, Raj was there to greet me. She didn't look nervous to talk to me so I took that as a good sign. However, a big part of her job is to show her game face to patient's families, so that blows my theory right out of the window.

"Hello, Mr. Douglas, how are you today?" she said as she came out from behind her desk.

"Tell me my wife is awake and I'll be just fine."

"She's still sedated but is improving. Dr. Amsterdam is in with her now. She will be out soon and give you an update."

"You don't know?"

"I really can't say but please, don't worry."

They wouldn't let me back there so I had no choice but to wait in the waiting room. I was giving it five more minutes and then I was going in no matter what. Raj must have sensed my anxiety from earlier and walked over with a cup of coffee for me.

"Not exactly what I need at the moment but I will take it anyway, thank you."

"You are welcome. Dr. Amsterdam has finished with rounds and will be out in a minute to speak with you. My shift is over Mr. Douglas, stay strong and I will see you tomorrow."

"That means my wife will still be on the ICU floor tomorrow?"

"Not necessarily. It means as long as Dr. Amsterdam is her doctor, you will see me too."

I placed my hand over my heart to calm my nerves. I was never a fan of hospitals. You had to see me when Renee had the kids, I was a complete mess with almost passing out once when she pushed out Rogan.

"Good morning Mr. Douglas, I've just come from examining your wife, and I'm happy to say she's doing well, so much that she's fighting the vent. I just removed it and hopefully in a matter of hours she will wake up."

"Oh, thank god! Can I see her now?"

"Absolutely. She's in room 4115."

I nearly dropped my coffee after the doctor told me about Renee. She's always been strong and she would never give up without a fight. When I entered her room, I was thankful she was the only patient in here. I closed the door behind me and grabbed a chair to sit beside her. The sounds of the monitors all beeped in a synchronized rhythm. One would stop and another would sound off. The side of her face was marred by road rash, and she had bruises and abrasions lining her arms and her hands. Where are her rings? Pangs of guilt hit my heart like a baseball bat. My wife never took her wedding rings off and to see her hand bare made me feel sick. I hated myself for hurting her and even angrier for not being able to save Renee from getting struck by that car. I was too far away from her and all I could do was to watch in horror as my wife got hurt. I held her hand in mine and leaned over to kiss her forehead. She had multiple IV's in her arms and was careful not to get in the way of them.

"Hey baby, I'm here. Yeah, that's stupid. Where else would I be? When I saw you last night standing on the other side of the street, you took my breath away. You looked so beautiful and your smile, your smile righted every wrong in my life. All I wanted to do was reach you, hold you, and love you for the rest of my life. So, in order to do all those things, you need to wake up for me and put me to the task, okay?"

I kissed every mark on her battered skin and then prayed for God to hear me and make her well. "Renee, please come back to me. I love you." I stayed by her bedside the entire day and through the night forgoing the hotel. They tried to kick me out but this time I refused. I would camp outside the door if I had to but it didn't come to that.

So this is how I spent the next three days. The "team" kept reassuring me that she was getting better and stable but to me, she was in a functioning coma and every day I sat here watching her broke me down a little more by the day. This was killing me and I had no idea what to do. Both Rogan and Emily have been texting me which I have been ignoring to the best of my ability but I know them and they have to be wondering what's going on with their mother and me.

I have to call them but what will I say? Emily helped me plan this entire surprise for her mother. My beautiful girl is such a romantic and all she wants is for me to fly in on my magic carpet and fly her mom away to paradise.

By the fourth day, I was climbing out of my skin after spending the last 48-hours at the hospital. I had returned to the hotel after her doctor forced me to leave to get some rest. My energy was depleted and as tired as I was, I didn't believe I could sleep. The room had been cleaned and the sheets didn't smell of Renee anymore, so I took out her favorite perfume and sprayed the bedding just so I can have a piece of her with me.

I only had a duffel with me with minimal clothing so once again I called down to the concierge to help me with a few things. This time I didn't forget my manners and asked him his name which is Franco. He was more than happy to assist me in the shopping department. The hotel has personal shoppers on call from Saks, so one phone call later to confirm my sizes and I had a new wardrobe delivered by the afternoon.

Once I had eaten and showered and dressed for the day, I took some time to go through Renee's things. She had her papers strewn all over the desk and I had just finished putting everything in her briefcase when I saw her speech with red markings all over it. It was supposed to be the original speech she was going to give. I looked around for another copy but I didn't find one. My interest was definitely piqued and I looked through her papers again and found a business card of the event coordinator from the conference. Jacque Gillespie, I immediately called her and thankfully she answered on the second ring.

"Hi, my name is Lawson Douglas, and my wife is Dr. Renee Douglas. Yes, thank you for that. She's in stable condition and still in the ICU. Thank you for the flowers, unfortunately, patients can't have them in there but the nurses love them. Anyway, let me get to the reason for my call. I found my wife's speech with her things and it seems to be heavily edited. I was wondering if you had a copy of what she delivered to the conference?"

"Oh, Mr. Douglas, do I ever! The keynote speeches are always recorded and streamed for the members that are not able to attend. I can send you the file and you can see your brilliant wife in all her amazement. I am telling you, sir, she just floored me."

I let out a frustrating sigh before interrupting her banter. Did this girl ever stop talking? "I truly appreciate it, Jacque, but I need to go. Yes, I will send your best." My phone beeped right away with the incoming file. I clicked it open and watched my wife. She always looked beautiful but she seemed nervous standing at the podium. She bounced on her feet for a moment or two and then began her speech.

"Please welcome, Dr. Renee Douglas, your keynote speaker." She received a standing ovation.

"Thank you. Thank you. I truly appreciate your warm welcome. I'd like to also extend my gratitude to The Elliman Wellness Foundation for inviting me to join all of you here this evening. I have to say I was surprised to hear what topic I would be addressing this evening. So, let's talk about communication."

"That is one subject that I don't believe not one person in this room has mastered, including myself. I may have many degrees that line the walls of my office that prove I know what I'm talking about most of the time, but I have to be honest here and admit to you that I wish some days could just be silent. I can be silent and just listen. Yes, communication is key to any successful relationship we have in our

lives. From marriage to friendships, it's a key component and one we can't live without unless you want to spend your life in a world of silence. I've recently learned a valuable lesson on this very subject. You see, I've been married for 25 years and so much in love since I was sixteen years old. Along the way of getting everything we ever wanted, some things in our lives were so loud that we actually went silent."

"It took a major wake-up call in my life to realize that I was too busy and wrapped up in my career and putting the needs of my patients first, then my children, and lastly, my husband. It's very easy to exert power and control over others when you're the one at the top of the food chain. The truth of the matter is, I stopped listening. I never knew how much my avoidance of certain things in our lives was costing my family, especially my husband. But I certainly did know on the night he finally had enough and reached his breaking point with me. Of course, I was totally taken off guard and played the victim and blamed him for everything."

"Why did I do that? It's a question I've been asking myself for weeks now and have come up with this answer. I got used to my own rules and totally disregarded the ones I had promised to my husband. I stopped listening. As I look around this room, I see the shock registering on your faces because I'm sure you were not expecting to hear this kind of speech from me. I guess I surprised myself too because I've never found myself in a situation that I couldn't control. A problem that I couldn't solve. Yes, all new territory for me, so this is not my usual speech that I give at conferences to a room filled with my peers. Right here and now is my confession. I'm not perfect."

I watched my phone screen and focused on my wife and then she did something I wasn't expecting, she laughed. I smiled at the sound of the carefree tone in her voice, a sound I have missed.

"Wow! The world didn't stop with those words, did it? No, I'm not perfect, far from it and it feels damn good to finally admit it. You can

open any medical textbook and look up the definition of communication and you will find many answers to this very complex subject. Look, let's be honest, it's not pretty. We make our living using our fine communication skills to help others but I am here to say, the real work begins at home. We can only be our best self when we acknowledge our faults first, and I intend to work on mine the minute I can board a plane and have a real conversation with my husband. One where I will listen and allow someone else the chance to speak because I now know I can't always take the lead."

"I'll leave you with this. You ever hear the reference a good painter is only as good as his paintbrush?" Yes, I know, I shuttered the first time I heard it too, but it has merit. A good communicator is only as good as their last conversation. Think about it and give youself time to really believe how it will apply to you, your patients, and your life. And while you're doing that I will say, "Thank you for your time."

Her speech had ended but the recording went on for a few minutes of unending applause and standing ovations. I saw a woman rush the stage and hug my wife hard. Her expression was classic Renee, I loved it. Renee wanted to see me as badly as I wanted her. She called her speech a confession but to me, it was an apology, and one she didn't say to me but to an entire room of her peers. This took courage for her to put it all out there and I have never been prouder of my wife.

My tears wouldn't stop. I paused the screen and it was frozen on Renee's smile. I let out a roar of pain and never prayed so hard in my life for my wife to come back to me. I had reached the hospital just in time for the evening rounds. Dr. Amsterdam had already been in to see Renee and was waiting for me at the nurse's station when I arrived.

"Good evening Mr. Douglas," greeting me warmly.

"It's Lawson, please. How's Renee?"

"The same. I ordered another MRI and the results are clear. I can't imagine how you feel being on this nerve-wracking timetable waiting for your wife to wake. All I can say with my complete medical assurance is, in fact, she will wake up. I believe something is holding her back and that's a mystery but if anyone can bring her back, it's you, Lawson. I've only known you for a little over a week, but I can tell you love her dearly."

"You have no idea."

"I think I do. Why don't you go in and sit with her? Maybe tonight is the night."

She looks so small in this big hospital bed. Most of her wires were now gone with just her IV line remaining. I kicked off my shoes and gently slid in beside her holding my wife and sending her all my love for her to feel.

"Have I told you how magnificent you are? I'm sure there had to be a few times through the course of our marriage but I figured I'll tell you again. I listened to your speech. It was wonderful and real. I don't know how you can stand up there and feel even a small sliver of the doubt when the masses you spoke to would not stop applauding. It was like you were a star up there speaking to your public. I am so very proud of you and I wish I could have been there right in the front row. I probably would have been competing with Jacque, your biggest fan. Yes, I didn't meet her but I sure got an earful from her on the phone."

"I haven't called the kids yet and I really don't think how much longer I can avoid them. I just don't want to worry them and you know Emily is going to freak and jump on the next plane to be here. I miss them both terribly but I know the minute I see them, I'm going to fall apart."

"Don't worry, I won't let you. I'm here, Daddy."

I looked up to see Emily standing in the doorway of Renee's room. I got up from the bed and sure enough, I lost it the minute I saw my daughter begin to cry. She walked right into my arms and buried her face in my chest.

"Oh, Em, I'm so sorry for not calling you sooner, I didn't know how to tell you."

"Rogan is here too, and grandpa. They couldn't stay away, so don't be angry. And before you ask about work, Alison has everything covered along with Ty and Paul."

"Work is the last thing on my mind but thank you for telling me. How did you find me here?"

"Well after you didn't return my calls, I called the hotel and found out mom was still registered. Before I could make any more inquiries, I got a call from Jacque Gillespie. She told me about the accident and of course, I called Rogan, and then he told grandpa, and now we are all here. Daddy, why didn't you call us right away? That's my mom in that hospital bed and we had a right to know our mother was nearly killed."

Before I could defend myself and my reasons for not calling her, Rogan rushed down the hallway with my father following. "Dad!" he called out.

"Em, let's continue this after I speak with Rogan."

"Oh, yes we will. Hey bro, give him hell."

"I got it, sis. Dad, how's mom?"

"She's stable. Let me say hi to grandpa and then we can all go somewhere quieter to talk." I walked over to embrace my father and he patted my back in return.

"How's our girl? I want to see my daughter in law."

"Let's go talk and I will give you all an update on Renee," Emily was peering over my shoulder with her eyes focused on her mother. Our kids needed to see her and spend some time with her. I gave them some time to do that and I just quietly waited in the corner of the room while listening to my kids cry over her still body.

They both kissed her hands and wiped away their tears. Emily had noticed right away that her wedding rings were missing. I explained to our daughter that after I located the rings with the rest of Renee's belongings, I discovered that they were damaged in the accident. As soon as I could, I would repair them and vow to see them on her hand again. I watched my father lean over and kiss her forehead before wiping away his own tears. They all surrounded me and we stood in silence hugging each other and praying for Renee to wake up. I spoke to Raj and told her that I would be returning to the hotel with my family for a while and would be back later. She had printed passes for the kids and my father to return with no issue even if it was beyond visiting hours. The cab ride was quiet back to the hotel. I knew they would have many questions about Renee.

"Is anyone hungry? I can order room service."

"Dad, we're not here for a vacation and a day at the spa. I want to know about mom."

"Okay, Rogan, Emily, and dad, please take a seat and I will explain. As you know, I flew here to surprise your mother and make things right with us. I arrived shortly after she finished giving her speech which was amazing by the way, and I was just standing across the street and that's when I saw your mother on the other side. She looked so beautiful and happy, more like at peace. I called out to her and she saw me and your mom smiled. The light had changed and we began walking toward each other. I don't know what happened but she fell down to the street and I tried to get to her but then a taxi ran the light and struck your mother head-on. All I heard was screeching tires and the sound of crunching metal leaving your mother in the middle of the street."

"Oh my god, poor mom. Daddy, we need to be with her."

"And you will. Let's take this time to talk and then we can go back." The kids agreed and I continued on with my explanation.

"The taxi driver was drunk. After the ambulance took your mother away, I wanted to kill that bastard but I was held back by the cops."

"Dad, you should have called us immediately. She's our mother and she could have died without us being here. Are you that fucking selfish that you don't know that?"

"Rogan, calm down," my father admonished him for his outburst.

"I know you are angry and have every right to be. I wanted to call you but I just didn't know how to find the words. This is your mother's department. I just couldn't do it. I have never been so terrified in all of my life. What I experienced, I will never be able to unsee. I'm sorry if you think I was being selfish but I needed those moments with your mom." My son wiped away more of his tears and lunged forward to hug me.

"I'm sorry dad, forgive me. We can't lose her."

"We won't, Rogan."

"Son, we understand but how could you believe you could take all of this on by yourself? We are your family and we love Renee just as much as you do."

"Yeah, I don't think so. She's my life dad and I need her to wake up and come back to me."

"She will daddy, she just has to."

"Okay, if you're ready, let's go back to the hospital. Dad, do you want to rest for a while and then I can send back a car for you?"

"I'm fine, stop worrying. I want to see my girl."

I guess I couldn't argue with my father when he got like this. It's not like I couldn't blame them. I just need Renee to wake up and we can begin to put this nightmare behind us.

"Okay, I'm going in first to check on mom and then I'll step out and you can go in."

"Daddy, why can't we just go in now?"

"You're right, go in and see your mom."

I watched Emily and Rogan each take a side with their mother, and my dad standing at the foot of the bed. My heart was aching taking in the scene before me. I couldn't do it and had to get some air. I walked down the hall and stood by a window placing my forehead against the glass.

Of course, he followed me. "Are you alright, son?"

"No, far from it. I'm out of my depth here and have no clue on what to do. What if I lose her dad?"

"Talking like that will not help you or your family. She's fighting son, it's just taking some time."

"How much more? The waiting and pacing these hospital floors is exhausting. The hours seem to just tick by at a snail's pace and it's so quiet, I can't even think straight."

"Let's go back in there. Emily has probably cried a bucket's worth already and Rogan has seemed to take over the pacing for you. They need you son. You need to be strong for your kids."

"I need Renee."

"I know and she needs you too. Go to her and tell her that. She'll come back to you. I know it, Lawson. This is not the end for you and Renee not when you have so much more to experience with one another. She's fighting her way back, I know she is. Now you go and be strong for her."

"Thank you, dad. I know this can't be easy on you, especially after losing mom."

"Don't worry about me, I'm fine. Your mom is watching over all of us right now. I know you may believe you get all of your strength from me. It's easy to think that way with fathers and sons, but it's really from your mom. She was the strongest person I knew and the way she fought in her final days was a miraculous testament to the person she was. You have that same fight in you and now you need to pass it to Renee."

I hugged my father so hard, I feared I may have hurt him but then he returned the same force of hug back to me. It wasn't easy for a man like Roman Douglas to express what he was feeling but he did it for me tonight because he knew it was exactly what I needed.

CHAPTER
Sixteen

PAST...

Renee

"Do you like this house?" My husband excitedly asked as he practically bounced on his heels.

"Lawson, it's not a house, it's more like a mansion."

"Yeah, maybe, but if we are going to fill it will kids then we need a lot of rooms."

"Can we afford this?"

"Baby, I run my own company and the last time I looked at my bank statement, yeah, we can afford this."

"So what you're saying is this is the house that we are going to raise a family in."

"Exactly. Let's get started."

Before I could even blink, Lawson had me over his shoulders and running up to the house. "Did you already buy this house and this is why you have a key and now are opening the front door?"

"Oh, baby, I wouldn't buy a house without you seeing it first but I did charm the panties off the real estate agent and she's allowing me to get a feel for the house before I sign, no we sign the contracts later today. Let's go check out where our master bedroom will be, maybe we will make a baby today."

"You are crazy," I said as I swatted his ass.

"Crazy for you," he responded and swatted mine in return.

He carried me all the way to the top of the landing and did not put me down into we were standing in the middle of the vast bedroom with French doors leading out to a balcony. Natural light radiated throughout the room. It was lovely and all I could imagine was sitting in the corner rocking our baby with Lawson playing the guitar.

"This is beautiful, I love it and I want the house."

"You sure?"

"Yes, this house is everything I want and every time I look at it, I can't help but imagine we building our life here together like we always promised each other. Yes, let's do this."

"Yes! I love you, Renee. I promise to always make you as happy as you have made me."

"I love you too. Let's make a family."

PRESENT...

"Dr. Amsterdam, here are the results from her latest labs."

"Thank you, Raj. Let me take a look. This is so frustrating. Everything is normal and in perfect range. Her MRI is normal with no bleeds and her leg is healing. I just don't understand it, Raj, why isn't my patient waking up? I don't know what to tell her family at this point. It just doesn't make sense."

"Why don't you talk to her husband? Maybe he can help?"

"At this point, I will try anything. Do you know where he is?"

"Yeah, they went to get coffee and should be back in a few minutes."

"Okay, page me when the family returns."

Is Lawson here? I wanted to open my eyes and find out what the hell was going on but they felt heavy and my body wasn't cooperating at the moment. I heard the door open and close as I tried to come up to the surface but again I felt as if a heavy weight was keeping me down.

"Dr. Amsterdam, it's been five days since the accident. Why isn't my wife waking up?"

He's here. I wasn't imagining him. Yes, I remember. He came to New York to see me and I got hit by a car trying to get to him. OMG! Wake up, Renee. Your family is here sobbing over you and you're just laying here doing nothing to help them.

"Medically speaking, she is recovering. Something has to be holding her back, I just don't know what that is."

"So, this could be all in her head?"

"Something like that. I have to get personal here, Mr. Douglas, is there a reason why your wife may not want to come back to you and your children?"

"Why would you ask me that?"

"I'm sorry, I don't mean to pry but in this case, I have to for the sake of my patient's recovery. I don't know you or the past you share with your wife. I've seen how worried you've been. Having said that, I still have to ask questions that may make you feel uncomfortable. More importantly, I have no medical reason to offer you and your family as to why she is not waking up. The only reason why I am even entertaining this line of questioning is that I've seen it before in other patients. It's like they are blocked, maybe even afraid to face something in their life before the accident."

"I don't know how to answer you, doctor, she was practically run over and maybe the trauma of almost being killed is keeping her asleep."

"Maybe. I'll check back later."

PAST...

"What do you want from me, Renee?"

"What do I want? How could you ask me that? I want you, Lawson. I want our marriage. What the hell do you want? Oh, that's right, I remember. You asked me for a divorce. Tell me, Lawson, is that what you really want from me?"

"Stop pushing me, Renee, you know that was a mistake and one that I will forever regret. I know I hurt you deeply and I am so sorry for that."

"You always said apologies were just words and actions were the real apologies."

"I know and I still believe that."

"Okay, so what's it going to be, Lawson?"

"Meaning?"

"The grand gesture. The big over the top moment to win me back?"

"I have no idea, Renee. I know I love you and I wish that was enough right now but I know it's not. You don't know how much I hate myself right now, so much that I just want to punch myself in the face and knock my stupid ass out."

"Okay, that's a start. Listen, I have a plane to catch, New York, is waiting for me."

"Knock'em dead."

"I will, I always do. Is that where I went wrong with us?"

"I don't know what you mean."

"Sure you do. It's my over-confidence, right? I behave as if I have all the answers to every single problem and I doctor you too much instead of being a wife because that's what you have needed me to be."

"Renee, I'm sorry."

"Yeah, you've said that. See you, Lawson."

CHAPTER
Seventeen

PRESENT...

Lawson

"Daddy, I'm going to say good-night to mom and then head back to the hotel with grandpa and Rogan."

"Spend as much time as you need, I'll be outside."

While our kids were in there with Renee, I lit some candles in the chapel and prayed for my wife. I didn't have a clue on how to fix my life. All I knew is that I want my wife back and she needs to wake up so I can do everything in my power to make things right between us.

I said goodbye to the kids and my dad. They got rooms in the same hotel so we could all be close to one another. It's been a super long day and I was worried that my father was overdoing it but he basically told me to kiss his ass and be quiet about it. I love my father and his bluntness way of setting me straight.

I took my wife's hand in mine and held it to my heart. "Renee, is it my fault that you are not waking up? I know I hurt you and maybe this is your way of protecting yourself from the pain I caused you. I wouldn't blame you if this is my punishment, I deserve it but the kids don't. Our kids need you to come back to them. I need you. I need my wife to forgive me and just open your eyes. I would do anything to be able to return to the night of my birthday and instead of being stupid, take you in my arms and love you."

"You're not stupid." *What?*

"Renee? Come on baby, keep talking to me."

"I'm here, Lawson, and I'm not going anywhere." She coughed a few times clearing her throat. I reached for the pitcher of cool water and poured some in a cup. I held it to her lips as she slowly took a few sips.

"Thank you," she softly whispered.

"You scared the hell out of me. Oh, my god, Renee, I thought I was losing you. Please tell me I haven't. There is nothing we can't conquer as long as we are together."

"That's my guy, dive right into the hard stuff."

"I'm sorry, I'm just so grateful I'm looking into your beautiful eyes. The kids are here and dad is too. I'm going to call them right now and they'll come back." She reached for my hand to stop me from leaving. Her eyes were warm.

"Lawson, slow down. It's late and they need their rest especially your father. If it's okay, I just want you right now." I visibly relaxed.

"Yeah, it's okay. Anything you want, baby, I will do for you."

"Will you kiss me?"

I cupped her face and kissed her chastely at first and then she beautifully opened up for me and it turned passionately. "God, I love you. I love you so much. Thank you for coming back to me. I swear to you, Renee, I will never ever hurt you again for as long as I draw breath."

"Lawson, please, let me come up for air and say something to you."

"Okay, go on."

"I had a lot of time to process everything that happened between us and to tell you the truth, I'm kind of over it. You made a mistake and I punished you for it. I vilified you and made myself blameless and that was wrong. I've been going back to the past and the here and now and you know what?"

"What?"

"We've had more good than bad and a few hiccups along the way, but nothing so bad that justifies divorce. We promised that we would grow old together and even die on the same day. I never gave up on anything in my life, and neither have you. So, I'm not going anywhere and if you are, then I'll follow you."

"I promise I will never..." She placed her fingers over my mouth and then kissed me again.

"Lawson, no more promises, okay?"

"I don't understand?"

"We don't need any new ones, not when the original ones are still intact."

"Really?"

"Yes, really. You are the one I love and I would have to be deaf and blind not to know how much you love me. Can I ask you a question?"

"You can."

"When I was asleep, I had so many dreams of us and our life together. Some of it was fuzzy but I pretty much understood where my memories were taking me to. I remember asking you before I left for my trip what your grand gesture would be to win me back. So, I guess my question is, were you coming to New York to sweep me off my feet?"

"Yeah, something like that. I expected our reunion to be a little more graceful than watching my wife get hit by a car. That was the scariest moment of my life and I wanted to kill the driver that hurt you."

"Yeah, I imagine you did. I remember hearing your voice and me turning around looking for you. At first, I thought I was just missing you so much that I wanted to believe you were there and then you were and I was so happy. Remind me to never wear five-inch heels again."

"Never, not when they make those legs of yours look so damn sexy."

"You're the sexy one, I'm just trying to keep up."

"Oh, baby, no it's me that's been trying to keep up with you. You never knew how beautiful you are and not just on the outside, but on the inside too. I see you practically kill yourself with all those crazy diets and work-out routines, and I'm like, what is she doing? You are gorgeous and I think it's about time you begin to believe it."

"Okay, I'll try."

"Thank you, my love. Renee?"

"Hmmm"

"What's next for us?"

"You come home to me if that's what you truly want?"

"With all my heart, baby. You really forgive me?"

"Yes, and if it's all the same to you Lawson, I don't ever want to talk about it again. It's over and in the past, let's keep it there where it belongs."

Even in the face of crisis, my wife was so strong and honest about her feelings. I loved her so much. I took her face in my hands and kissed her ever so gently. Dr. Amsterdam came into the room shortly after and checked on Renee. She was relieved that Renee was sitting up and talking. She was hopeful with a few more day's rest and help from a physical therapist, Renee would be strong enough to fly home.

"Do you have any questions for me, Renee?" her doctor asked.

"I know you said you're confident I will make a full recovery but just look at my leg. I have plates and screws and more tubes than I have ever seen in my life. How am I going to be able to do this?"

"Simple. You are going to follow my orders down to the last bolt in your leg. The tubes will come out once the sites are completely drained and I see no sign of infection. Recovery can take up to four months to the latter six months, but I promise you, Renee, with hard work in physical therapy, I'm confident you will be able to resume your routine again."

"Will I have a limp? Or need to use a cane?"

"You may at first through the recovery process but once you are strong enough and making positive progress, the helpful aides won't be necessary. Try not to worry about all you may or may not need. Let's focus on what we have right now. Your wound sites need to drain. I need to get you on your feet after that, and then we will get you home. I've met your family, and your husband here never left your side, I think you are in good hands."

"You got that right," I interrupted the pep talk she was giving to my wife. "I'm here Renee, and I will get you through this."

"Okay, that's enough for tonight. How's your pain level?"

"I'm managing." She hesitantly answered.

"Renee, you don't have to brave it and it's actually counterproductive to fight against the pain while you're recovering. So I'll ask again, on a scale of 1 to 10, how's your pain level?" my stubborn wife closed her eyes and sighed.

"Renee, tell the doctor."

"Fine, it's high right now, probably a solid 8."

"Thank you for telling me. I'm going to give you ten minutes more with your husband and then you get some good night medicine and by the time you wake in the morning, you will see the rest of your family."

"Thank you, Dr. Amsterdam," I said for the both of us.

"A solid 8? Baby, why are you being so stubborn?" I asked her as I crawled back in beside her.

"Lawson, it's a miracle I woke up at all. I'm not so eager to go back to sleep."

"Okay, I can see how you would feel that way but your body needs the rest to heal, and I want you home. Isn't that what you want?"

"Yes, of course, it is, but…"

"What? Talk to me, babe."

"I'm scared."

"Nothing is going to happen to you, not on my watch. Please take the pain medicine and I promise you when you open your eyes, I will be here waiting and loving you."

"Fine. Will you kiss me first?"

"Try to stop me." I kissed my beautiful wife and I had never been more thankful to have her in my arms. As I kissed her and told her I loved her, Dr. Amsterdam came in and added the sleep-aid to her IV bag. A few moments later, she was sound asleep.

"I love you, Renee."

CHAPTER
Eighteen

PRESENT...

Renee

After I finally gave in and stopped fighting my doctor, I willed my body to accept the medicine. Lawson must have forgotten but I have an extreme tolerance for pain and I know what my body can and cannot handle. I had only been sleeping for maybe four hours when I woke up to feel Lawson asleep beside me.

I knew he wouldn't leave, especially after promising to be here in the morning. I miss the kids and want to see them. I miss everything about our life and I can't wait to get out of this bed so I can return to it. He stirred a bit but remained sleeping. I felt around for my phone and once I had it in my hand, I opened up the camera and snapped a selfie of my beautiful sleeping husband. I moved my head to one side to hide my cuts and bruises. I sent the picture to the kids with the caption, "Look who's awake. I love you and I will see you soon."

I wish I could turn and snuggle with Lawson but my leg was still braced above the bed and being hooked up to monitors didn't help much. I closed my eyes and slept for a couple of more hours and then I was done with resting.

"Okay, I'm up," he mumbled against my shoulder. "I'm proud of you for lasting this long. How do you feel?"

"I'm fine and need to get out of this bed."

"Yeah, fat chance at that happening but I love your positivity."

He kissed me swiftly and then got up from my bed. I watched Lawson give his body a deep stretch with moving his neck from side to side. "Feel better?"

"I'll be better when I get you out of here. I'm going to get some coffee and then call the kids."

"Already handled. I suspect the kids are on their way."

"What did you do?" he smiled as I handed him my phone.

"I should have known. Tell me you slept a little bit?"

"I did, and I promise if I was in any pain, I would have woken you up."

"Okay, I believe you. Now give me a proper greeting." He was so handsome even more so with his day-old beard. It was just the right amount of dusting that just made Lawson Douglas so unbelievably sexy. He held my face, I loved when he did this and caressed my cheeks with his fingers.

"Mom?" our kiss ended when our daughter called out. Oh my Emily, she looked beautiful but sad at the same time with tears glazed over.

"Come here baby, I'm fine," I said. Emily rushed over to my bed with Rogan quickly following behind her. They each gave me a hug and held on to my hands with Rogan leaning his head down. Lawson stepped up behind him and rubbed his shoulder telling him I was going to be fine, but I don't think he really believed it. It took me a little time to convince him that I would be coming home soon.

"Don't cry son, I swear I'm okay. Yes, I'm banged up and my leg doesn't look that great but I will recover."

"Mom, we almost lost you."

"There was no way of that happening. No more tears, okay?"

"How are you so calm?" asked Emily.

"They give some good drugs here."

"Yeah right! You wouldn't even take an aspirin for a headache."

"Where's Roman? Dad said he was here with you."

"He is. He's downstairs in the gift shop probably buying out the florist."

"There's my girl," sure enough they were right. Roman walked in with a huge bouquet of roses. "How are you darling?" he asked and then kissed me on the top of my head.

"Sore but on the mend."

"Don't you scare me like that again, you hear me? I don't want to live in a world without you in it." He kissed me again and then wiped away his falling tears.

"I promise, no more scares with New York taxies. Speaking of which, what happened to the driver?"

"He's in jail after he was denied bail," said Lawson. "The bastard is lucky he's behind bars. I wanted to beat the hell out of him but New York's finest held me back." *He's still my protector.*

"I'm happy for that. I don't need you in jail too."

So my doctor may have stretched the truth a bit about the recovery process. I ended up staying in New York for an additional two weeks until they removed all my drains and got me on my feet to begin physical therapy which royally sucked.

It was days filled with pain and I feared I was going to become dependent on the pain meds so I said no more to the pills and focused on what I know, and that's my inner strength to get through it. I have been through tough situations with my patients and now I'm the patient, so it's best to follow my own advice at least from time to time. I laughed quietly to myself because doctors make the worse patients ever.

Roman and the kids went home to Georgia two days after I woke up after I insisted they return to their lives. Emily and Gus were in the middle of planning their wedding, which now has been postponed because of me. I felt awful and argued with my daughter to no avail of my stubborn daughter changing her mind. *"You are not going to change my mind on this mom, it's done and Gus agrees."*

"Emily, it's a cast, and there is no reason why you have to postpone anything because I have a broken leg. Your father can twirl me around in a wheelchair."

"No! it's not good enough and the wedding is off until I can watch my parents dance with each other."

"This conversation is not over, only on hold until I can get back home and talk some sense into you and Gus. I'll tackle the two of you and use my best power of persuasion."

"Don't forget, you mentored me on those skills."

My head pounded remembering that fight knowing how stubborn our daughter can be. Emily would not concede on anything which drove me absolutely insane. Rogan was easier. He knew I wasn't lying when I said I was okay and had enough with Lawson staying with me. He gave me a kiss on my forehead and a huge hug followed before leaving for their flight. He is so much like his grandfather and Lawson. What he was doing was good work that would help so many families and their farms. I understood it and so did Lawson.

I would be going home tomorrow on a private plane Lawson had arranged for us. He wanted me to be as comfortable as possible. A flight nurse and a member of my physical therapy team were also accompanying us on my return home trip. Lawson spared no expense to my aftercare and if I had any problems with my leg, I would have medical staff to step in and help.

Lawson went back to the hotel to pack our things and get some sleep. I wanted the night to myself to clear my head and figure out what comes next for us. He's coming home to live under the same roof again, that's one thing we established right away. Every once in a while he still slips in an apology but I keep telling him it's over and we will move on together and be stronger in the end.

"Knock, knock, how's my favorite patient doing?"

"You know, I believe I heard you say those exact words to Mr. Murphy yesterday."

"Well, he is handsome," we laughed. "So, tell me about you. How's the leg?"

"I'm okay and I was okay yesterday and the day before that."

"I'm just being thorough, habit." She shrugged her shoulders and examined my leg one more time before leaving for the night. "So, I've already spoken to your physical therapy team that will continue the program we started here for you. My only advice and I'm sure it may be tough for you to follow but pace yourself, okay? I know you have a busy life and a lot of people depend on you but you will be useless to all if you don't take care of you."

"It's funny you say that because that's the way my life has been like since I created one with Lawson. I've put my needs on the back burner and tended to my husband, our parents, our kids, and everything in between before myself. I figured because this is what I do for a living, I can manage my personal life just as well as my professional life."

"And? what does that look like?" Dr. Amsterdam questioned.

"Well, if you ask my husband, he would say a well-oiled machine."

"And you? what do you say?"

"It's a puzzle with a lot of scattered pieces that you try to fit in its perfect place. On most days, I would say Lawson has me all figured out right down to the way I organize the fine china, but who knows? The one thing I do know is that I need to change in a major way if I'm going to save my marriage."

"I'm not married at least to a person, for me, it's more my career. I've heard it's about give and take and a lot of compromise in between. You'll find the middle ground. You would have to be blind not to notice how much he loves you. Begin there and I think you both will find your way."

"Thanks, Dr. Amsterdam. I appreciate you saying that."

"My pleasure, Renee. Get some rest, you're going home tomor-row."

CHAPTER
Nineteen

PRESENT...

Lawson

They didn't know I was there and I shouldn't have been listening to their conversation but once I heard the sadness in Renee's voice, I knew I wasn't going anywhere. When I heard Dr. Amsterdam say goodbye to Renee, I ducked out of sight so she wouldn't see me. Once the coast was clear, I stepped inside of her room and she smiled when she saw me.

"Somehow, I knew I would be seeing you again tonight. Lawson, you are so tired and haven't slept since the night before my accident. You need to go back to that fancy hotel and get some rest."

"I'm fine and all our things are packed, I just need you." I kissed her gently but my wife wasn't having it. She pulled me down to her and crushed her mouth down to mine. I moaned with every slide of her tongue that touched mine. "Should I bust you out of here right now? Because you know I want that more than anything."

"I do too, but I promised my doctor one more night."

"Are you sure?" I asked her and then kissed her again.

"Sure about what? Going home tomorrow?"

"No, not about home."

"Then what?"

"Me, Renee. Are you sure you want me? because there is no one I want more in this life than you, and I promise you as long as I draw breath, I will never hurt you again."

"I want you, Lawson, how could you possibly believe otherwise?"

"I heard you talking with Dr. Amsterdam, and I know what doubt sounds like and maybe a little brokenness too."

"The only thing broken about me is my leg and that is healing as we speak. I love you and want nothing more than to go home with you and be with our family."

"Good. I like it when we are on the same page." We both laughed and shared a light moment between us. "Do you want me to stay? Because I can."

"No, go back to the hotel and pick me up in the morning."

As the limo ascended the hill that led to our home, both Renee and I began to feel the excitement and apprehension of being home and home together. My birthday party feels like a lifetime ago and the argument we had that drove me away feeling lost and confused. I hated that my personal confliction made me feel weak and not good enough for Renee or my family.

This life is the life I chose and the one I have always wanted with Renee since I was eighteen years old. I know she hasn't said much about it since we decided to put the past behind us and forget the past couple of months, but tell that to my heart or hers for that matter. She is incredibly strong, always has been and that's what scares me. I know she can take anything life throws at her, even surviving a car accident that nearly killed her. A blip in our marriage should be a piece of cake.

"Lawson, will you look at that," tapping me on the shoulder brought me back to the present. "There are welcome home signs everywhere, oh, I love our kids." She clapped her hands and was careful not to bounce up and down, not that she could do much with her injured leg.

The car came to a stop and then Rogan, Emily, Gus, my father, and Renee's parents all came charging at us waving their signs. It's been a long time since we all gathered together in one place. Her parents had retired and moved to Florida. They wanted to come to New York to be with her but once she woke up and I told her about it, she asked me to hand her a phone. That was a fun day listening to her father grump and of course, blame me. Yes, we had to overcome a lot of indifference in our relationship but I know they love me. I think he just gives me shit now just out of habit.

"Baby, you have to be tired. It's been a long day."

"I'm okay but I agree with you. I'm ready for bed."

"Is that an invitation?" I winked but secretly hoped it's what she was thinking too.

"You never need one but tonight would you mind just holding me?"

"You never have to ask, I'm just thankful you still want me there."

"Always, Lawson."

"Forever, Renee."

Yes, the cast was the biggest hurdle to overcome to get a decent night's rest but once we were in a comfortable position, it was bliss for the rest of the night. Renee was completely off her pain meds and managing her pain level on her own. I hated ever knowing she was in pain but she never would tell me. It's that invisible strength that lives and breathes inside of her.

CHAPTER
Twenty

PRESENT...

Renee

"Dammit! I can do this," I shouted at my therapist and felt frustrated.

"Renee, you are rushing the process and if you don't slow down, it's only going to impede your recovery."

"Robert, I can do this. I know my body and I know what I can and cannot do. Now, please hand me the weight and let's go again."

"No, I'm done for the day and so are you," he said and then put away all of the weights I use in my physical therapy.

"You're fired."

"Yeah, okay. Put your arm around my neck so I can move you to the couch."

"No, I am staying here and doing one more set."

"Renee, I'm a patient man and I will say you busting my balls three times a week is not fun but I endure it because I like you and want you well."

"But?" I asked.

"Today, I've reached my limit and you are starting to piss me off. So, put your arm around my neck or I may have to take extreme measures and haul you over my shoulder."

"Um, that won't be necessary. I think that's a job for her husband." I looked beyond my captor, Robert the tyrant and smiled brightly at Lawson who was impeccably dressed in a gorgeous three-piece suit. How did I miss that this morning? He practically stalked me with his sexy eyes until he could get his teeth on his prey—me.

"Hey baby," he said and leaned down to kiss me. "Why are you giving Robert a hard time when you know he is only trying to help you?"

"He's mean to me and he beats me," I couldn't even say that with a straight face before I gave up and just laughed.

"I'm guessing you can take over for me?"

"Yes, Robert, you can go. Thanks, man for everything."

"You are welcome, she? Not so much. See you on Wednesday, Princess."

"Nope, you're still fired."

"Sure, I am," he said over his shoulder as he grabbed his bag and walked out the door.

"Renee, he's right you know, this is not a race."

"It feels like one. I'm sorry but I can't help it. I hate that I have to use this stupid wheelchair when I'm too damn tired to use anything else."

"I'm not going to say I know what you're feeling because I don't but I'm here to vent to anytime you need to."

"Lawson, I know you are not going to want to hear this, but I need to get back to work."

"No, you're not ready. You need to take more time to heal. Renee, it will kill me if you get hurt again."

"Unless you hit me with a car, I'll be fine."

"That's not even remotely funny."

"I'm sorry but I need my work and I have to get back to my practice."

"Emily and Gus have been doing a great job and managing all the day-to-day along with Jeanie, it's fine."

"It's my practice, Lawson, and I need to get back to it," I said as I let out a frustrated huff.

"And you're my wife and I need you to be healthy." He countered.

I wanted to scream as loud as my lungs would allow and then pound my fists on his chest. I wasn't really angry with him, I just wanted to get back to me again.

"Talk to me, please."

"I want to say mean things to you."

"And?"

"Scream a little."

"I love you, Renee, and this to shall pass."

"I love you too and I'm sorry for being difficult."

"Yeah, okay we will go with that."

Without saying another word, my husband knew what I needed and carried me up to our room where he gave me the best massage that lulled me into sleep. With every knead to my sore muscles, I felt my body slowly relax. I felt the bed shift just slightly, probably Lawson changing out of his suit. I decided to be good and remain where I was.

One month later...

I was free. Free from the Lawson Douglas prison for one. Yes, it was okay for my husband to return to his empire but not me, especially when I was still in pain. I tried to hide it from him but to no avail, he knows me too well.

I refused to take the strong meds and ate the over the counter ones like candy until my stomach kicked my ass and said, no more. It's been three months since my accident and I am a star patient for my therapist. Robert is so pleased with my efforts and since I no longer complain, he has cut me back to two days a week. I've been slowly walking around the property and doing light yoga with a lot of assistance. At least my arms look fabulous.

Lawson kissed me goodbye and left me on my own to get to the office which means my driver awaits. I haven't been cleared to drive yet but that's okay, at least I'm going into the office. Today would just be about reconnecting with my assistant who has been so amazing throughout this entire ordeal. Emily and Gus will be there too.

Emily helped me do some online shopping for my post-accident wardrobe since my usual pencil skirts were out for now. I have a selection of comfy form-fitting maxi skirts in a ray of colors. I still have to wear a support brace but no more wheelchair or walker. To be walking on two legs is a miracle in itself, so this girl is not complaining. As I rode the elevator up to my office my phone has pinged twice. I just smiled knowing it was Lawson. I texted back that I was fine and powering down for a while so I could enjoy my morning with my staff. He texted back that wouldn't stop him from bugging Jeanie on her cell.

"Welcome Home" was all I heard as I walked through my office. I guess it was fitting since this was my home away from home with many hours spent here. I loved what I do but it was time to make a change. Recuperating at home allowed a lot of thinking time to decide on what comes next in my life. Lawson has cut back on his work and has given Rogan a lot more responsibility along with Ty and Paul. We've been talking more and trying to focus on the now instead of the past. Yes, we agreed it's important, but we can't live there like we used to. So, knowing all that has brought me here today and hopefully, my news will be welcomed and a step in a new direction not only for my daughter but for me too.

"You guys are wonderful. I love the signs and the balloons. I love you."

"Oh, mom, we are just so happy to see you here," Emily said as she pulled me close for a hug.

"That goes double for me," I said as Jeanie gave me a hug and then Gus too."

"You look, fabulous mom, I swear you are glowing."

"Thank you, Gus, but you just saw me a few days ago. Have I changed that much?"

"I guess I mean just full of life happy."

"Yes, I am happy to be back here but I'm not sure for how long. Listen, let's dry up the tears and get right to it," I said as I walked as poised as I could manage to my desk.

"What is it, mom? What do you mean by that? Are you not ready to return to work? Because we have it covered and your patients seem to have acclimated to me, and even Gus has taken on a few new clients."

"Everyone take a breath, especially you, Emily. Let me get a coffee and settle in and then we will order some lunch and talk."

"Mom, I—" My happy daughter was slowly crumbling before me until I raised my hands up to stop the tears I knew would come next.

"I'm fine and I wouldn't be here if I wasn't. I just need some time to myself and then when I'm ready, I will call you all in."

"Fine, I'll be in my office. Gus, are you coming?"

"Jeanie, please stay."

"Okay boss, what's going on?"

"Nothing extreme as my daughter believes. This," I gestured my hands all around the room, "is great. Thank you."

"You are welcome. Now talk to me. What's going on?"

"I guess it started in New York, and way before that stupid taxi hit me. Aside from that unfortunate incident, it was great."

"Yes, I love the highlight reel that Jacque sent me. Your speech was awesome. You never veer off the script."

"You're right, and that's the problem. I never do anything out of my comfort zone and I truly believe that is why Lawson exploded at me on the night of his birthday."

"What do you mean, Renee? I'm not following where I think you are going with this."

"Living apart from Lawson opened my eyes to a lot of things that I was blind to, so to speak. My entire life is a schedule and for a long time, I loved it that way until something got missed and I was alone. When I asked Lawson to leave, I thought he would take a day or two to calm down and then practically crawl back to me on his knees, but he didn't. Maybe deep down he wanted to but he needed to stand on his own for a while and I had to do the same. And now he's home and it feels like everything is new and shiny and I'm afraid if I go back to the 'old me' then what we are trying to work on is going to get tarnished and I will lose him for good."

"I can't believe I am hearing this, and from you no less. If the roles were reversed and a client was saying the same words to you, I know you wouldn't be so eager to just advise him or her to just forget who they are and pacify their partner. I mean, is that what this is? Because Renee, it's going to backfire in your face."

"Jeanie, it's not what I am doing, and need I remind you that I am the doctor of the mind here, not you. I'm still me for fuck's sake! I have realized that I am not above changing and if I'm being honest, I treated my marriage like an object I could control and I'm so angry with myself for doing that I just want to punch myself in the face until I knock myself out." *I paused for a minute and smiled remembering how my husband told me that he wanted to do the same thing to himself when we were apart. I guess we are more alike than we realize.* "Lawson deserves better than what I've been able to give him and that's what today's meeting is about."

"Okay, go on."

"I've built this practice from the very first patient that trusted us enough to treat, coach, whatever they needed and now with Emily and Gus on board, I don't have to do it all."

"Okay, but they are not doctors like you, and we need a 'you' to make this practice work."

"I agree and I'm not going anywhere but I will significantly be cutting back. I can't work fourteen-hour days anymore. Emily and Gus are doing a fabulous job with their coaching clients and gaining more by the week. I met many up and coming therapists in New York that are looking for a change and I think our practice may be what they are looking for. I have three in mind and I sent their information to your e-mail. Read it over and set up some interviews for next week."

"Wow, okay, I'm officially stunned."

"Yeah, I think Lawson will be too."

"You haven't told him yet?"

"Nope, and I'm not going to until I see how my choices work out."

"That's where I come in, right?"

"Exactly, you are my secret weapon to weed out the bad and bring in only the best. Can I count on you?"

"You know that you can. I will always support you, Renee, I guess I'm just worried that you may be jumping into something for the wrong reasons. He's not going anywhere. Hasn't he proven that already?"

"Yes, without a doubt. The point you are missing is that I am not just doing this for my husband's benefit, I'm doing it for me too. Jeanie, it's so easy to blame your partner for anything and everything wrong in your relationship because the other is afraid to take responsibility for their contributing part. I was that person. I didn't know Lawson was conflicted about his career and the direction his life was taking until the night of his birthday."

"My incessant need for control drove my husband away that night long before I asked him to leave. We are on solid ground again but I truly believe this is a right move for not only me but for the practice as well. All that I am asking is for you to be by myside and help me through this transition."

"Okay, I'll be here for you."

"That's my girl. Thank you."

"Yeah, you're welcome."

I hugged Jeanie with everything I had. Her reservations came from a good place and I understood why we needed to talk before I could move forward with my plans. Three months ago I would have never entertained this idea, but I'm also not the same person I was back then. This is right, I know it is. Now, I have to explain it to my husband.

CHAPTER
Twenty-One

PAST...

Lawson

"**K**eep your eyes closed or I will be forced to blindfold you," I said as my curious wife giggled in my arms. "We just have a few more steps and then we will be there."

"You know I love surprises, but the best ones always come from you."

"That I know my wife, and we're here," I kissed her on her lips before giving her permission to open her eyes. "Okay beautiful, you may open them."

I watched in wonder as Renee slowly opened her eyes to our picnic under the stars. It was a gorgeous night here in Savannah, and it seemed like the sky was lit up just with the twinkling stars shining on us. Who needed the moon when we had our own light show up there? "Oh, Lawson, this is beautiful. I love it and I love you for always giving me moments like this."

I turned her around and held her in my arms kissing her passionately until we were out of breath. "I love you so much and I know our lives are busy with two careers, two kids, two dogs, but I wouldn't change it for anything in the world to have this night with you."

PRESENT...

"What do you want for lunch? The guys were talking Thai, but pizza works too. Hello? Earth to Lawson."

"Excuse me, what?"

Alison laughed and handed me the menus. "You seemed a million miles away. I was talking about lunch. Choose something fast, we have a hungry group and they are waiting for you."

"Order anything you want, I'm not hungry."

"You okay, boss?"

"Yes, I'm fine. Will you excuse me, Alison? I have to make some calls."

"Sure thing. You're free for the next hour and then you have a meeting with the deputy mayor of Savannah."

"Cancel it, better yet, cancel the rest of my day. And for the future, I only meet with the mayor and not his lackey."

"Lawson!? What has gotten into you?"

"Please just do as I ask."

"Yes, sir."

I scrolled through my contacts and found the number I needed, dialing right away. "Yeah, it's me. I need to see you."

I stopped my knock in mid-air when the door swung open and he stepped aside to let me in. "Wow, I thought my ears were bleeding when I heard your voice on the other end."

"Yeah, well the feeling is mutual but what can I say? I needed to talk and you are the only one that I can basically say anything to and if I don't like your reply, I say fuck-off and we're still friends."

"You can tell me to fuck-off when you are paying me by the hour, and starting right now, you are."

"Thanks, Dalton."

"So, tired of getting analyzed by the misses? You call her biggest competition?"

"Oh, yeah? If that's true, then why did Renee give the keynote speech in New York, and you didn't?"

"Fuck you, okay, now that the usual pleasantries are done. What can I do for you, Lawson?"

"Renee hasn't called you, has she?"

"As a friend, yes. If you're asking me as a client, you know I cannot tell you that."

"Yeah, I know."

"The clock is ticking and I moved my day around for you, so talk."

"Why did I do it, Dalton?"

"Do what exactly?"

"You're really going to make me say it?"

"Oh, yes, I love it when the great Lawson Douglas screws up so badly that he ends up on my doorstep."

"Are you done? because I really need some advice and I'm not kidding here."

"I'm sorry. You and Renee have been so stressed and it's like a game of chess. Both of you are afraid to make a move without calling checkmate. She's been through hell these last few months trying with everything she has to recover and get back to where she was before that dreadful accident."

"And what about before? Is she trying to get back to Renee before her husband of twenty-five years shattered her entire world by asking her for a divorce, or just the walking/running Renee before a New

York taxi plowed her down and almost made her roadkill?"

"Let's dial it back for a minute, okay? You fucked up and it was huge but not unfixable. Renee knows that and for all that's holy in the world, she is trying to move on from it, and you should too."

"She said that?"

"Come on, Lawson, what do you think? I have talked to both of you as a couple, individually, and as a friend. My advice is still the same. You two love each other more than all the gold in the world. You have been together since you were just out of puberty for all intent and purposes. You are allowed to make a mistake or two and I think you've paid enough for yours. Lawson, Renee has forgiven you, now you need to forgive yourself."

"I'm trying."

"No, you're not. You think Renee has always been the fixer in your relationship because she has a degree on the wall that says she gets paid to solve people's problems, but it's not true. Don't you know that she depends on you just for breathing? You stole that girl's heart when she was just sixteen, and I can promise you without a shadow of a doubt that it still beats just for you my friend. And if I was a betting man, I would say it doesn't work without the matching half."

"Thank you. I don't know why I keep putting myself through this. It was a slip, that's all it was, and I've been regretting it ever since."

"Yeah, but it's time to let it go for good. Believe me, she has. She needs her husband and best friend back in her life and not just for show. If you are in, then you have to be in all the way because she deserves nothing less."

Dalton was right, he always is when it comes to me and Renee. He's been our friend for a long time and one of the few that we both get to vent to without judgment. I wanted to see my wife. I needed her. "Hey, you busy? Good. I'll be there in twenty minutes."

I practically sped away from Dalton's office like a race car driver. I was eager to get to my wife but more importantly to make her night in the best way possible. It just came to me as I was listening to Dalton go on about me and Renee.

I had phoned Alison to make the necessary arrangements I needed to pull off quite the surprise for my girl. She needed this and if I was being honest, I did too.

"Okay, sir, I got it. They will tell me at least two hours but that's their way of getting it done under an hour and looking for a bonus tip in their payment."

"Whatever it takes, I just want it all to be ready to go by the time I arrive with Renee."

"It will be and you have the perfect night for it."

"Thank you, Alison. I appreciate you dropping everything to make this happen."

"No problem. I was reminded earlier that you are the boss."

"About that, I didn't mean to be so curt with you."

"I'm sorry, I shouldn't have overstepped. It's my job to make sure everything runs smoothly for you but sometimes I can be a little overbearing."

"Preach, you and me both. Thank you, I'll wait for your text."

I parked my Lexus right out in front of Renee's building and told the valet to keep it close. I wanted to run in, get Renee and begin my night with her. Unfortunately, everyone knows me here and it never fails for at least one or two or more staff members to stop and say hello. I was prepared this time and made a run for the elevator waving at one of the security guards. By the time I reached her floor my body was buzzing. I was so excited to see her.

"Dad! What a great surprise. Chris called and told us you were on your way up."

"Hello, Emily, I have no time to chat right now. I'm here for your mom. Where is she?"

"She's in her office and you would be happy to know she's resting. It's been a long day and I think she's worn out."

"Okay, let me go check on her. I love you and we will catch up soon."

"Love you. You're up to something, right?"

"Stay tuned," I said over my shoulder as I walked down the hall to Renee's office. When I walked in she was on her sofa with her leg up. "Renee, time to wake up."

"I remember hearing those same words a while back."

"Yeah, well I said them every other minute for five days until you did."

"Thank you for that. So, what's up?"

"First off, how are you feeling?"

"I'm good. I took it easy and listened to my body when it was tired."

"Excellent. So, are you up for a little excursion?"

"Depends on what you have in mind."

"I have many things on my mind but first we need you to get up and off this couch and into my arms. I'll carry you out of here if I have to, but I need your body pressed up against mine for my next breath."

"Well, if that's not incentive I don't know what is. Let's go."

The smile Renee wore on her face was transcendent. She never looked more beautiful. She was carefree and happy, a look and a feeling I never wanted to go away again. We have spent a lifetime together and it has been an amazing one. Yes, I know it has taken a few hits these past few months, but it has also made us stronger and better for it. I guess there truly is a silver lining in every storm cloud.

"Our apartment? You brought us here?" she surprisingly asked as I helped her out of the car.

"It was the closest and highest place I could think of in a short amount of time. Come, you'll see once we get there. Can you make it? Or do you want me to carry you?"

"You are the most gallantry man on the planet. I don't want to break your back, I'll manage."

I growled at her comment as I lifted her protesting body into my arms. "What did I tell you about putting yourself down? I don't want to hear that kind of deprecating talk come from your delectable mouth again, do you hear me?"

"Yes," she answered quietly.

I held my wife in my arms the entire elevator ride up to the top floor. Once I stepped out to our private rooftop garden, she knew exactly what I had re-created for us. She happily squealed in my arms and lovingly kissed me. I placed her down and her eyes scanned the entire roof strewn with twinkling lights and candles encased in glass mason jars where I had a blanket arranged for us.

"Oh, Lawson, it's wonderful," she said and then wiped away her tears before I could. She wrapped her arms around my neck and kissed me senseless until I had her lifted off the ground holding her against me. I never wanted to let her go.

"Can you set me down? I need to."

"Oh, my, your leg?! Are you okay?" I asked as I placed her down on the blanket and pillows.

"Yes, stop worrying. It's been a long day and the leg is stiff. I need to take my brace off and let it relax and I think this is perfect to do so." She gestured to the multitude of floor pillows I had all around her.

"Okay, I guess I got carried away. I just wanted to make you comfortable."

"And, I am. A massage would help loosen up the muscles."

"Your wish is my command." I began a slow rhythm massaging her calf and working my way up to her thigh. Her hand stopped me from going any further but I pushed it away and kept going. I knew what she was doing and what she didn't want me to see but I didn't care.

"No, Lawson, I'm fine."

"Baby, it's just a scar."

"It's so much more than that. It's ugly and I hate when you see it."

"Stop it right now. I don't give a flying fuck about your scar. If anything, it's going to remind me for the rest of my life to treasure every single second I have with you and not take what we have for granted. You are alive because something bigger than the both of us decided your fate and kept you here with me. Please, let me touch you. Let me love you, scars and all."

With a smile that set my heart on fire, she slowly lay back on the blanket and allowed me to keep massaging her until I reached the inside of her thighs and placed a path of kisses leading up to her soaked sex. It had been a while since we made love with Renee recovering from the accident, I improvised on what I could do to bring her pleasure. We had gotten the all clear from her doctor but still hadn't made love. Well, that changes tonight.

I loved that she was wearing garters and stockings clipped to her barely-there underwear. It was like unwrapping a Christmas present. Layer by layer, I released her from her bindings and then she was on full display for me to ravage and I did beginning with my mouth. Her hands immediately found my hair and she forcibly tugged at first until lessening her hold. Reaching her first orgasm was effortless. She was already over the edge screaming out my name as waves of pleasure raced through her body. I wasn't done with her. My explorations of my wife's body were just the beginning. I ripped my shirt off and tossed it to the blanket as she sat up to begin to unbuckle my belt and remove me from my pants. I kissed her and did it myself.

When we were both naked, my body covered hers and we just got lost in the other's eyes until she reached up and kissed me. "I love you, Lawson, make love to me, please."

We said nothing more and began to make love under my version of the stars and were surrounded by burning candles just like our love. My heart only burned for my wife, I thought as I picked up the tempo and thrust deeper into her sexy wet pussy. Her one leg was wrapped around my waist as the walls of her vagina tightened around my dick. She was close as her eyes closed. "Baby, open your eyes and stay with mine. I need to see you as you come. Hold on, baby, and try to wait for me."

"Oh, my god, Lawson, I have to come. This feels so fucking good, damn, I missed this," she said as I kissed her passionately and commanded her to let go. She did, we did in spectacular fashion. Our bodies were soaked in sweat as we clung to each other.

"Holy shit! Lawson, you sure don't fuck like you're fifty." I laughed before descending to her neck.

"I love you. I love you. I love you. You were magnificent," I said as I continued to kiss my wife still connected with her.

She contently sighed. "I love you too, now feed me."

"I just did."

"Caveman, and you most certainly did."

"I don't want to let you go, Renee, but your wish is my command. I pulled out from her body and I couldn't help but notice how she winced. "Did I hurt you, baby?"

"No, just a little out of practice but nothing to worry about." We cleaned up and dressed in minimal clothes while we dined on strawberries and champagne. "These are amazing, and the champagne is perfect."

"I'm glad you are pleased. Do you remember the last time we did this?"

She didn't answer right away and then the recognition of the memory had come flooding back to her. She leaned over and kissed me. "Yes, Lawson, I remember everything and for you to do this for us just means the world to me."

CHAPTER
Twenty-Two

PRESENT...

Renee

"Why has it taken us so long to do this? Picnics and lovemaking under the stars should always be on our calendars. New rule," I said as my husband wrapped his arms around me. I moved as close as I could to his body. I wanted to feel every part of him.

"Thank you for this. I will never forget it. I'm sorry it's been so long, totally my fault for making feeble excuses putting our time together off. I promise I will not do that again. I've turned over a new leaf and I am going to stay true to my new promises. You want to hear them?"

"Yes, I do." He laughed and kissed my temple.

"Well, it was why I needed to go into the office today. If this accident has taught me anything is life is too short. We all know this but yet still behave as if it's forever. The accident changed that line of thinking for me. I was scared, really scared that I wasn't going to wake up and I would die listening to desperate cries and pleas for me to come back to you. When I did wake up and you were there, it was like I had a do-over to right all the wrongs I have made with us. So after careful consideration, I am going to scale back from the practice."

"Are you sure? Because I don't want to be the one that holds you back from anything you want to do, especially your work."

"Oh, Lawson, isn't that one of our problems that drove you to ask me for a divorce in the first place?"

"No! Renee, I was stupid and behaved so badly that night. All you were trying to do was give me a good night and I broke your heart in the process."

"No, I accused you of that, but you didn't. And I didn't bring this sore subject up to hurt you. You have always given me the room to grow and shine and you never once complained. I would be incredibly selfish if I allowed you to keep doing that for me. My practice has grown by leaps and bounds over the last few years and now with Emily and Gus on board with running the Yoga Wellness Center, I can scale back. I want to do this for us. I'm not giving up my career, but I can take a break once in a while and that break is now."

"Thank you, baby. I love you so much."

After our rooftop picnic and another round of lovemaking, I was pretty much toast and in need of sleep. Although I protested and could walk on my own, my husband carried me once again to our waiting car and drove us home.

He massaged my entire body including working overtime on my leg. My entire body was Jell-O and I never slept better. It could have been a combination of things to why that is, but I wasn't going to overthink it. Lawson and I were in a better place and I was just excited to complete my physical therapy and burn my brace once and for all. I still had a couple of months to go but like me, Lawson also promised to scale back and give our son more responsibility at the helm along with the fieldwork he was doing.

My father in law has been a godsend with his mentoring of Rogan.

They are two peas in a pod and practically attached at the hip. I sometimes worry about our son because all he wants to do is work, which is a good thing to a point. He tells me all the time not to worry about his love life or finding the perfect girl for him. He said his little black book suits him just fine for now and he's happy just dating. Okay, I know when I'm outnumbered but I'm a mom and I just want my kids happy. As for Emily, her wedding is back on and I am giving it my all to be able to dance with Lawson.

"Come on, Renee, one more set and you are done." said my sadistic trainer standing above me as he placed the bar in my hands.

"Robert, I didn't injure my arms, it's the leg that needs the work."

"For once, stop arguing with me and just do the reps. You are almost there, I promise."

After I finished working out, he gave me a health assessment of my progress and my leg. "You know you are a pain in the ass, right?"

"Yes, I know. Tell me something I don't know."

"I'm clearing you and releasing you from my care."

"What?!" I shouted, startling the other patients.

"Yes, you heard me. I spoke to Dr. Amsterdam and viewed all your recent scans. We are confident that you can be released and continue on with maintaining exercise on your own. I worked you hard, Renee, but that was the reason to get you back to where you were before the accident. I'm proud of you."

"I don't know what to say, Robert," I hiccuped between my happy tears.

"I think thank you will suffice and stick to your program to continue to gain strength."

"I will, I promise," I practically leaped off the table and into his arms to give him the biggest hug I could manage. "Thank you for giving me my life back."

"It's my job, and you're welcome."

After a rest in the sauna and a shower, I felt ready to take on the world but I decided I needed to celebrate and knew exactly who I wanted to call. Yeah, you're probably thinking my sexy husband, right? Well, you wouldn't be wrong but today it's about Emily. She has been amazing throughout this entire ordeal. She put her wedding on hold for me and worked a million hours at the office while I was away recovering. Now with the wedding only two weeks away, it's time for the mother of the bride to treat her daughter.

I called her from the car and told her that I would be picking her up, yeah, that is so Lawson. I guess I learned a few things from my over-the-top husband. She was bouncing with excitement when I pulled up in front of the building. Gus was with her.

"Hey, this is girls only."

"I know mom. I was just keeping her company. Have fun babe," said Gus, and then he leaned in once more to kiss Emily goodbye.

"Thanks, I will. Love you!" she called out from the window as I pulled away.

"Okay, mom, I'm here, now where are we going?"

"Spa day!" I said as I shifted gears and sped on.

"What's the occasion? Or do we really need one?"

"Today we are celebrating my official release from my sadistic but loveable physical therapist, Robert. I am 100% recovered."

"Oh, my goodness! That is fantastic but why am I here and not daddy? I would think you would want to go out on the town and celebrate."

"Oh, we will and there will be plenty of dancing but I'm saving my grand entrance for your wedding young lady. I told you I would not miss my chance of dancing at your wedding."

"You are amazing, and for the record, I never believed otherwise."

"Okay, I'm happy you agree. Time for some major pampering."

With cucumber slices on our eyes and champagne in our hands, both Emily and I were in a blissfully relaxed state. We just had our massages and were currently soaking our feet in lavender waiting on our pedicures. It felt like heaven.

"Mom, can I ask you a personal question?"

I removed the cucumber slices from my eyes and tilted my head over to Emily. "You can ask me anything, you know that."

"It's about you and daddy. Do you think my marriage to Gus will be as wonderful as yours is with daddy?" I let out a deep sigh after hearing her question because our Emily was simply a hopeless romantic and always wanted everything to be perfect.

"Em, when I look into your eyes, I can almost see stars dancing in them. You remind me so much of myself when I was a young girl falling in love with your father. My goodness, what did I know at sixteen? Your grandfather hated the fact that I, too, had my head in the clouds when it came to your father, but I fought him at every turn until I broke him down and made him accept my choice."

"Why did grandpa give you such a hard time?"

"I guess he was just so protective and only wanted the very best for me."

"And he didn't think dad was the one?"

"In a way, yes. When your father got deployed overseas, I think a lot of his early reservations for him just shifted from hating to supporting him. A military man is a big deal and Lawson didn't hesitate to honor his commitment to our country and to me. He promised he would come back and marry me. To give me the future we always talked about when we were lucky enough to have those stolen moments without interruption. Yes, your father was my first and only. My girlfriends back then told me I was crazy for not experiencing multiple boyfriends and the thrill of falling in love over and over again but Emily, I had all I needed with your father."

"You make this insane choice to love someone for who they are before you can even figure out who you are yourself. Let alone what you will become as a couple. My best advice for you and Gus is this: Marriage is about choices. You have to keep choosing to fall in love with each other, even in those moments when it may not seem to be the best choice at the time when you may be struggling."

"Falling in love seems so complicated but wonderful all at the same time."

"Yes, you're right about that but it's also the best thing you'll ever do. You just have to make sure the man you choose to fall in love with is worth it to you, okay?"

"I got it mom, and I have never been happier with my choice. Gus is the one and I know he will make me happy for the rest of my life, just like daddy is for you."

She got up from her chair not caring at all about the spillage of water and hugged me tightly. I returned her love and closed my eyes saying a prayer for my daughter for a happy and loving marriage. She didn't want to hear the statistics of divorce, or the ups and downs when you fight and how quickly you will resolve the issue.

Emily is a bright and intelligent young woman. I'm confident she has made her pros and cons list with over a thousand reasons why marrying Gus is the right choice. I love her so much for her mind, spirit, and her heart which she always leads first with. My girl wants the fairytale she believed I had with Lawson.

We have had our share of troubles over the years and this year was probably our greatest test, but we made it to the other side and are stronger for it. Lawson Douglas still remains my choice. I choose to fall in love with him daily but not with the same promises I made when we were younger. No, they were all wonderful back then but we're older now, more experienced and growing and moving forward in a new direction.

At this point in our lives, we don't have to compartmentalize our hopes and dreams and make them look great on paper. We've done that and have this twenty-five year plus relationship to show for it. The next chapter in our story is to simply choose us. To make every single day count loving one another and grabbing a backpack, a map, and see where life takes us. This is what I want with Lawson. I just want to leap really high with my hand in his and see where life takes us next.

A few hours later I wasn't traveling the world, but I was nestled close to his chest as he held me in his arms. "Hey baby, I missed you today. How was spa day with our daughter?" he asked as he continued to kiss me.

"It was wonderful. We had a long talk and cleared the air about a lot of unfinished conversations."

"Everything okay?"

"Yes, it's perfect. Emily is so in love with Gus and is bursting at the seams to marry him. She's so happy, Lawson. I want that for us."

"You don't have to want. We have it, baby. We've always had it. Don't ever forget. Not ever."

"Always," I whispered, and my husband held me for the rest of the night in his arms. Perfect.

CHAPTER
Twenty-Three

PAST...

Lawson

"I love this bed. I love this belly. I love my wife and I can't wait to meet our baby," I whispered to Renee, as I rubbed small circles on her growing stomach.

"Do you regret not finding out the sex of our baby?"

"Not a chance because when we found out with Rogan, I know I was over the top crazy getting everything ready for his arrival that I think I missed a few things along the way."

"Such as?"

"I guess what I mean is the anticipation of his pending birth. Once we knew he was a boy, all I wanted was to decorate the nursery in baseball gear and buy out the toy store."

"You were there for me always, sometimes too much. Do you remember the day I kicked you out and I made you call a friend and do something fun?"

"Yeah, I remember. I ended up calling my father which was a big mistake because he had a list a mile long and I did repair work in the hot sun all day out in his barn. Yeah babe, thanks for that."

"Okay, I'll admit it wasn't my best idea but you made your father happy and your mom ended up coming over here to our house and brought over all your baby clothes for me to go through. It was the best day of my pregnancy. We cooked and we sure did laugh a lot. Your mom is so cool."

"That she is and can't wait to meet this one. I say it's a girl."

"How are you so sure?"

"Because I know women, and I know without a doubt that this baby is a girl. And I already know what I want to call her."

"You do? Oh, wise one, enlighten me."

"Emily."

"After your grandmother?"

"Is that okay?"

"Yeah, it's okay. It's wonderful. Whoa, that was a big one."

"Is she kicking?"

"Yes, put your hand right here." As instructed by Renee, I placed my hand on the bottom of her belly and just enjoyed the rapid kicks from my little soccer player. It was amazing for me to experience.

"Hey little one, it's your daddy. I feel I already know you, but only because I feel you kicking mom from the inside. Now she has the inside track on all of this amazement but I'm here too. We can't wait to meet you. I love you."

PRESENT...

"Dad, you up there?" I heard Rogan call for me.

"Yeah, son, I'm here."

"Mom says it's time to get ready. The photographer is going to be here in twenty minutes."

"Okay, I'll be right down."

"Hang tight, I'm coming up," I swear my son was like Tarzan. He made it up to the top of the tree house in thirty seconds.

"Wow, it's been a while since I've been up here and yet it still looks and feels the same as when we were kids. Em and I loved this tree house, we played up here every single day."

"It's a good place and it holds many memories."

"What are you doing up here anyway?"

"Just doing a little reminiscing. I can't believe your baby sister is getting married today. Have you seen her? Is she okay?"

"Yeah, she's great. Mom looks amazing. I just caught her twirling around the room testing out her new shoes. She's so excited to dance in them. Maybe just the thrill that she could after everything she's been through."

"She's a walking miracle. So, how are you? We haven't had too much time to catch up."

"I'm great. Work is amazing."

"Yeah, how about the other part of your life. Are you at least trying to have a social life?"

"Dad, I have it covered and the ladies are not complaining. Don't worry so much about me, okay? I am not an obsessed workaholic. I just enjoy what I do."

"Okay, I'll drop it. What do you say we get your sister married?"

They say you have moments in life that you will never forget right down to the smallest detail of the day. I couldn't agree more because it's exactly how I felt while walking our daughter down the aisle that was covered in rose petals left by Gus's niece. My girl never faltered in her step. She was ready for the next chapter she was beginning here with Gus. They remind me so much of Renee and me when we were younger and all we had were dreams.

When I lifted her veil and righted the lace and silk material behind her head, she leaned in and kissed my cheek whispering in my ear, "I love you, dad. It was your love with mom that got me here today." I kissed her back and placed her hand entwined with Gus's before giving my blessing to the priest to go on.

"You okay?" she asked as I took my seat next to Renee with her hand on my lap.

"I'm perfect," I replied. Who would have thought it would be Gus breaking down before Emily while reciting his vows. He was a towering foot taller than her but she beamed as she listened to him profess his love for her.

When we heard, "you may kiss your bride" the church erupted in a thunderous applause for the happy couple. I held Renee back for a moment as our family and guests left the church.

"What's wrong?" she asked.

"You're so beautiful."

"Oh, Lawson, you don't have to say such things."

"No, I do. The entire time sitting here and watching our daughter marry the man she loves just makes me love you even more. I know we are not perfect, but we come pretty close to amazing in my book. You, Renee Canton Douglas, you are my entire life and there is not a day I want to live without you right beside me. We have had a wonderful journey that has led us here to this moment and I guess my question is, are you up for more?"

"Yes, name the adventure."

"How about marrying me again, right here, right now."

"You're not serious? Are you? can we do that on our daughter's wedding day?"

"You sure can!" we both turned around to see Emily, Gus, Rogan, and my father standing at the back of the church.

She lifted the hem of her dress and practically sprinted toward us. "Yes, let's have a double celebration. Father Weilly is right outside."

Renee looked over at me and then back to Emily. "Are you sure? This is your day, your moment. Your father and I do not want to steal your thunder."

"Nonsense, you two will just make it more special," Gus added.

"Well?" I asked Renee. "What do you say? Marry me, again?"

"Okay, I would love to marry you again, Lawson Douglas."

The wedding planner and her team brought the photographer back inside and instructed him to take some photos of our family before he headed out to the venue for the reception. After closing the doors, it was just us. Emily stood next to Renee, and Rogan was at my side as I married their mother again. I held her hand and brought it up to my lips to kiss. I touched her rings that had been beautifully restored and then I found my words.

"Who knew a choice, a calendar, and a marker would have led us here to this moment. It was so simple back then. I asked a question and without hesitation, you answered and we made the one decision that would set the course for our future. It was a decision that I have never regretted and it is one that I will be thankful for all the days I have left in my life. This ring symbolizes my heart and all the promises I gave to you on that day. I told you that my heart would be your shelter and my arms holding you would be your home. I love you, Renee, and if you would be so generous to allow me one more promise, It will be to give me the chance to make you smile every single day for the rest of your life. You deserve nothing less. You are my queen and all I want to do is kiss you madly showing you how much I love you. You made my life complete simply by trusting me to keep my promise. The only regret I have is that I made you doubt for the smallest measure of time before I came to my senses and returned to that man I was when I asked you the first time. Let today be the beginning of the next chapter in our story. Write it with me and let's see where the next page will lead us to."

I leaned in close to Renee and wiped away her tears. "I love you." She closed her eyes and exhaled a deep breath before beginning.

"You are a pretty tough act to follow but I will certainly try to convey what my heart has known since I was sixteen years old. I don't believe that there is one person on this earth that can truly define the word 'love' until you live it, feel it, and lose yourself to the power of it. As I stand here with you today, all I can remember is a quote by the great F. Scott Fitzgerald." She placed a kiss on my wedding band and said, "I love you, and that's the beginning and the end of everything."

CHAPTER
Twenty-Four

PRESENT...

Renee

“It's just that simple. I love you, and that's the beginning and the end of everything. You will forever be my everything, Lawson Douglas. Now, if you would be so kind to fulfill one of your promises now and kiss me madly, we can celebrate our beautiful daughter's marriage to Gus, and what comes next for us.”

With applause all around, Lawson stepped closer and took my face in his hands kissing me in the only way he knew how. It was a kiss I would feel for days and Lawson wouldn't have it any other way. He quietly whispered in my ear how much he loves me and can't wait to celebrate our 'reunion' of getting married. I giggled because as if a renewing of vows would stop him from consummating our marriage then and now.

After we took the thousand obligatory wedding photos for Emily and Gus, and a few of our own, we kicked our shoes off and partied into the night. Emily had changed from her formal wedding gown to a more down to earth party dress that she could easily move in. This was her moment to shine and I wanted her not to miss a minute of it.

The tear-jerker moment of the evening was when she danced with her father. She was always a daddy's girl and now has grown into this amazing woman who's now married. Her grandfather Roman had stepped up once her dance with Lawson was over. He twirled her around with ease and never stopped smiling. I wish Becca had lived to be here with us but we know she's watching from heaven and sending her love to all of us.

"Are you ready to get out of here?" asked Lawson coming up from behind me as I stared happily out to the dance floor.

"Yes, lead the way, my love." We said our goodbyes and wished Emily and Gus a fabulous honeymoon. They would be leaving in about four hours on a private jet to Belize, where they would spend a few days before moving on to Europe where they will travel to a number of cities before returning home. Not too many couples take a month for their honeymoon, but we insisted they do since they waited patiently for me to recover, and once Emily returns, I would be officially on my own break from the practice. I can't wait.

CHAPTER
Twenty-Five

Lawson

O kay, so hijacking our daughter's wedding wasn't on the schedule but I'm known for my over-the-top romantic gestures and renewing our vows here today may have been my very best. The look on Renee's face was priceless. The minute I asked her, you knew she wanted to just say yes but was cautious because it was Emily's day.

We have an amazing daughter who would do anything for us and her selfless act today was just one testament to many of how much she loves us. I took one more dance with my beautiful bride before leaving the wedding venue to have a private celebration of our own. This wasn't planned so I had to quickly improvise for a special night with Renee.

Our penthouse apartment was just as luxurious as a five-star hotel but for my night with Renee, I would need all the amenities a hotel could offer and on short notice. I phoned the manager I knew personally at the Ritz-Carlton. I had known Deacon for a number of years and considered him a good friend too. I bypassed the hotel and called his private line. He answered on the second ring.

"A little late for a social call, don't you think?" he said, as I heard ice clink in a glass. No doubt I was interrupting his night.

"Hello to you too, Deacon, and what makes you think this is a social call? I can do those during the day, tonight this all about business."

"I'm intrigued, tell me more."

"I need your best with the works. Candles, strawberries, champagne, and the couple's spa basket to be ready in thirty minutes."

"And? If I deliver which you know I can, what will I get in return?"

"Deacon," I said curtly. "I just renewed my vows with Renee, and my honeymoon re-do night has to be perfect. Yes or no?"

"Yes, a thousand times yes. You know I love Renee more than your ugly mug. I'll have it ready in twenty."

"Thanks, man, I owe you one."

"Your Aspen house for Thanksgiving."

"Done."

"Wow, that was easy."

"No, it was necessary, and you've come through for me on a lot of occasions. I'll throw in hired help for you too. Gotta go, my woman is waiting."

"Have fun and congratulations."

I practically sprinted back to Renee and the moment I saw her, I lifted her in my arms and kissed her until I was out of breath. "Lawson, you're practically vibrating with energy. What are you up to?"

"You know better not to question the master of surprises. Now, I trust you said your goodbyes?"

"I have. I was just waiting for you."

"Perfect. I hope you're ready to be amazed."

"As long as it ends up with me under you, I'm good."

"Atta girl." I kissed her and then led her to our waiting car.

"Wow, this is gorgeous. How did you manage this?" she asked in complete wonderment.

"Do you doubt my mad skills?"

"Not in a million years but this is just amazing. You are the most thoughtful man on the planet. You never cease to surprise me, Lawson."

"No, you're the one that keeps surprising me. When I asked you to marry me all those years ago, you just accepted with complete trust never knowing what would come next."

"Now who's the one doubting. Lawson, your one promise was all I needed to believe in and I have never regretted a single second. So, if we are done with the talking part of this magical evening you have arranged for us, how about you take off your clothes and mine too and make love to me."

She just took my breath away standing there looking as gorgeous and carefree as the last time we were like this. It's pure magic knowing the love that began this incredible life we have shared is strong as ever and I am just the lucky bastard that gets to be with this beautiful woman here in my arms. I didn't pause for one moment and turned her around to undress her. She shivered under my touch as my fingers grazed the top of her back to begin slowly unzipping her dress making it fall to the floor in a pile of fabric.

I instructed her to lift her long slender leg and step to the side. Once she was free from her dress, next was the sexy as sin bralette set she was wearing underneath. On my knees ready to worship her and it amazes me that she doesn't believe how fucking sexy she is. I'm almost nervous about how fast my heart is beating.

"Baby, it's not our first time you know."

That earned her a love tap on her ass. "I'm just taking my time if you don't mind."

"I actually do because I want you so badly and now is not the time for your teasing." She turned and lifted my chin so I could look up at her. "What are you waiting for?"

"I just love you, baby." I worked my fingers up her leg caressing every part of her until I reached her garters and unfastened them one by one. The silk material only made me harder for her. She turned with her hands twisted in my hair pulling me closer to smell her arousal. I ripped her underwear off and entered her slick folds with my tongue making her tighten her grasp on me.

"Holy shit! I'm going to fall over," she shouted out.

"Shhh, I've got you, Renee," I whispered and took her wet pussy again until she shouted out her release. Practically limp in my arms, I carried her to the extravagant bed layered with rose petals. It took me a second to get naked and climb over her. My hands were on the sides of her head watching her glazed over eyes look back at me.

"You are so beautiful and under me where you belong. I hope you don't plan on sleeping because I intend to be buried deep inside of you until the sun comes up."

CHAPTER
Twenty-Six

PRESENT...

Renee

Two amazing months later, I was standing before my staff and saying goodbye for a while. We conducted a rigorous search for the perfect partner to join my practice and be the new "me" until I was ready to come back. Casey Davidson was the perfect fit for what we were looking for. She specialized in the same field as I do. I almost laughed out loud when I was interviewing her because, in another life, we could be sisters sharing the same likes and dislikes. She was well rounded with an easy-going flow to her personality, perfect for this office.

It was a Friday, spent going over every last detail before it was time for me to leave everything I worked so hard for in their capable hands. Emily and Gus were thriving with building up their client list and making their own mark in the practice. I'm so proud of the both of them. Okay, this is it. The part where I walk out those doors and trust that all will be well upon my return.

"Stop stalling, mom," Emily said as she stood close to her husband.

"I'm not, I'm just so incredibly proud of what we have built here. To work alongside you amazing people. We have learned and grown with each other helping so many individuals who have trusted us to help them, and by doing so, making our lives so richer in the simple knowledge of that. You're going to be great, just not too great where you all forget me."

"Not a chance, boss. We love you. Now go find that handsome husband of yours." said Jeanie.

"Yes, I second that, but eww to the handsome part. Don't you two ever stop gushing over each other?" I laughed as Rogan walked in and joined us.

"No, and I hope we never do. You should be so lucky son in hopes you will find your someone special someday."

"I'm working on it, mom. You never know? Someday may just be around the next bend. But today is not about me, it's about you and dad who is waiting for you. Are you ready?"

CHAPTER
Twenty-Seven

PRESENT...

Lawson

"O kay, I believe that covers it. Thank you, Alison."

"Hey, what about me? I helped her."

"Right, and the sky is purple. You just be brilliant in what you know but leave the managing of the office to the boss here." I pointed to my longtime assistant who was practically bouncing on her feet. It wasn't often I displayed such emotion, let alone high praise but I'm a changed man and I know what I have and promised myself I would not be taking anything in my life for granted again and that includes my staff. She's had to put up with a lot from me over the years and never has let me down, it's only fair to be awarded with not only words but a huge raise too. She deserves it and so much more.

"You have an amazing time, son. Give my daughter a hug and kiss from me. We will be here when you two return."

"Thanks, dad, I will. Don't work too hard, okay?"

"Yeah, and the sky is purple." He took me in for a long strong hug and a slap on my back. He wasn't always the most affectionate man but I knew and felt what he was saying.

I stood at the top of the stairs of the company jet watching Rogan open his mother's car door. She stepped out under the late day sky getting ready to set and begin the night. Her smile was warmer than the late day sun. She gave our son a hug and began walking toward me. I took her in my arms and said, "Are you ready for the next adventure?"

"As long as we're together, I'll follow you to the ends of the earth."

"That's what I hoped you would say." Kissing her passionately, I scooped her up in my arms and carried her to our private quarters hearing Rogan call out "have a good time" I was in bliss and couldn't help myself. I felt younger than my fifty years and so strong in body. Her love made me feel this way and I never wanted it to stop. We divested of our clothes in record time and made love 35,000 miles in the air locking out the rest of the world.

Just us two.

Back then, the only thing we were sure of was the knowing and feeling of being in love. Yeah, it's the stuff that makes up fairy tales in the romance novels my wife and daughter love to read.

I kissed the top of her head as she slept soundly beside me. I breathed her in knowing just how lucky I was to be the man she chose and trusted. In our beginning, we had our doubters. Young love is just that. It's built on infatuated emotions and unrealistic dreams. I let out a small laugh causing her to stir.

"You okay, baby?" she whispered nuzzled into my chest.

"Yeah, I'm good. Go back to sleep," I said and kissed her again.

Sometimes in life, the book is judged by its cover, never knowing the story inside, and that's okay. Not everyone has to believe in love but we do and it was that love that has sustained us throughout all these years together.

Although I loved her from the time she was just sixteen, and watched her wave from her porch as I left her there to wait for me to return. The real story of Lawson and Renee began the moment she circled the date on the calendar. It's when I knew she was truly the one then as much as she is now.

Now that's a wrap for Lawson and Renee's love story.
Now moving on to Rogan and Alexane.

HERE & *Now*

PART TWO

Rogan and Alexane

CHAPTER
One

"You got another postcard from your father," I hear from Alison, his longtime assistant and my saving grace since he's been traipsing all around the world with my mom. I peer up from my monitor and she never misses an opportunity to tell me how tired I look.

"Where are they now?"

"Thailand," she replies. "It's getting late and you are the last man standing. Do you want me to order you some dinner before I go home for the night?"

"Nah, I'm fine," I say as she hands me the card. "They are crazy. Who knew they were global adventurers? Did you read it?"

"I couldn't help it." She smiles and tries hard to stifle her laughter.

"It's okay. It's hard not to when it's written with a bold black marker. I'm happy for my parents."

"We all are but I really need to get home. See you in the morning, and please do not sleep here again, okay?"

"That was a one-time occurrence and I appreciate you not telling my father how many hours I've been putting in. The project is now done and the only thing we are waiting on is the inspections to come through which should be any day now."

I worked for another three hours before heading home. I was beyond exhausted but so freaking proud of the completion of the new water systems for the farmers that were affected by land deals that went bad, weather, and just bad luck.

I climbed the stairs to my old bedroom back at my parents' home. I had been staying here while they were away on their trip and enjoying the perks of using their huge hot tub. Yes, casa Douglas had its advantages after a long day spent at the office. I swam some laps in the Olympic size pool and then soaked my sore muscles in the hot tub for a while. When I was finally relaxed, I collapsed on my bed and managed to sleep to almost eight which is a new record for me. I knew I didn't have anything pressing to deal with this morning, so I took the time to get a work-out in and eat a real breakfast for a change.

My phone was vibrating with one call after another, all from my father. I knew he was checking up on me, no thanks to Alison his spy.

"Hello dad," I answered with a sigh.

"Good morning, Rogan, I see you are making good use of the pool while we are away."

"What!? How do you know that?" I questioned.

"The house is monitored, you know that. And before you ask, I wasn't spying, your mother was."

"Gee, that makes me feel better."

"Watch the tone. She was worried about you because you haven't returned her calls and have been avoiding mine, so we checked the feeds on the cameras. What gives, Rogan? You are practically living at the office which you promised you would not do."

"I know and I'm sorry for that. I'm sure you have checked in with Ty and Paul about the project completion."

"I have and I am extremely proud of all the great work you have accomplished."

"But? Come on, I know it's coming."

"No, it's not. You are a grown ass man and you have your own life. You have done incredible work over at Douglas, and I'm proud of you."

"Thanks, dad, I appreciate you saying that."

"No, thank you, Rogan. You, grandpa, and the team have made it possible for me to have this time with your mother. It saved my marriage." He paused after he said that maybe not wanting to reveal something so personal to me.

Mom and dad always sheltered us from any real problems not that we really had any growing up until they took their small window apart. "You're welcome but I think you are exaggerating on the saving part. You two are amazing and perfect role models on what a marriage is all about. Don't be too hard on yourself. You just had a blip, that's all."

"Maybe, but it still makes me grateful for all of you. We have a few more stops before we head home for good. Let me know how the inspections go. I hear the new inspector down in Fleming's office is tough and doesn't cut corners. I think his name is Depry, yeah, Alex Depry. He just doesn't just hand out green tags until completely satisfied with the work."

"Well, we are too, and I'm not worried about a newbie still wet behind the ears inspector. We will have our green tags and then it's back to business. His name is not familiar to me, have you worked with him before?"

"I have not. He's new with the Agricultural Division at the EPA. Take my advice and work with Ed, and play nice with the new inspector. You don't want to make an enemy down there. Okay?"

"Yes, I get it. I've been around these guys long enough to know how the game is played. I'm not worried about our jobs."

"Very good. Keep me posted if that's not the case."

"What? No daily reports from Alison?"

"Smartass, and no. She's not your babysitter, she's my P.A. and a good one at that. Don't give her a hard time and get one of your own. I don't like to share."

"Bye, dad."

"I love you, son."

"Good morning, Alison," I said as I stepped off the elevator.

"If you want to call it that," she said grimly. "Here, you need to take a look at this. Ty and Paul are already at the site."

I took the file and dropped my bag on the chair before taking a seat. The minute I opened it, I knew my day was fucked. "The dipshit red flagged us? How is this possible?"

"That's what the team is trying to figure out. You should get over there."

"No, I have a call to make first. Will you give me the room?"

"Of course. I'll be outside if you need me."

I continued to read on before throwing the file across the room. I hit #2 on my desk phone and hoped I could get this misunderstanding worked out before lunch. "Are you fucking kidding me!?" I shouted into the phone receiver. "No, I won't calm down until you get me Ed Fleming on the phone. I don't care if he's in a meeting. One way or another, he's going to talk to me."

Well, that went well with his assistant hanging up on me. "Alison, I'm going over there, I'll be on my cell if you need me," I called over my shoulder as I took the elevator down to the parking garage. I was so fired up, I could spit nails. This is bullshit and I will get to the bottom of this. My phone buzzed in my pocket and I looked down to see it was Ty calling. "Hey, you still over there?"

"We are and it's not good. The new inspector is a hard ass and will not budge until we pull the lines from Harrington, Stallings, and the Jefferson farms. I'm telling you, Rogan, these lines are sound. I don't know what made this guy fail us but it's not our fault."

"Don't I know it. I'm going to speak to Ed in person."

"Yeah, good luck with that. The bastard has been ghosting us all morning."

"Me too, but that ends right now. I'll call you back."

Thank goodness for boring routines. My grandfather Roman was dead on when it came to Ed Fleming. He leaves his office every day at noon and eats lunch in the same spot at the Promenade. I didn't waste my time going up to his office, so I waited for him to come out and then I followed him. Sure enough, he sat down at his usual table and then when he was about to take his first bite, I sat down taking him by surprise.

"What the fuck, Douglas. Isn't it enough that you harassed my secretary all morning, now you stalk me on my personal time?"

"Why was I flagged?" I slammed my hand on the table.

"I wish I knew but I don't. Rogan, I have worked with your grandfather and father for years and I never once red flagged anything that had the Douglas name on it, and I never will. I have a few more years left and then I retire. We got new blood up in there and I was pulled from this and replaced with Alex Depry."

"How is that possible when you're in charge?"

"Yeah, that may be true but I'm not an army of one. I have people to answer to as well, and it wasn't my call."

"None of this makes sense, Ed."

"Listen, keep your head about you and give me some time to look into it. I'll call you this afternoon after I make some calls."

"Ed, these families have waited a long time for this victory. Please do everything in your power to help us make this right. Our lines are good. I worked those lands myself and helped install all of them. Make this right, Ed."

My chair skidded behind me and I left Ed to his lunch. Meanwhile, I drove over to the farms in question and met up with the guys. My grandfather was talking to Mr. Harrington when I pulled up.

"Hey grandson, what did you find out?"

"Hi grandpa, not too much right now but I have Ed Fleming working on it."

"Rogan, how is this happening? You assured me all would be okay with the lines. I trusted you."

"Look, I know you're upset and have a right to be but I promise you, I will get to the bottom of this. I can't tell you why we were red flagged because I have no idea, but I will."

"Okay, I guess I have no choice. Let me know what you find out." I watched Mr. Harrington walk away with his head cast down low in defeat. *I have to help him and make this right for the farmers, or all our hard work would be for nothing.*

"He's just upset, don't take it personally."

"Grandpa, how can I not? This was the first project I was given the lead on. It's my responsibility."

"Yes, but grandson, you are not the lone ranger here. We are a team and work as a team. Just because you carry the Douglas name doesn't mean you are the solo act. Now, let's get out of here so you can buy me a beer."

"I have to get back to the office."

"No, it's beer time and that's an order."

CHAPTER
Two

"**S**eriously, grandpa, what are we doing here?" I grumpily asked as I twirled around on the swivel bar seat.

"Will you stop it! And what does it look like to you?"

"Sorry, I don't mean to be a jerk but I have to get back to work. This red flag issue is driving me fucking crazy and I need to ring the neck of Alex Depry."

"Watch your mouth and down your shot. Here, drink," he handed me the tequila and I did what I was told. "You see? It helps on a bad day. Bartender, another round."

"Grandpa," I said as my head began to slowly spin. I wasn't a big drinker and my father would have my ass knowing I was in this dive bar with my grandfather. Sometimes I don't know who's scarier, Lawson or Roman Douglas. "One more drink and I'm out of here."

"I think you need to get laid." I spat out my beer all over the bar countertop.

"Grandpa! Are you for real right now?"

"Yes, are you? I swear the younger generation makes me sad. You are not hurting in the looks department, thank you very much. You can grate cheese off that stomach of yours. Seriously, what is the issue?"

"Right now, it's work. I'll figure the rest out later. Oh, and thanks for the advice but I think I'm good."

"Yeah, you're good? So why haven't you noticed the leggy blonde over in the corner checking you out for the last ten minutes? Yeah, I'm old but I'm not dead yet. From what I can tell, she looks like she's drinking a martini. Send one over to her, the dirtier the better."

I held my head and counted to ten. I feel as if I have entered the twilight zone sitting here with my grandfather but I can't help but love the guy. He's freaking awesome and right. I flag down the bartender and send the martini over but not before confirming that yes, I'm looking too.

When the bartender handed her the drink, she looked over his shoulder and nodded appreciatively to me. I did the same in return and continued the lively banter with my grandfather until we were interrupted by the mystery girl.

"Hello," he said in a flirting tone.

"Hello to you too. Thank you for the drink, it's my favorite." *WTF? She thinks the drink was from my grandfather? Omg! I need to go before I embarrass myself more than I already have.*

He lifted her hand and chastely kissed it. "You are most welcome but it was from my grandson. You see, he's had a really bad day and is in need of company, would you be so kind to take my seat and give him that?"

Kill. Me. Now.

"I would love to," she said and took his vacated seat.

"Grandpa, you don't have to go."

"I think I do. Don't worry about me, I'll call for a car." And before I could say another word, he threw down some money on the bar and left. As she sipped the martini, I could feel her trying valiantly to hide her laughter behind the glass.

"Yes, this is embarrassing, probably my finest hour of humiliation."

"Ha! I think it's wonderful. He obviously cares for you and is the perfect wingman for you."

"You think so?"

"Absolutely. He's great."

"He's crazy but definitely made a crappy day better. So, what's your name? I can't keep referring to you as the leggy blonde which would be in bad taste."

"Do we really need names? Why don't we have another drink and just be here in the moment?"

"Suit yourself. Another round?"

"Yes, please," she crossed and uncrossed her legs making my dick painfully hard. She was beautiful with legs that I would love seeing wrapped around my shoulders as I feasted on her pussy. *Shit! It's got be the tequila. I left my player days back at the frat house. I keep waiting for her to slap me.*

"You know, my day wasn't great either until I came in here and a nice man sent me a drink. It's getting better by the minute but there's always room for improvement." After she downed the last of her drink, she placed the glass down on the bar and stood up nose to nose with me. "You coming?" she asked.

"Not yet but you can bet when I do, it will be all over your sweet ass."

I hadn't been back to my place in weeks, not when I had mom and dad's house to play in. I can't bring her back there for obvious reasons. My apartment is practically bare because it's a temporary living space. My dad keeps telling me it's time for an upgrade but who has time to house hunt?

"Hey, I can see the wheels practically turning in your head. My apartment is not too far from here unless you've changed your mind." Her words broke me out of my reverie.

"No, it's not that. I guess I was just figuring on where to go."

She laughs, "In between places?"

"Yeah, something like that."

"Well, no worries. Take the next right. I'm up on the left with the red mailbox."

"Nice place, you live here long?"

"For the last four months, I'm still getting used to it. Drink?" she offered.

"No, I'm good."

"Let's hope by the end of the night, you will be great." Grabbing my face to pull me in closer, her lips were on mine taking a sweet and savage kiss. She didn't breakaway as she led me into her bedroom falling back onto the bed and taking me with her. My body had settled over hers with my erection pressing in between her legs which she opened for me without hesitation. Once I ripped my mouth away, our clothes were next. Her body was curvy, and her naked legs did not disappoint. They were full of muscle but sexily lean and long. Just as I imagined when I saw her at the bar, her legs felt strong wrapped around me.

"You bench press or something?" I asked before feasting on her.

"Amongst other things, but yeah, a woman has to stay in shape."

"I'm not complaining, just the opposite. Stick figures don't turn me on." After my comment, it was like her body naturally melded into mine. "Do me a favor and grab on to the headboard."

"Why? Are you into kink or something?"

"Who isn't? but that's not why I want you to do it."

"Okay, I'll play," she extended her arms high above her head and positioned her hands in between the wrought iron bars which were just about perfect. "Happy?" she asked with a sass to her voice.

"Extremely, now I'm going to make you fucking scream," I spread her legs even wider as I plunged my tongue deep inside of her.

Her hips immediately bucked up and she shouted, "Oh, shit!" I thought silently, *exactly right.* Her body tightened as the evidence of her arousal slowly seeped out of her dripping pussy. I lapped it all up on my tongue as she continued to come. I took her mouth again making her taste what I just devoured, she was delicious. I didn't give her a minute to breathe inserting two fingers inside of her. Her hands were off the headboard and I stopped. She screamed in frustration.

"What are you doing?"

"I can ask you the same question. You took your hands off the headboard, did I say you could?"

"Sorry, it was intense."

"I've only just begun but I won't continue until you place your hands back on the headboard."

"Okay, I promise. I will not move them until you say so, okay?"

"Yes, right answer. My thumb was rubbing teasing circles on her clit as my two fingers continued to work her sex. She was writhing beneath me as she reached her second orgasm. I reached for my wallet and grabbed a condom coating my dick quickly not wanting to waste a second with her. "You can let go now. Put your arms around my neck and don't take your eyes off mine. She did as she was told as I plunged inside of her body. This feeling was incredible and she was so much more than a one night stand. I wouldn't worry about that at the moment. All I wanted to do was give her undeniable pleasure and listen to her come gloriously as she got closer to her third orgasm.

"Hold on for me, I'm so close."

"I'm closer," she panted.

"Control! Come with me," I finally was the one shouting. Her fingernails clawed into my sweaty back as we both found our euphoric release. I practically collapsed on her. I couldn't move and didn't want to. She felt amazing under me and I would give myself a quick breather before I would take her again.

"Thank you, I needed that." She let out a few breaths before getting up from her bed.

"Um…you're welcome. Come back here."

"Sorry, I have an early day tomorrow and need to get some sleep."

"Are you serious right now?"

"Quite." I frowned at her comment.

"Oh, don't feel so dejected. I really do have work in the morning."

"Yeah, me too, but do I really have to leave right now?"

"Yes, you do."

"Can I at least have your name?" I asked as sudden unsettled feelings began to rage through me. I didn't like the brush off. I tossed the discarded condom in the wastebasket by her bed and then pulled on my briefs and then jeans. I was usually good at reading women but this one was an enigma of sorts and I couldn't help but be turned on. I asked her again and she still didn't reveal her name to me. Once I was completely dressed, I turned and pulled her into me with her hands reaching around my waist.

"I've never been asked to leave before and dejection is not what I'm feeling right now, quite the opposite you fucking tease."

"Good to know. I'm happy I can elicit such emotions but I'm tired."

"Can I see you again?" I asked with hopefulness to my voice. Name or no name, I wanted her.

"Let's just call this what it was, okay? I'm good with that, I promise."

"Maybe I'm not. Why won't you tell me your name?"

"Why is it so important to you? Haven't you ever just wanted to let go for once and just live outside of the box?"

"Yeah, I have and being here with you, I did."

I was getting tired of the back and forth and didn't want to get pissed off in front her because my dick had other ideas. I conceded and kissed her again before releasing her. I didn't believe for a second she didn't want me again but I wasn't going to push her any further. I grabbed my wallet and keys and left her bedroom without another word. I heard the shower turn on and knew I had a minute or two to look around before she finished.

Her place was just as bare as mine but with a little more flair. I looked around her desk for a piece of mail telling me who the hell she was but I came up empty. I'm not that much of a stalker, so with her address already programmed in my phone, I hoped I would see her again.

I drove home back to my place with blue balls and in need of a cold shower. The parents are always telling me to take advantage of life's unexpected moments. Tonight with the mystery girl definitely comes close to that. Decision made. I need to find out more and see her again.

CHAPTER
Three

I gave my body a good stretch before getting up from my bed. I tossed and turned half the night struggling to catch a few hours of sleep. All I could think of was that girl and the need to take her again and make her mine.

It happened. It finally fucking happened. I met someone that I actually enjoy being with but the catch is—she won't tell me her name and once was enough for her. It's like love karma laughing in my face. Love? No, let's not get crazy right now. Yes, the interest is there and that's where I'm going to go to—for now.

I hit the button on the Ninja and waited for my coffee to brew. This contraption was sick with lots of features to choose from. A gift from Emily when I moved in here. It's cool and everything but I'm good with my old Mr. Coffee one a cup. Yeah, I think that got chucked into the trash with the rest of my dorm/graduate school necessities. Even with high tech gadgets, this place kind of sucked and maybe it was time to go house hunting or at the least, spruce this place up. My apartment was in the same building as my parents, but the one they owned was the penthouse. I have the less than the luxury model. It has everything I need. I thought as I looked at the bare walls and minimal furnishings. I sighed. I guess I do live like I'm still in college.

"Okay, mom, you win. I will redecorate but hand over the pleasure of the shopping to Emily." I shook my head knowing my sister will absolutely love the idea of spending my money. I was given full access to my trust fund once I turned twenty-five and finished graduate school. My parents have always been generous with both Emily and myself at the same time keeping us grounded. I dialed her number and Gus answered it.

"Hey brother, what's up?"

"Not too much, is Emily there?"

"She's sleeping and so was I before you called." By the sound of his voice, he wasn't all that happy and then I knew why. It was barely six am.

"Shit, I'm sorry. I didn't even look at the time. Go back to sleep and have my sister call me later."

"I'm up, tell him to give me a second." A groggily Emily said in the background.

"Okay, that's better. Gus is making me coffee. Sorry if he was a grump, we got in late last night."

"It's my fault, don't get mad at your guy. Anyway, the reason for my call is to enlist your help on a project."

"Oh, yeah? What kind of project?" she asked. "Thank you, honey. I love you."

"Love you more. I'm going to take a shower."

"Okay, love. I'll make this quick and then join you. Don't use all the hot water up." Her voice went from groggy to sex kitten in under a minute.

Ewww! If I hit my head hard enough against the wall, do you think I can erase what I just heard from my baby sister?

"Hey!" I shouted into the phone. "Earth to Emily."

"I'm here, sorry. I'm a newlywed for cripes' sake. Oh, and don't act like a freaking prude."

"I'm not, I just don't feel like hearing my sister sex talk with her husband. It's gross."

"No, it's fucking awesome and I have to go, so tell me what you want."

I let out a frustrated sigh and then asked her. "Will you shop and decorate my apartment?"

A thunderous squeal sounded on the other end of the phone making me hold my phone away from my ear. "Is that a yes?"

"Hell yeah, it is. When can we start?"

"Today, if possible. I'm going to have Alison call over to the Galleria and set up my account. Everything can be billed to me but let's not go crazy."

"Oh, big brother, I've got this. Don't you worry about a thing."

"I will try not to. Thanks."

"No worries, I love spending other people's money. Now I have to go. Gus is waiting to give me some pleasure."

"You suck! You know that, right?"

"I do, and Gus loves it." She giggled.

The call dropped and I think I just threw up in my mouth. Shaking off the racy images of my sister, a thought you should never have, I took a shower and got ready for work.

Once I was relaxed all my thoughts went back to Blondie, yeah, that's what I will call her until I know her real name.

I filled my travel cup with more coffee and headed down to the garage. The doorman greeted me and wished me a good day. I waved back and once again thought of Blondie. It will be a fantastic day if I get to see her again.

"Morning," I called out to Alison who was directly behind me as I entered my office.

"Good morning to you too. Okay, before we get started, I want to introduce you to your new assistant. Think of her as another version of me."

"And? why would I do that?" I asked as I placed my stuff down and turned on my computer.

"Because she is my niece and is amazing."

"I guess it was too much for you working for my dad and me, huh?"

"Not at all, it's just time for you to build your own staff. Your father insisted and I had to move things along for you."

"Good old dad, okay, when do I get to meet her?"

"She's here taking a tour around the building with Jan from HR, and once she's finished, I will make the introductions."

"Okay, sounds good. Any messages from Ed? Or anyone down at the EPA?"

"Radio silence, sorry."

"No, the only person that is going to be sorry is Alex Depry, once I get my hands around his neck. Okay, please get Ed Fleming on the phone for me and patch him through to my private line."

Instead of going drinking with my grandfather last night, I should have been reading through these inspections again. My mind was in a haze as I tried to read but all my thoughts kept going back to Blondie. I started searching on Google for anything that would help me locate her and coming up with zilch. Grandpa knows the bartender pretty well, maybe I can take a look at the credit card receipts to find out who she is.

Will you get a grip? This is just crazy. I have to focus on work and not this girl.

"Rogan, I have Ed Fleming for you."

"Hey, what do you have for me?"

"I tracked Alex Depry down. His record is spotless. I thought maybe I would stumble across some backdoor dealings but nothing. He's a straight shooter climbing the ladder. I've heard aggressive but fair. He's supposed to be assigned here but I haven't met him yet."

"That's odd. Do you know why that is?"

"He's a transfer from back east and is kind of in limbo at the moment until getting permanently placed. The Harrington Farm still has an operations trailer on site and I heard he may be going down there this morning to check the lines to back up his report."

"Perfect. I guess my day just got better because he can run but not hide forever. It's time to meet the elusive Alex Depry."

"Watch yourself, Rogan. He's still a government employee."

"So fucking what. He's screwing with our business for no cause and I want to know why that is. I'll get back to you. Thanks, Ed."

"Alison, I'll be back."

"Okay. Any idea when?"

"Nope! But it will be after I squash the bug."

The drive over to the Harrington Farm didn't take too long. I kind of ran every single light to get here. This trip would be worth the speeding tickets if I had been pulled over. I don't know what would make this new guy flag us but his reasons are unwarranted and any member of my team including my grandfather can back it up.

When I parked near the trailer, it looked like the guys were packing up their gear. They all knew me well and said hello. I found the foreman that runs Harrington Farms and asked him if the EPA inspector had been by. John said not to his knowledge but he just got here himself. I said okay and walked out to the fields that contained the new lines to make this farm great again. It would always be a thorn in my side knowing that greedy mother fucker Lockhart screwed over these farmers. My father took care of it and told me to let it go. He lost and we won but I can't really celebrate the victory until our work gets the passing stickers.

I was wasting my time here and began walking back to my car. I saw Mr. Harrington on my way out and not looking all that happy.

"Hey, what's up?"

"Rogan, maybe you need to take a look at this," he handed me what looked like a summons. "I can't believe this is happening. It says that our lines need to be moved and relocated to another area that's not in the protected zone. My family has been working these farms for five generations and not once did we ever come to know that we were breaking the law on protected property."

"Okay, slow down. Let me read this." I took a few minutes to peruse the documents and nearly shredded them on account of being so angry. This screams corruption and when I find the person responsible for this, I'm going to hang him by his balls, beginning with Alex Depry.

"Keep it together, Mr. Harrington. I am going to fix this."

"How? Son, you are cashing checks when you know the well is dried up."

"I won't believe after everything we worked for it's all coming down to a threat. Give me some time to track this inspector down and I will get back to you."

I sped away from his property and headed directly to Ed's office. Someone has to know where I could find this guy. You can't just wreak havoc on someone's life and business and be a ghost. He has some explaining to do and I will not leave until I get one.

It didn't take long for news to spread. My father had already left two messages and was currently leaving a third. I couldn't deal with him right now. Before I could talk to him, I needed more information.

I walked right past Ed's secretary with her chasing after me as I barged into his office. He didn't look surprised by my sudden intrusion. "I'm sorry Mr. Fleming, I couldn't stop him."

"It's fine, Dolores, he's cleared." She closed the door behind me and I took a seat in front of Ed's desk. "I had a feeling I would be seeing you. I'm sorry, Rogan, I just heard about Harrington."

"Ed, I don't want your apologies, I want answers. Where the fuck is Alex Depry?" His eyes went as wide as saucers and then we heard.

"Standing right behind you and there is no need for that kind of language." *My words were caught in my throat because the voice I just heard sounded familiar to the goddess whose legs were wrapped around me last night as I fucked her.*

I slowly turned around and everything I refused to believe came crashing to the surface with the truth. The person singlehandedly trying to take me down was no other than Blondie. "You?" I shouted. She was obviously caught by surprise because she said the same words back to me.

"It's you."

"I guess I don't need to figure out who you are anymore." The sudden coldness to my tone was a distant memory to the one I used with her last night. I was so lost in shooting cold daggers at her, I didn't hear Ed interrupt us.

"Do you two know each other?" he questioned. Still dumbstruck, she remained silent where she stood.

"Yeah, you can say that." I looked back at Blondie who I now knew was Alex Dupry.

"And?" asked Ed.

"Yes, we've met, quite intimately. I met her last night in some dive bar my grandfather took me to for a drink. We left to fuck, nothing more. What I didn't know last night is that she is the same person that is hellbent on destroying me."

"Oh, shit!" mumbled Ed. She had the nerve to look embarrassed when I stood there not giving a flying fuck to her feelings.

"Rogan, get a hold of yourself and let's start from the beginning."

"So, you're Rogan Douglas of Douglas ECO Systems?" *And she speaks!*

"Yes, in the flesh, or do you need a reminder of what I look like with my clothes off."

"Rogan! That's enough." Ed bellowed from behind us.

"No, we are just beginning. I need a minute alone with your inspector." I demanded instead of asking.

"Keep yourself in check. I'm going to get a coffee and I will be right back."

"Don't worry, this won't take long."

I waited until he closed the door and then practically rushed her until her back thudded against it. As angry as I was, I wanted just a taste of what she gave me last night. She's standing here with her mounds of hair piled high on her head and wearing the tightest skirt ever leaving very little to what was hiding underneath.

"Did you shower after I left? Or just turned on the water for effect? Because I can still smell me on you and it's making me want to explore your body and take what was so easily given up for me last night." I practically hissed in her ear as I sucked her neck between my lips.

She moaned and tried to move out of my grasp but it was no use. My hands were already at the junction of her thighs and confirming what I had suspected—she was dripping with wetness. I moved in and out of her sex while her arousal coated my fingers. I could take her right here and she would let me. As much as I wanted to, I stopped and brought my hand close to her lips before I licked them clean. Her face hardened and that's when I let her go.

"Frustrated much? Yeah, I know the feeling lady."

"Fuck you!" she shouted as she tried to right her skirt and get control of her breathing. Her face was clear of being scandalized. A look not even Ed would miss.

"No, fuck you and the game you're trying to pull on me." I didn't give her another chance to flee and again, I was on her before she could run. This time her perfectly round ass was pressed against the desk with me caging her in. "Answer me this, did you know who I was last night?"

"No, and I wish I never met you," she hissed.

"Liar! I don't believe you. Try again," I said as I pushed my hard erection against her mound.

"What? Not knowing your name or letting you fuck me?"

"It's definitely not the latter. If it wasn't for Ed coming back here, I'd have you spread out all over his desk. Now, did you or did you not know who I was?"

"I didn't know who you were."

"Why did you red flag us?"

"I think the report speaks for itself."

"No, what it is, is crap. You know it and I know it. These reports have already been sent up to the head of the EPA, so unless you want to be brought up on charges for fraud and any number of charges I can hit you with, you better start talking to me. I'm a pretty patient guy but when I'm fucked with, there's no telling what I'm capable of."

"Okay, but not here." She continued to struggle against me, but it was no use. The more she moved, the more she felt my erection against her.

"Very well. I expect to see you at this address in one hour." I pulled out my card and tucked it in between the fullness of her breasts. Before I let her go, I took her mouth in a punishing kiss, not asking for permission as my tongue entangled with hers. "One hour. Don't be late." I whispered in her ear but not before taking another taste of her neck and then leaving a mark, my mark where anyone could see.

"Better clean yourself up, we don't want Ed thinking we fucked on his desk. I can smell your arousal from across the room and it's taking all my control to make my legs move so I could walk out of here while I still can."

I kind of expected a wise-ass comeback but instead, she remained where she was and panted while her eyes bore holes in my back as I walked out of Ed's office. He passed me on the way to the elevator as I tried in vain to tamper down my erection.

"Is everything okay? It looked pretty heated back there."

"Just a misunderstanding that will be rectified by the close of business today." *Or tonight in my bed, either choice is fine by me.*

"I'll be in touch," I said as the elevator doors closed.

CHAPTER
Four

Yeah, I've experienced a few surprises in my life but discovering *my* hot Blondie was actually the evil inspector I've been trying to meet nearly knocked me on my ass. My first reaction should have been to chew her deceptive ass out but my treacherous dick had other ideas.

I received a text earlier from Emily telling me that she had turned my apartment into decorating central so I knew I couldn't meet Alex there. Instead, I instructed her to meet me upstairs in the penthouse where I knew we wouldn't be disturbed. It also had staff at my service which was a plus. I called Hildy and had her prepare some treats and make sure the bar was stocked. I had a feeling I would need a lot of liquid courage to get me through what I had in mind for Alex Depry.

I took a shower and changed into something more comfortable than my suit. It wasn't really my style but my father insisted on it if I would continue to be present in the office. The sound of the doorbell rang right on time. When I opened the door the very reason for my discomfort in my lower region was standing looking as tempting as she was when I saw her for the first time in the bar.

"You showed," I asked surprised by the tone of my voice. She didn't look too amused.

"It wasn't like you gave me much choice, so yes, I'm here. Are you going to invite me in? Or are you going to continue to undress me with your eyes?"

"Yes, and yes, but I prefer a more private setting. Come in and make yourself comfortable."

"Why are you being so nice?"

"Do you think this is nice? Hmmm, I guess I have to work harder on my betrayed look a little better. Have a seat, please." I gestured to the sectional where she stomped over to. She was quite adorable, I'll give her that. "Let's start over, shall we?"

"Yes, that would be great. The sooner we can get this over with, the better." The look on my face must have screamed sarcasm, to say the least, because she hauled off and smacked my shoulder.

"Stop it! What the hell is so funny?"

"I guess it's the thought of you believing what's between us will be over once we get to the bottom of your deception. No, sweetheart, you are mistaken because we are just beginning. Get comfortable because I don't intend on allowing you to walk out that door," I pointed over my shoulder. She crossed her arms over her chest in defiance but who was she fooling? I know women and this woman is clearly sexed up and ready to jump me any minute now. I shifted on the couch leaning my head on my hand so I could look at her when I asked her why she would sabotage everything I worked so hard to accomplish.

"You say you didn't know who I was when we met in the bar, is that true?"

"I believe I have already answered that question."

"I'm asking it again. Did you know who I was? Because if your answer is yes then the hole you have dug for yourself just got bigger. I don't appreciate being played."

"I did not," she said through gritted teeth. You know, you are an arrogant asshole. No, I didn't know you last night and now I wish I never was in that bar, and definitely regretting accepting that drink.

The only thing I don't regret is meeting your grandfather, he was nice, and you are an asshole."

"You wish you had regrets but you don't. Come on, you can do better than that. Where is my wild Blondie that rocked my dick all last night until we both collapsed?"

"Yeah, you wish. What an overactive imagination you have. You're hot and definitely know what you are doing in bed but you are not God's gift, so don't fool yourself, pretty boy." I couldn't help but smile. She was refreshing and I dug that about her even being mad at her.

"Again, with the laughing? Am I that amusing to you?"

"Yes, and you're right. I know who I am, where I come from, and what I look like. It affords me certain advantages that some men may not know. You're honest and say it like it is which is another quality I do like and respect. So, aside from what I just said which is probably making your head spin, what I need to know is why you waged war on my work. You can't be working alone and you have no plausible reason as to why you would do this. I need a name so I can go after the real person responsible for fucking with my company."

"I can't tell you. If I do, someone in my family will be hurt and I will not risk that."

"But it's okay to hurt someone in mine? My family's reputation is at stake along with the innocent farmers that can't work their farms. Now, as much as I have enjoyed this banter between us, it's time for answers and you will give them to me."

"The report you submitted is clearly false and every red flag is superfluous. Any amateur new to the game will see the difference. Now, before I take that report and send it directly to Washington, I want you to tell me the truth."

"I thought you said you had already done that?"

"I was bluffing but this time I am not. Who the fuck are you? And why did you do this? As much as my dick wants to be inside you again, no pussy is worth my legacy."

"Fuck you! Your arrogance knows no bounds. Your legacy? Give me a break. Do you want to talk about legacy? I'll tell you mine. My father taught me everything I know about hard work, ethics, and yes, legacy and what it means when it comes to family. My father worked his entire adult career answering to the top dogs in his company. He tried to play the game and climb the corporate ladder but when it came to backstabbing and underhanded deals, he took himself out of that circle. He watched from the sidelines as the dirty players benefitted and got rich but at least he could sleep at night."

"When he was about to retire a few months back, an envelope with a large amount of cash was left on his desk with instructions to sway the right people to side with Winston Lockhart and his company."

"Creekside Orchards."

"Yes, the very same. I'm sure you know what great lengths Winston did to hold on to those farms but there was a bigger player in the game that stopped him before my father could."

"Lawson Douglas. My father."

"Right again. My dad, Ernest, by the way, was his name."

"Was? You say that like he's no longer with you."

"Because he's not, Rogan. When my father refused and turned over the envelope to his superiors, he was ostracized by the department that should have had his back. He lost what friends he thought he had and was under a great deal of stress. I was up and coming and doing well in my current position which made him happy in his final days but it wasn't enough. He never got to officially retire because he suffered a massive stroke and died on the way to the hospital. I remember saying goodbye to him that morning over cold coffee and a bagel. I didn't even hug him, I just ran out the door and told him I would see him later."

Clearly, the conversation between us had shifted to a direction I never expected. I was at a loss here and wasn't sure about what to do next. Her back was stiff and instead of trying to comfort her, I got up and poured her a drink. She accepted it and nursed the bourbon while continuing to tell me her story.

"After my father died, I was inundated with the mountain of bills from his funeral and household expenses. His pension is buried under red tape and I don't know when I will see that money. I know this must sound far-fetched to you but it's the truth. This is not unheard of in Washington, it's practically the norm up there. I still believe there are honorable people that work honestly like my father but this was so much more than that. He was targeted and when he didn't comply, they made him suffer. I just wanted a fresh start only to find out that my fresh start was bought and paid for by Winston Lockhart."

"I don't know how he did it but he was responsible for me being in the job I hold now. He threatened me and promised to destroy my father's reputation and mine if I didn't agree to help him. I was like, come and get me. My father was dead and I was drowning in debt. What more could he do? Well, I was wrong. He falsified documents and painted a not so colorful picture of my father's life. It would be a total embarrassment and would ruin any legitimate chance at me working anywhere in a federal position."

"It was too late to stop your father and the motions he had in play, so another plan was formed which involved me red flagging the farms. If I did this, it would buy Winston some time to plan yet another hostile take-over on those properties and ultimately buy back what he believes your father took from him. Essentially, he did but your father and your company did it the right way. This is just a businessman scorned and is out for revenge to even the score."

"And use you to do it."

"Yeah, that's pretty much it."

"Okay, so if all you said is true then why the phony report? You had to know that my team of lawyers who I employ at my company would not just sit quietly and accept the failed inspection. We have a stellar reputation and rarely fail at anything."

"Yes, I know that Rogan which is why I did what I did."

"Okay, I know that now, but your plan failed. I'm guessing because and don't take offense by this but you are not seasoned yet. You haven't been in your position for long and may not understand everything that happens in front and behind the scenes."

"You submitted your findings that was quickly disputed. You had to know we would do that. Having said that, once the failed project in question was re-inspected, we would be issued a new report resulting in your negligence."

"I know," she said with no doubt to her tone.

"So let me understand this. You were okay with deceiving Winston? And further infuriating him?"

"I knew the risk."

"Oh, baby, don't you know it's the same play your father did and sadly, lost."

"It was a gamble but I thought if my work was judged then my bosses would reprimand me in making the mistakes I did and then Winston wouldn't have anything left to hold over my head because I would have been removed from the job and it would be handed off to Mr. Fleming."

"I guess that's why Ed is so in the dark over this matter. I believe you, Alex, and I am very sorry for your loss. I know it can't be easy living with what you have been through and now to be blackmailed into committing a crime."

"A crime?"

"Yes, what did you think you were doing? Do you even realize how many laws you have broken here? Forget about your career, you may face jail time over this."

"Oh, my god, I can't go to jail. This is not my fault, Rogan. I was trying to do the right thing without blowing my cover to Winston. Don't you see that?"

"I do but tell that to the same pricks that destroyed your father's career. They can't be trusted but I can, and so can my father. We can help you."

"How? When the mighty have already fallen."

"You haven't met Lawson Douglas, and you need to have a conversation with my grandfather, Roman. They are fearless and very badass."

"Come here, Alex," she did without hesitation. All my earlier anger was now gone. I wrapped her close in my embrace and brushed the hair away from her face.

"Tell me something. Last night in the bar and going home with me, is that something you do often?"

"No, never. I told you, it was me experiencing life outside of the safe box I have been in. I never did anything reckless in my life. My father raised me all by himself and I was sheltered for most of my teen years. The one and only time I snuck out of my bedroom window to go to a party with my friends, I was caught with a blaring flashlight in my face. I never made it out of the backyard."

"Wow, sounds like he was pretty tough on you."

"He was but he always said it was for my benefit and one day I would thank him for it. Now, back to your question. I wasn't lying. Last night was me looking for an experience I never had and I always wanted. I didn't want to overthink it, just free my mind and go with it."

"For what it's worth, I don't regret being with you. And whatever happens next, I promise to face it with honesty. I never lied once until I was forced to. I won't be making that mistake again. I'm sorry and I will turn in my resignation tomorrow to Mr. Fleming to face any consequences he deems appropriate for my actions."

I moved her on to my lap and held her face in my hands. This was probably the craziest thing I was about to do but life is about taking chances and for some reason, mine begins with her. I didn't take my kiss hard this time. I wanted her to feel my touch and not be afraid of it or pretend to be into it because I now had the power over her. This was me being real and showing her that I wanted her. We kissed once and then again and again until she pulled back to look at me. Her blue eyes were glazed over with lust and her hair was tangled in my hands.

"What happens now? She asked all breathy and so fucking sexy.

"I think you know," and by that, I picked her up and carried her into the spare bedroom where I intended to be buried inside of her for the rest of the night. The morning light crept through the floor to ceiling windows as I began to waken from my long night with Alex who was still asleep beside me. I was almost surprised by that. I may have thought she would have fled from my bed and life once she knew I was asleep but that wasn't the case. I was actually happy she didn't and stayed.

Knowing what I know about her and her past and how it directly affects my life, I should have had her arrested but after I listened to her story, I knew that was not an option. I still don't know how the powers at be will react to this latest development, mainly my father. I'm almost nervous to call him not even knowing where the hell he is at the moment.

Her long and out of control blonde locks were covering her face. I swept them off her and placed a kiss on her warm cheek. She was too much of an enticement to remain here with her.

I got up and grabbed a pair of lounge pants from the tallboy dresser before closing the door behind me. The coffee maker was already brewing as I made my way downstairs. I have to make sure to send Hildy my thanks for doing this and on short notice.

I checked my phone for messages, most of them from Emily. The others were all from my father asking me to call him. Do I have coffee first? Or bite the bullet and just call him? I could always forgo the first two and just go back upstairs and wake the beautiful creature asleep in my bed. Yeah, that's the only choice I could get on board with and judging by the tenting erection in my pants, he agrees.

"Fuck! just dial his number," I say aloud and hit number one on my phone.

I don't even get the chance to say hello when he begins to shout into the phone. "It's about fucking time you return my fucking call," I hear my mother in the background trying to calm him but to no avail, he keeps yelling at me.

"No, I will not. He's lucky this conversation is happening over the Atlantic instead of face to face." He says to my mother before continuing on with me. "Rogan, where the hell have you been? And why has it taken this long to ring me back? Is this responsible behavior? Answer me!" he continues to shout.

"Dad, if you would stop yelling at me for a damn minute, I would be able to get a word in and explain. Where are you by the way?"

"We are in London waiting for the jet to refuel and then we will be coming home. To a disaster no less. I can't believe I had to hear this news from Ty and Paul, and not you."

"And what news would that be?"

"I'm not in the mood for games right now and when it comes to business, I'm even less inclined to fuck around. So, tell me who the fuck is Alex Depry and why has this douchebag flagged our jobs?"

I looked up to see Alex standing in front of me wearing my t-shirt and twisting the hem of it. No doubt hearing every word my father just said. "Dad, first of all, Alex Depry is a female and far from being a douchebag. Great language, by the way, do you kiss my mother with that dirty mouth."

"Rogan, my patience is walking a very fine line. You need to stop messing around and talk to me."

"I'm not trying to piss you off, and I'm certainly not playing any games. You know everything I do at Douglas ECO, I take seriously. I know you are upset but I promise you that I am on top of this issue and it will be resolved once you are home.

"I can't fly all the way home not knowing what is going on," his tone was softer and then I heard him whispering to my mom. She never liked when he lost his shit with me, which was pretty often when I was growing up. I know I have given him reasons to doubt me but not when it comes to this. "Please, talk to me."

"Dad, do me a favor and remember the reasons why you put me in charge when you left for your trip. I haven't let you or this company down. Believe me, please. I have to go. Call me when you land." I hit end on my phone and then turned it off so I could put out another fire with Alex, who was about to burst into tears.

"Come here, baby," I said and then opened my arms for her. She accepted the invitation and allowed me to hold her while she buried her face in my chest and wept. "I'm sorry you had to hear that."

"It's okay, I deserve it. Your father hates me and probably will want to bury me once he learns the truth."

"No, he won't. He will want to bury Winston and anyone else that caused you a single day of pain. Listen, with my father flying home today, I have to get into the office and meet with my team."

"What about me? do I just go into work today and act as if nothing is wrong?"

"It's exactly what you are going to do. As for anyone directly involved in this matter, they believe we are still red flagged. Ed knows I have our lawyers working on resolving the reasons why we were flagged in the first place."

"What about the farmers?"

"Another day is not going to matter. They are fine for now. I do have to ask you a question and please don't get upset at me for asking it."

"Okay, go on."

"Did you tell me everything I need to know? Because if not, you need to tell me right now."

"Yes, there's more," she sniffled and then gestured to the coffee maker.

"Yes, you may have a cup and would you mind pouring me one?"

"It's the least I can do," she said sadly. Hildy had left pastries, rolls, and muffins for breakfast but she declined food. I grabbed a muffin and began peeling back the paper while I listened to her explanation.

"Rogan, the failed inspection was just a stalling ruse to buy Winston more time."

"More time for what? He didn't have any rights to those farms."

"Yes, but he's claiming he owns the mineral rights that lay below the Harrington Farm, and if he can accomplish shutting his farm down for good, he will move forward and try to drill on that land."

"No way, what you're saying is just not true. This is a bed of lies he has been feeding you to get you under his thumb and to sabotage me."

"How can you be so sure, Rogan? I mean, he was pretty convincing."

"Yeah, well he's a wolf in sheep's clothing. And a bastard that would sell out his own mother for profitable gain. Wildcatters have been trying to find oil since the 1950s and I know this to be true because my grandfather used to tell me stories. About ten years ago, all the wells which equal to be around 160 are all dry and have been capped off. I'm not disputing that there is no natural gas to be found because there is. The bottom line is, we don't have enough of it and that's why this issue has been dead in the water. Whatever Winston is up to is simply his way of sticking it to my father and I'm sorry he hurt your father to do it."

"Can you tell me what happened to your home?"

"I sold off pretty much everything we had after my dad's funeral. The house is paid off but it's the taxes that I struggled to pay. I didn't have time to sell it, so I ended up renting it to a nice family with two kids. She's a stay at home mom, and he works in the city."

"And the pension? Why has that been delayed?"

"Beats me. My mom died when I was young, leaving me my father's only beneficiary. Do you think this is Winston?"

"It could be, I'm not sure. Listen, I really have to get ready to go. Would you mind coming by the office this afternoon and talking with my assistant? I need to get some more information to look into this for you."

"After everything I've done, you're still willing to help me? Is this a trick or something?"

I pulled back in astonishment not believing what she just asked me.

"I can't believe you would ask me such a question, and especially after last night. Alex, do I look like I'm laughing?"

"No, you're quite serious at the moment."

"Yeah, I am. I wouldn't say something and do another. I promise I will work this out and free you from Winston and his manipulations."

"And? what will happen after that?"

"I know what I want to happen right now," she laughed and then I cupped her face to kiss her. The rest we will figure out later. I just want to hold on to all the moments I can with you and not worry about anything else right now."

"Why? When you can have any number of women on your arm and in your bed."

"There's only one woman I want, so if you've changed your mind about me, it's best to tell me now."

"I haven't changed my mind. I guess whatever this is between us doesn't happen to me very often, if ever and I was just hoping I didn't lose you when I only just found you. To the shower!" I shouted, causing her to jump right before I threw her over my shoulder in a fireman's hold and carried her all the way upstairs. Yeah, Blondie is not getting rid of me so easily. After this mess is over, she is someone I definitely want to know better. For now, the shower will do just fine.

CHAPTER
Five

I was beyond late getting into the office but a part of me wasn't even sorry. I know this is crazy to even be entertaining such a possibility of starting something with this girl, but I can't help but want her.

I don't know where these feelings are coming from or how I can begin to understand them but why do I need to have it all figured out in one day? According to my grandfather, youth is wasted on the young. He may be right to a point but not in my case. He practically pushed me into the arms of Alex, and yes, he didn't know who she was either but now I do and she is worth giving a chance to. I just hope my father agrees with me.

By the time I got upstairs to my office, not only was a fire-breathing dragon aka my father waiting for me, but joining him was my grandfather, Ty, Paul, and Alison. She looked over at me with eyes as wide as saucers silently giving me the signal to get out when I still could. I kind of stood there for a moment not sure what to really do and then my father pinned me with his not so subtle cold stare and I froze. Shit! He looked pissed.

"Nice of you to join us, take a seat. We have a lot to talk about."

My father stated. "Hey dad, would you mind showing Ty and Paul the latest projections on the Laramie property? Alison has everything on her drive." My grandfather looked at me and then back to my father shrugging his shoulders but agreeing to give us the room.

"I thought you were in London," I said as I dropped my stuff down to the empty chair.

"I was and now I'm home."

"But I just talked to you. You said you were refueling the jet and on your way home."

"Again, true but that was yesterday. Your mother and I arrived home early this morning and to my surprise, you weren't at home, or at your apartment. Now, you are a grown man and can come and go as you please, but when you host booty calls at our apartment that's what I have a problem with."

"Look, dad, I needed the privacy. It's no big deal and I don't understand why you are making it one."

"It is a big deal especially when you are with the one person responsible for causing our company and our customers a lot of unneeded stress. What the fuck were you thinking taking an EPA inspector to your fucking bed? Or shall I say, my bed?"

"It's clear you know more than you have let on, so are we going to continue to dance around this or really talk?"

"Okay, we will talk. Rogan what you need to understand is that although I left you in charge to oversee operations and keep all the cogs running smoothly, it doesn't mean that I am out of the loop. I have eyes everywhere and I always have to keep the company's best interest first."

"Dad, I know that! Our interests are the same here. I want the best for Douglas ECO and I want to prove to you that I can do the work and keep this company moving forward. You just have to trust me here. I know what I am doing."

"And by you having sex with Alex Depry, that's keeping the company moving forward. Come on, Rogan, I thought you were smarter than that?"

"Dad, before another word is spoken here, you need to know that I care about this girl. And, no, I did not know that Alex was the person who red-flagged our farms. Grandpa took me to some dive bar that he loves so much and kept shoving tequila shots down my throat until I loosened up and thought about anything besides work."

"Ha! No shit. Was it Raggy's?"

"Yeah, I think that's the place."

"He used to take me there all the time especially when I was home on leave. Wow, I haven't been there in a long time. I didn't even know it was still standing."

"Well, it is and it's a cool place. It's where I met Alex. Grandpa told my ass off in his own and unique way and pointed out the beautiful woman that was checking me out. He sent her over a martini and when she came over to us, she actually thanked grandpa who shamelessly flirted with her."

"I love it. Not bad for an old-timer."

"Yeah, don't count him out just yet. I know he will miss grandma forever but I also believe he's lonely and needs someone he can spend time with."

"Okay, not ready to talk about my father's sex life or lack of one, let's get back to you."

"It's pretty simple. Two strangers meet in a bar and are attracted to one another which leads to the cliché one-night stand, or so it seems until a real connection is made and I can't stop thinking about her. We didn't exchange names, it's what she wanted. She wanted to just do something out of character with no regrets. Although I knew where she lived, that's all I had. A couple of days later and still nothing from the EPA and our jobs flagged, I went down to see Ed, and yes, I was pissed."

"He told me some background info on Alex, and at this point, I still believed Alex was a guy. I was mad and running my mouth and then a familiar voice was behind me and I knew our mystery inspector and the girl of my dreams was one in the same. Ed gave us the room and I lost my shit. I felt like I was being set-up or something and then it just totally shifted to something else. I asked her to meet me at your apartment and once she was there, she gave me the truth and it's quite a story."

I continued on and told my father everything Alex had shared with me. My father remained quiet for a minute and then paced his office until stopping at the bar. I might have thought he was going to pour himself a drink but then he just went for the coffee instead. God! he is so frustrating using the silent treatment while sipping his coffee. He finally sat down behind his desk.

"Her version of the truth. Come on, Rogan, you're smarter than that and I raised you better to know the difference. You got played by the oldest trick in the book."

"I am smart and I didn't get played by anyone especially Alex. She's being blackmailed and not just by anyone but Winston Lockhart. You fucked him over and now he wants to get back at us and using Alex to do it. Come on, is it really so far-fetched?"

"Let's say I do believe her story about her father and falling on hard times. I have her file right here which was not hard to get. Anyway, it says here her annual salary was $77,750 dollars. This is not a bad salary for a new inspector on the job. And already promoted in an even higher position." He shoved the file toward me gesturing for me to look at it but I don't.

"I believe her. And I don't really care if you don't."

"Oh, really? Well, you better god damn care! This is our fucking company she is messing with and I will not let anyone come between what we have built here. You need to get your priorities straight and until you do, you are hereby removed from the project and will no longer have any communication with the farmers or anyone down at the EPA. Have I made myself clear?"

"Don't do this, dad. I'm begging you."

"It's done."

I grabbed my stuff and took off for the elevator, totally ignoring my grandfather calling out to me. I couldn't face him and see another look of disappointment. I sped out of the parking garage not knowing where the hell I would go or what I would do. I knew who I wanted to see but I told her to go to work and treat it like just a normal day because that's what I was supposed to be doing.

My cell was going off and I didn't think it would be my dad and it wasn't. It was my sister calling. "Hey, Em, what's up?"

"Hey bro, ghosting my calls? Wasn't it you who asked me to help you?"

"Yes, I did and I'm not avoiding you. It's been a crazy morning and I just didn't have time to return your calls."

"Well? What about now? Can we meet at your place? I want to show you something before I have to get to work. You know I have a career too."

"Okay, I'm on my way."

"Thank you," she laughed in victory. I didn't want to be a jerk, especially to my sister who drops everything for me when I call. I shoved aside my earlier anger and focused on getting home to Emily. When I unlocked my door, I didn't think I was in the right place. It looked so different.

"Emily? How did you do this?" I asked as I took in my surroundings. The bare walls were now full of modern art. The black leather furniture is now gone and replaced with a sectional in lighter tones. Big floor pillows were around a huge center table covered with different shaped vases and art books. Bar stools were now at the breakfast bar and the countertop was decorated with red place settings. I was stunned and in awe of my sister. She was amazing.

"So, you like it?"

"More than like, I love it. Come here," I opened my arms up wide to hug my sister. "You did great. Thank you so much."

"I'm happy you like it. I was happy to do it."

"So, I have to go to work. Mom's back and I'm guessing she will be making an appearance today. Have you seen dad yet?"

"Oh, yeah, I've seen him."

"Uh-oh, your tone suggests the reunion didn't go so well. Do you want to talk about it? I can push back one of my appointments."

"No, don't do that. I can handle dad. I just need to take some time to think a few things through and then I'll go back later."

"What? Why are you looking at me like that?"

"There's something different about you, I just don't know what it is yet but give me time, I'll figure it out."

"I'm the same guy I've always been."

"No, you're not. You have this confidence in you that you didn't have before and it looks amazing on you big bro. I love you."

"I love you too."

"Good. I want you to remember those words because here is the final bill. Don't look at it until I'm gone."

"You are worth every penny."

"Okay, keep on saying that. Love you." she stood on her tippy toes to smack a kiss to my cheek and then sprinted for the door. My sister has the ability to make a cloudy day look like sunshine. Sometimes I envy her. She is so carefree with this incredible zest for life. It's no wonder why she is so good at what she does and has found the perfect partner in Gus. Damn, I want that too. I want to be able to share my life with someone special.

I know I was the one who always put off the idea of something permanent with someone else. How many times would my mom try to fix me up on a stupid blind date that I knew would go nowhere but I did it to make her happy? Sure, I slept with a lot of girls back in college, but that's all it was. Strings of just girls looking for a good time and that would be it. I was too focused on getting my degree and working for my dad. I didn't want anything more because that would come later, and now it's here. I want Alex, and I pray to god she still wants me too.

Dad: You've had enough time cooling off. Come back to the office.

Now.

Shit! "Sorry, dad but you are the last person I want to see right now." I grabbed my keys and headed for the one person I did need.

CHAPTER
Six

I sent Alex a text telling her that I was at the Promenade, and if she could come down to meet me that would be great. It didn't take long for her to answer me back telling me that I had perfect timing and she was on her way.

I chose a table away from peering eyes and waited for Alex to show. Fifteen minutes later, the beauty walked in and joined me but not before greeting me with a kiss. I savored it and wanted more but out in the open wasn't an option at the moment.

"Hey, thanks for meeting me."

"Thanks for calling. How's your day going?"

"I'm in hell." I dropped my head and reached for her hands.

"Rogan, what does that mean?"

"My father is home and he's not too happy with me right now. He kicked me off the project."

"This is my fault. I'm so sorry, Rogan."

"No, it's not your fault, and it's not mine either."

"I thought he was in London?"

"Yeah, I thought so too but he was already home and checking up on me."

"That's kind of a dick move."

"I'm not disagreeing with you but that's dad. Don't get me wrong, he's fucking fantastic on a good day but that's not today. Today, he's angry and wants someone's ass for making things difficult for our company and because I was in charge, it's my responsibility."

"No, that's bullshit and you know it. This is because of me and the deception that I created. I have to come clean to my superiors and make this right before it's too late. I can't sit on this and the longer I wait, the worse it's going to get for me. If I'm lucky, I may still have a career after all is said and done. If not, I guess I deserve what I get."

With her hands in mine, I pulled her close to me and on my lap not giving a shit who was looking. I wanted to hold onto her and keep her with me. I touched her face bringing her lips to mine. She tasted like fresh strawberries.

"I want to keep kissing you but it can't be here. Please come home with me." I felt her body tremble just by my touch alone. Her arousal was even stronger. It was like smelling blood in the water and I was ready to feast at any moment.

"Sir," I heard someone say. He cleared his throat and tried getting our attention again but my entire focus was on Alex. "Excuse me, sir, but I've taken the liberty of boxing up your order," he hesitates, "to go." We both laugh but we just don't care. She gets up off my lap and carefully fixes her skirt. I grab the to-go bags and fold two-hundred-dollar bills in the waiter's hand.

"Thanks, man," I say and then lead Alex away from the restaurant and straight to my car. "I can have someone pick up your car but for now, you're coming home with me."

"And where's home exactly?" she asked.

"The same building you were in last night but a few floors lower."

"Lower? Really now. And just how low exactly?"

I chuckle. "As low as you want baby," I say before I kiss her hard, raging war with her mouth. "I actually prefer southern regions the best."

"Welcome to my home. Please, make yourself comfortable. I kept my hand on the small of her back as I led her inside.

"Wow, your place is gorgeous," she said as she walked further inside and looked all around the wide-open space.

"Thank you, I'm happy it pleases you," I say smirking a bit watching Alex take in all the new additions Emily arranged in here. It felt right having Alex here with me. I stepped closer and pulled her into my arms. "All of this," I gesture around the room, "is thanks to Emily. I wish I could take the credit but I don't know anything about interior design. It needed a woman's touch and now it feels like a real home." Her eyes changed and all I saw now was jealousy, like the green-eyed monster. Oh, this was fun. She suddenly looked nervous and unsure if she was invading on someone else's turf.

"Um, is Emily someone important to you?"

"Yes, very much so. I love her very much."

"Oh, I see. Maybe I should go?"

"And why would you do that? Have I said something wrong?"

"Look, I've messed up your life enough for one day, I'm not about to be the other woman in a relationship that obviously means something to you. I just wish you would have told me from the start. It would have saved us both a lot of time and trouble." She began to leave when I pulled her back into my arms and easily lifting her off the ground and into my arms.

"What are you doing?" she asked in a huff. I couldn't stop laughing, she is downright fucking precious.

"Stop laughing! What is it with you?"

"Sorry, baby, you bring it out in me."

"Do you call Emily baby too?" she smirked with all the fight leaving her.

"Only when she's being annoying. But then again, if I even caused my '*baby*' sister to shed one little tear, my father would have kicked my ass."

"Oh, my god! I am so embarrassed. I feel stupid," she buried her face in my chest but I made her look at me.

"No, you're beautiful, Alex, and I want you so much."

"Rogan, you don't have to say that."

"What? That you're beautiful? Yeah, I do. I don't care about the reasons that brought you into my life, I just care that you're in it and I want you to stay."

"Um, am I getting heavy?"

"Not a chance," I laughed and placed her down on my new couch that I have yet to sit on. "Alex, my parents have been in love with one another since they were sixteen and eighteen years old. When my dad came home from his last tour of duty, he was honorably discharged and free to marry my mom. He did as soon as they could and built an amazing life together. This year they had one moment where that life was interrupted and questioned. In that time, my sister and I were devastated because our parents could do no wrong. We always believed they were perfect, at least in our eyes."

"No one is perfect," she says caressing my face.

"Yeah, I know that now. Here's another thing I know. They are stronger than ever because even with that small pause in their relationship, it only proved how much they love each other and are completely devoted to the other. Alex, meeting you has made me want that too. I can't explain it nor understand it. I just know I have all these feelings that are new and I have never felt before until meeting you."

"And what about your father? You already told me how angry he is? How will he ever accept me as the person you care about?"

"No, you're wrong. I just don't care, Alex, I love you."

She got up from the couch and far away from my reach. "You don't love me, Rogan, you can't."

"Why? Because you say so?"

"No, it's a fact. We come from two very different backgrounds. We might as well be on opposite planets. My father was a low-ranking federal employee that worked his entire life. He didn't go for the big promotions and tried his best to follow the rules. He raised me as a single dad, and he was amazing at it too. I loved him very much and miss him every single day. When he told me what they were doing to him, I accused him of being weak. I hurt him more on that day than any one of those assholes ever could."

"You made a mistake, it happens."

"And what about the rest? I allowed myself to be blackmailed by another rich asshole who believed he could do anything he wanted and get away with it." I was now up on my feet and standing in front of her.

"Let me ask you a question. Is that what you see me as? Another rich asshole? Because I'm not like Winston Lockhart, and far from the bullies that hurt your father. My father raised me up to be a man. To stand as a man and be proud of who I am and where I come from. Please don't judge me because of all of this." I pointed to my apartment and all of its new things.

"Look at me, Alex," I turned her around by her shoulders. "I am so much more than this apartment. I'm just a man, a good man who believes he has found his soulmate. The one person he wants to share his life with. The one who one day will surprise with a wedding proposal that will blow her mind, probably make her cry, but then when she says yes to him, she will make him the happiest man in the world."

"I love you, Alex Depry, and I'll say it again. I don't care how we were brought together. The only thing I care about is that we are here now and it's where I want to be." I released her arms and just waited for any sign that she felt the same for me. Her shoulders began to shake, and she began to cry silently. It hurt my heart to see it, so I took my thumbs and wiped away her tears. More fell and I wiped them away too.

"You know something," she said.

"What?" I asked as I stepped closer to her proximity.

"You are some kind of wonderful. You know that right?" she continued to cry.

"No, I didn't know that but thank you for telling me. What else are you telling me?"

"I love you too. I know this is fast and maybe a little crazy reckless, but I don't care. Let's be together." I rushed her and lifted her in my arms taking her mouth.

"Dinner could wait. I want dessert."

CHAPTER
Seven

How did I get so lucky to have found her? I thought as I continued to watch the only person who managed to find a place in my heart. The living breathing organ inside my chest that beats a little faster every time she's near. You can't get any closer to where she is right now. She's in my bed and in a perfect world that's where I want to keep her.

She stirred a little and contently sighs as her lips curve into a smile. That right there is what I'm talking about. She doesn't even know it but she's making me so incredibly happy just by dreaming. I wish I could look inside of her mind and see what she sees. It has to be pretty awesome to make her look that beautiful even in sleep.

"Hey, how long have you been up? Or shall I say staring at me?" she says and then gives her body a long stretch causing the sheet to shift just enough to expose her breasts. What a sight.

"Not too long, how are you?"

"Thanks to you, I'm pretty good."

"Well, I aim to please."

"Oh, don't worry about that part. You certainly pleased me and more than a few times. I stopped counting after the fifth orgasm."

"Stop, you're making me blush, and you are so good for my ego."

"Okay, you sucked."

"Now you're going to get it!" I pounced and pulled her on top of my body so she could straddle me. My hands caressed her naked body as she seated herself on my cock. "Fuck me, you feel amazing."

All sexy with panted breaths she said, "I am fucking you. Oh, Rogan, I'm going to come," she shouts.

I gripped her hips hard and held her to slow her pace but Alex had other ideas. She was riding the waves to her release and it was going to be explosive. "Holy shit! Rogan! Throwing her head back and crying out my name was all I needed to fucking explode deep inside of her. It was in spectacular fashion. Her hair was a tangled mess. When she leaned her head back, her long hair grazed over my knees.

"You are so fucking sexy," I rasp.

She leans forward to kiss me as I take her mouth and hold it hostage. My dick began to harden again as she already began to move. I flipped her to her back and thrust as deep as I could to make her feel every inch of my hard cock. Her nails clawed my back as we became one. It didn't take long for us to come gloriously with each other. Our sweat soaked bodies and the heady smell of sex that filled the air as we both came down from our high.

I couldn't move nor did I want to. We stayed connected for as long as we could until I pulled out from her body with my cum beginning to seep out of her. *Fuck! I didn't wear a condom. How the hell could I be so irresponsible and not take care of her? It's not like she stopped me so I could put one on. This is not good, unless she's on birth control then I don't have to worry about any babies arriving in nine months. Would that be so terrible? I can't begin to think about this right now. She's so fucking gorgeous laying underneath me as my cum continues to trickle out from her body and down her thighs.*

"You're staring again, stop it."

"I can't help it. You are easy to look at."

"Now it's my turn to blush. Your flattery astounds me and as much as I would love to keep hearing it, can we shower? Oh, and feed me too since you had your dessert first."

I carried her into the shower and was the perfect lover washing her from head to toe and finishing off with rinsing all the shampoo from her hair. By the time we finished, we were both so spent but very well sated.

"Hmmm, this is good even re-heated. Do you have secret powers or something?"

"No, why do you ask?"

"Penne Ala Vodka is my favorite Italian dish. I order it all the time."

"Good to know, I'll keep that in mind."

"Rogan, I don't want to be the buzzkill in the room but sooner than later we are going to have to talk about your father. Take it from someone who has lost both of her parents and would do anything for just one more moment with them. It wouldn't matter on any scale. A minute. An hour. A day. If I had any of that it would mean the world to me but it's just a dream in my story, it doesn't have to be in yours. Please, Rogan, I will not complicate your relationship with your father."

"Stop this right now, I know what you're doing and it's not going to work."

"Oh, yeah? What exactly am I doing other than trying to make you see reason here?"

"I think you are looking for a way to run and I'm trying to understand why that is. Did you not mean what you said to me?"

"What part? We said a lot to each other."

"The part where you love me. Don't fuck with my head, Alex, I can't take it. I'm in this too deep already."

"Are you always this dramatic? I would never say those three words so easily like I'm ordering a sandwich. And the only man I have ever voiced the words 'I love you' was to my father, and now today, it was to you. Please don't think I regret them or running like a scared little girl afraid of her own feelings. I was trying to protect you and your relationship with your family."

She looked remorseful which made me feel worse. I pulled her close and into my arms. "I'm sorry. I didn't mean to hurt your feelings."

"Hurt? No, bruised a little? Maybe."

"I'm sorry. I love you."

"I love you too," she whispered. "I have to go. My inbox is full of messages on account of my no-show back to the office today."

"Stay, I want you here. It's five o'clock somewhere and here in Georgia my clock says almost midnight."

"I don't have any clothes here."

"I can call my personal shopper and have everything you need to be delivered in an hour. Next."

"Why bother. You have an answer and a solution for everything."

"I try. Let's go to bed."

"To sleep?" she questions with amusement.

"Eventually," I say and lead her back to my bedroom.

"Call in sick," I almost beg as I continue to try to change her mind on leaving.

"I can't and you shouldn't either. Go see your father and make amends with him."

"Don't worry about it, okay? Can I ask you a question?"

"Of course, what is it?"

"What's your full name?"

"It's Alexane. It's actually my mother's maiden name and when I got to school it became too confusing for most kids, so my dad asked me if I wanted to shorten it. My mom was already gone and although I don't remember her all that well, I didn't want to disregard her memory by dissing her name."

"So, how did you reach a resolution?"

"My dad understood how I felt but then he sat me down one night for a talk. He showed me a video of their wedding and one titled 'the early days' they were so cute with each other. Watching my mom with my dad and then to hear her voice was just amazing. On the last part of the video, my dad got down on bended knee and asked my mom to marry him. She said yes immediately and then it was a few minutes of watching them kiss. My mom then said she couldn't wait to have babies and no matter what they had first, she would name him or her, Alexane. Here's the best part, my mom said she would call the baby Alex for short."

"It's perfect. What an amazing story for you to have. Thank you for sharing it with me."

"You're welcome. I hadn't thought of it for a very long time."

"I'm so sorry you had to grow up without a mom. May I ask another question?"

"How did she die?"

"Don't worry, it was always the first question I got every time I made a new friend."

"I'd like to think we're more than that."

"We are. Mom died from kidney failure. I was four. She suffered from diabetes at a young age and went against the advice of doctors and had me anyway. The strain from the pregnancy weakened her kidneys but with dialysis and medication, she managed until she couldn't. She was moved up the transplant list but then she developed an infection and wasn't strong enough to fight it. We lost her two days later."

"Oh, baby, I'm sorry." I wanted to hold her and never let go.

"I'm good. It was a long time ago. Rogan, by sharing that story with you should prove to you that I only did what I did because after losing my mom, the only person I had was my father. He was a good man and loved me beyond words. I know what I did was reckless maybe even a little stupid but I couldn't have my father hurt anymore in death than when he was alive. When you talk to your father today, please let him know how sorry I am."

"Babe, don't go.

"I have to. I'm fine. Go to work and maybe we can meet for lunch but for actual food."

CHAPTER
Eight

"I was wondering when I was going to hear from you," my grandfather says as he takes a seat at the bar. A little early for a drink but what the hey? You only live once."

"Thanks for meeting me, grandpa. I needed to talk to someone who would actually listen to me."

"Huh? Speak up son, I didn't hear you."

"Very funny. I wasn't joking when I said I needed you."

"Okay, I'm here and I will listen. And before you say another word, I've seen my son and I have heard his side and now I will hear yours."

"Grandpa, I tried to talk to dad, remember? You were there. He was totally unreasonable and only wanted to hear himself talk. I tried again, we argued and then he kicked me off the project. After that, all I saw was a haze of red and had to get out of there."

"Yes, I know and right into the arms of Ms. Alex Depry. Yeah, I know all about the EPA mole. So, grandson, let me ask you one question. Do you believe her?"

"Yes, I do."

"Okay, that's good enough for me. Finish your beer and then go see your father. He's waiting for you."

"I'm sure he is but I'm not ready to talk to him yet. Grandpa, I worked my ass off on those farms for months while he traveled the world with my mom. I lived and breathed for this project and when it was completed, I was so proud of what we accomplished. All I wanted was to prove to my father that I could do this job and do it well. I wanted him to be proud of me."

"I am," I turned around to see my father standing directly behind me.

"Took you long enough to show up." My grandfather said. He walked over to my father and pulled him aside to say something to him and then slapped him on his back and left the bar.

"Why does he do that?"

"Do what?" he asked.

"Slap you on the back."

"His version of a hug, I guess. Anyway, may I join you?"

"Yes, please." He unbuttoned his suit jacket and ordered a beer and a shot.

"I'm sorry, Rogan. I shouldn't have lost my temper the way I did, and certainly not direct any anger toward you. It was unfair and I apologize."

"Apology accepted. Thank you, dad."

"Wow, this place has not changed one bit. It brings back many memories for me and the moments I have shared with my father. He loves this place so much."

"He's told me all about it and how it will grow on me in time."

"Yes, it will. This place is part of him and I'm sure he wants you to love it just as much as he does. I should have known to come here sooner when he didn't show up this morning for work and neither did you."

"I needed time to think and sort everything out. I was hurt and confused by your actions and I felt staying away was my best option."

"And how is that working out for you?"

"Not very good but it's looking better since you showed up."

"I'm happy to hear that and so will your mom. I managed to stay off the couch last night but I was told this morning that if I didn't make things right with you, then I would find myself out in the pool house."

"Don't knock the pool house, it's awesome." I joked trying to lighten the mood.

"I agree but I would rather be in bed with your mother."

"TMI, dad!" I covered my ears. First my sister and now my father.

"Can we stay on topic?"

"Sure, go on."

"So, about Alex, she's telling the truth. I spoke to Ed this morning and along with some of his contacts, I was able to dig a little deeper into her past along with her father's. He was a good man with a solid reputation until Winston planted a lot of lies portraying him as a dirty inspector taking bribes."

"Dad, he didn't do any of that."

"I know this, but it was all fabricated to make it look like he did. When he refused the money and reported it, all that did was look like he knew his superiors were on to him and he was trying to cover his own ass. This is why his pension is frozen because it's under review."

"This is so messed up. We have to make this right for Alex, and her father."

"Yes, and we will. I have people working on it as we speak. It should be resolved relatively quickly because I also had Winston's private computer hacked and all the files copied and sent over to Ed and his superiors."

"You know a computer hacker? Shit! I think I need another beer for that story." I laughed and waved the bartender down but my father blocked my hand.

"No, you're done. We have to get back to the office. Your grandfather should be there by now. We have a lot of work to do and not a lot of time to do it in."

He threw some money down on the bar and put himself back in

order. I didn't move for a second because an overwhelming feeling of guilt flowed through me. I may have had my share of disagreements with my father over the years about school and my future but he was always fair. He always believed in me even when I gave him reasons not to. I shouldn't have stormed off and ignored him for two days. He's right, it's not the way we work out our problems.

"You okay?" he asked.

"I'm sorry."

"For what?"

"For leaving and feeling sorry for myself. I thought you lost your faith in my ability to do the work and take my place in our company."

"Listen to me, son. I would have never left for my trip if I didn't trust you. You have more than proven yourself worthy to continue what three previous generations have created. Douglas ECO is your legacy and your future. It will be yours to continue to build."

"Thanks, dad. What you just said—" I struggled with my words trying to figure out the right thing to say to my father but he did it for me.

"It's everything. I know this to be true because it's exactly what your grandfather told me when it was my turn to lead. I promise you, Rogan, you are everything I believe in."

"I will not doubt it again."

"Good. Let's go. It's time to take out the trash."

"Rogan, I'd like to introduce to you your new personal assistant, Cari Byers."

"Hi, Cari, a pleasure to meet you."

"Thank you, sir. I look forward to working with you."

"Look, it's going to be a little crazy around here today and I don't really have anything for you to do at the moment."

"No need to worry about me, sir, I have been compiling data all morning. I have everything here in these two files for you to peruse."

I took the files and walked around to my desk to sit down. "What am I looking at?"

"Everything you need to know to take down Winston Lockhart."

I placed the files down and looked up at Cari, who was just about bouncing on her toes. "I don't suppose you have special skills when it comes to computers, do you?"

"You tell me, sir. Read the files. I'll be at my desk if you should need anything else."

"Do you approve?" asked Alison.

"Yeah, she's good. Thank you."

"Hey dad, have you seen this?" I asked handing him the files.

"Yes, I have. Cari made me copies before giving them to you."

"Ha! Why doesn't that surprise me." I shook my head but my father didn't seem at all deterred by it.

"It appears Winston has been very busy, especially the last few months covering his tracks. Large amounts of money were deposited in the accounts of three federal workers all in the same department as Ernest Depry. Stupid mother fuckers! This is what happens when you allow greed to get ahead of your ambition. They took the money and planted false documentation on a man they once considered their friend. All for what? To take back the land he should have never acquired in the first place."

"Dad, what's the connection between Winston Lockhart and Ernest Depry? His main business is here in Georgia with interests all over the state."

"True but that doesn't mean anything. Winston owns the biggest orchards in the state and was looking to acquire more land to do what? We don't know yet. He wants the Harrington Farm back in a major way."

"You don't believe that bullshit about the mineral rights?"

"To early to tell but what we do have here is a valid reason to why he would need to go up to Washington. The process is extensive and most oil companies will not even look in your direction until they know for certain that the landowner owns the original mineral rights and then sometimes, secondary rights. This is Georgia, not Texas. I don't have a clue to why Winston is desperate to get this land back but it's not for oil."

"Are you sure Alex has told you everything about her father?"

"Yes, I'm sure. I believe her."

"So you've said."

"Dad—" I paused.

"I had to ask. Alison, arrange a meeting with Winston Lockhart, and right away."

CHAPTER
Nine

For the time being, I left my father to deal with Winston. I left him on his own while I caught up on some work in my office. I had a conversation with Cari and got a good feeling just talking to her. She's pretty easy going but smart as a whip. Her "alleged" hacking skills sure came in handy today but she wouldn't admit that she was the one. I wasn't going to press her about it, I was just thankful for the help and it seems she's a good fit.

"Okay, I've read over all your current projects and got familiar with the team. Here are the current standings where you are on your projects and your schedule for the rest of the month that is synced with my calendar. If you decide to add anything or delete, I will get an automatic update and an alert."

"Wow, my head is spinning. Thank you, Cari, for a great day. I usually work to at least seven during the week and may need you to work later if the situation calls for it. I sometimes get in by six am but I do not expect you to work those hours. I would say nine am is good but if you're needed earlier, I will give you plenty of notice. How does that sound?"

"Sounds perfect. See you tomorrow at nine." I waved her off and flopped back into my chair. I should work but I'm spent and feel like I could sleep for the next two days but not with Blondie around. Damn, how is it possible to miss her so much when I just left her this morning? I was just about to call her when my phone buzzed. It wasn't Alex calling but my mom who I could no longer avoid.

"Hi mom, yeah, I'm still alive. Sure, I'll see you soon."

"Oh, I have missed you," says my mom currently choking the shit out of me.

"Mom, can't breathe," I joke as I make a gagging sound. She gently shoves at my chest and laughs.

"I'm sorry, I just missed you and your sister so much. In all the years I've been a mom, I have never left you two for this long amount of time."

"Yes, this is true but we are also adults and you don't have to worry about me, and certainly not Emily. She's in married bliss along with yoga love and all that spiritual crap she does."

"Don't let your sister hear you speak that way and," she smacks me upside my head. Ouch! "I also do some of that work and if it makes your sister happy then it's a great life."

"Mom, you are a doctor, she's a life coach, two very different jobs."

"Enough! I didn't ask you over here to mock your sister's career which is amazing and that's the last I will say about that. Anyway, I want to talk about you. Grandpa Roman tells me you are in love. Is this true? I nearly fell over when I heard the news, and I want to meet her."

"Isn't there anything sacred and private anymore?"

"In this family? Yeah, think again. Rogan, this is amazing news. I am so happy you are happy. But love? I'm asking as a mom and not a professional, I swear." She crosses her heart for effect.

"Yeah, it's love. I know it's fast and you're probably thinking I'm totally crazy but it's the last thing I'm feeling right now."

"Come and sit with me," I join my mom on the couch and get comfortable knowing she's not going to allow me to leave until I tell her everything. Okay, maybe not everything. I smile.

"You and dad have been telling me for years that when I least expect it, I will meet someone that makes me feel something I have never felt before. When that day happens, I will know exactly what to do because my heart will tell me so. It did on the day Grandpa dragged me to Raggy's Bar. I was so caught up with work that I was oblivious to the fact that I was on her radar."

"I bet that hasn't happened before."

"You can say that."

"What happened next?"

"Grandpa made me send her over a drink and then she comes over and shamelessly flirts with him."

"Ha! I wish I could have seen your face." My mom says as she continues to stifle her laughter.

"It wasn't pretty and not one of my finer moments but then the old man takes off and leaves me alone with her. She was intriguing and I wanted to know her better. A few drinks later and I was back at her place. Need I say more?"

"No, we can skip that part. What happened after you met up with her again?"

"She ghosted me for a couple of days and then all hell broke loose at work and when I was down at the EPA with Ed, we met again. Only this time, I was the one taken by surprise. We both stood there in front of one another with this intense magnetic pull between us. A few moments earlier, I believed Alex was a he and all I wanted to do was rip his head off. When I found out the true identity of my nemesis, all I wanted to do was the opposite."

"Yeah, okay, I can piece the rest together. So, you sure do look happy and it's wonderful to see. After all the wedding hoopla surrounding your sister and then your father and I renewing our vows, it's all we wanted for you."

"But? Come on, just say it."

"Your father told me everything she's involved in and from where

I'm sitting, it's pretty deep. You have never had to deal with Winston Lockhart as your father and grandfather have. He's not a good man and will sell out his own mother if he knew he would get something out of it. Whatever he has on your girl must be pretty big for her to do what she did."

"No, you're wrong, mom, and dad was too. We talked today and he now believes her story."

"The story she told you."

"No, not you too. Please, mom, I thought you would be different and more understanding."

"And I can see that you have, but that doesn't mean I am just going to accept this woman into your life without at least having a conversation of my own with her. I am your mother and that role and responsibility do not end just because you become of age and move out of the nest. I love you and I just want to make sure you are okay."

"Done. I'm okay. You are off the hook." I got up and began walking to the front door.

"So, you're just going to walk out like a petulant child?"

"No, I'm leaving as an adult. Thanks for the chat, mom."

"Rogan, if you are 100% convinced that she is telling you the complete truth then I will believe her and welcome the woman you love into our family."

"Just like that? And if she doesn't measure up to your standards? What then?"

"Rogan—"

"Yeah, that's what I thought. I guess blind trust is only reserved for Emily."

"Rogan, that's not true and you know it."

I stood on the threshold of my family home and felt like a stranger. "No, it is. I know I was the family screw up for a while trying to figure out what I wanted to do with my life but I got there. All I have done is work and work fucking hard to prove to you and dad that I am so much more than your disappointment. And when I finally do meet that special someone, you treat her like a fucking felon. No, you will not be meeting her anytime soon. I'm not sure you ever will."

"You are not nor have ever been a disappointment. You're angry now, I get it but you saying the things you are saying right now are completely out of line and frankly, hurt my feelings. You and your sister are our entire world. We have given you both our complete heart, love, and trust. You want to be angry, be angry, but don't you ever question my feelings or commitment to you."

I didn't say another word and got into my car speeding off for the gate. As I was leaving the property, my father was arriving home. He rolled down his window and asked me what was wrong. "Ask mom" and then I sped off without another word. Fuck! this is not how I saw this playing out with my mom. Is she right? Am I just going on blind trust with Alex? I don't want to believe that I am.

A text message came through and it was from my mom.

Mom: *I'm sorry.*

I was stopped at a light and quickly texted back.

Me: *I know. I'm sorry too.*

Mom: *When will I see you again?*

Me: *When I'm ready."*

I shut my phone off and drove over to the one home I knew I would be welcomed in. When I got up to her place the door looked like it was kicked in. I shoved my way inside and called out to her in a panic. Her place was trashed with the little possessions she had were now knocked over and smashed.

"Alex! You here? Alex!?" I called out again and then I heard her call for me from her bedroom.

"In here," she said weakly. When I reached Alex, she was lying on the floor and bleeding from her head.

"Baby, oh, my god." I grabbed a t-shirt to apply pressure to her head that was still bleeding profusely. I reached for my phone and dialed 9-1-1.

"9-1-1, what's your emergency?"

"I need an ambulance to 137 Park Avenue right away. My girlfriend has been attacked in her apartment and is unconscious with a head wound."

"Okay, sir, I have your location and I am dispatching two units. E-T-A in five minutes, please stand by."

"Thank you, please hurry." I dropped the call and concentrated on Alex. The blood was not stopping even with using my shirt to apply pressure. What the hell did she get hit with? A hammer? A few minutes later I heard the paramedics call out. "We're back here, please help her." I cried out. I got out of the way so they could work on her. She was as still as a board. They were calling out all sorts of commands, I could hardly keep up with what they were saying. Thank god her apartment was close to the hospital. In a matter of a couple of minutes, she was accessed and loaded up into the back of the ambulance. I tried to join her but I was stopped by one of the responding police officers.

"Go, don't wait for me. Just take care of her."

"Listen, I have told you all I know. I got here and found the door hanging off its hinges. I rushed inside and found the apartment ransacked. I found my girlfriend barely breathing and then I phoned for help."

"Sir, do you know anyone who might have done this?" he continued to question me. I answered him, no but in the back of my mind, all I could think of was Winston and his thirst for revenge. Did he find out that his lies have been exposed? I never did check-in with my father, so I don't know what happened after I left the office. Fuck! He's a dead man if he did this to her. I raced to the hospital not caring about the traffic lights along the way. I just had this overpowering need to be with Alex. Once I arrived, I hastily parked my car and tossed my keys over to the valet and kept running toward the entrance of the ER department.

No one was at the information desk. Come on, I need help here. I looked around and then hit the bell and didn't stop until an older man came out to greet me practically snatching the bell from my hand.

"Can I help you, sir?" he asked with no humor in his voice.

"Yes, I need information on Alex Depry, she was brought in by an ambulance."

"Are you a relative?" he asked.

"Yes, she's my wife," I lie but I don't care. I will say anything to get back there.

CHAPTER
Ten

Three hours have gone by and still no word on Alex. What the fuck is taking so long? I checked in with the information desk every half hour on the hour and was told the same thing. She's in surgery and a doctor will come out and join me when there is news to be told. I'm going crazy here, like batshit crazy losing my fucking mind.

I was pacing the long hallway and that's when the double doors swung open and a man in scrubs began to approach me. "Are you the next of kin for Alex Depry?" he asked and my heart sunk. Next of kin? Is she fucking dead?

"I am. How is she?"

"She's stable. She suffered a blunt trauma to the back of her skull resulting in two brain bleeds in different sections of the brain. One was an easy repair, the other was more complicated. She's breathing on her own which is a very positive sign. She's been moved up to the ICU of Neurology. She's going to be closely monitored for the night and her condition will be assessed in the morning when the rest of my team joins me for rounds."

"I'm sorry, and you are?"

"My apologies to you. I'm doctor Bennett, head of Neurology. I was paged upon her arrival. We did a cat scan and quickly determined she would need surgery. I'm sorry that no one gave you an update sooner but due to the dire situation, we had to act quickly."

"No, I'm glad you did. Can I see her?"

"I'm afraid that's not possible. She's heavily sedated."

"I don't care, I just need to be close to her."

"Okay, five minutes and no more than that. You can get a special pass made up and be back here by six for rounds. We can meet up then."

"Fine, I don't care. I just need to see her right now."

"Follow me, I will show you to her room."

Her room was illuminated with a soft overhead light above her bed. Even in sleep, she was breathtakingly beautiful. I wanted to crawl up and lay beside her but she had so many wires coming from her arms and chest, I didn't want to hurt her.

Fuck! I swear on my life I am going to make whoever did this pay. I whispered in her ear that I loved her with everything I have and then placed a kiss on her forehead.

"I'll be back baby."

It was way past midnight when I arrived back at my parent's house. I rushed up the stairs to their bedroom and called out for my father.

"What is it, son? are you alright?" he asked half asleep.

"No, I'm not. I need you."

"I'll be right there. Give me a minute to get dressed."

I was at the bottom of the stairs facing the entryway when my dad came down. My mom followed close behind and as soon as she saw my expression, she quickly took me in her arms to hold me. It was taking everything I had not to break down and seek out my mother's comfort but it was my father who I needed more.

"Oh, baby, what's happening?" she asked with concern.

"I don't mean to be short with you but it's dad who I need. Please, mom, don't press me right now."

"Okay. I understand. Can I get you anything to eat or drink?"

"No, thank you. Dad, can we go somewhere and talk?"

"Sure, let's go into my office. Honey, go back to sleep. I'll take care of our son." She nodded and gave my father a hug and kiss before returning upstairs. I knew she wanted to stay but I was happy she gave me the time I needed with my father.

"What's happened?" he asked and closed the door behind him.

"Someone broke into Alex's apartment tonight and physically assaulted her. She had to undergo brain surgery and is in stable condition at the moment."

"Holy shit! It has to be Winston."

"My thoughts exactly. That mother fucker is a dead man walking. Let's go get him."

"Rogan, it's not that simple."

"The hell it isn't. This has gone on longer than it had to be. And? For what? Some fucking land? Mineral rights that are just that? He's deluded if he believes he has oil on those lands and no land is worth hurting my girlfriend!" I shouted out my anger.

"Rogan, will you calm the hell down and take a breath. I know everything points to Winston but we need unyielding evidence first. Hopefully, that will come tomorrow when I meet with him."

"You can't be serious."

"After you left the office yesterday, I did some digging of my own and found out the original mineral rights did indeed belong to Creekside Orchards but they were in the name of Winston's father. They never got transferred over to the new owner which would be Harrington."

"How can that be? Doesn't the new owner take possession when he acquires the property?"

"Yes, in today's times, they do but this is going back over five decades maybe more. The laws were different back then to what we have in place now. Harrington could not have known and all he wants to do is work his farm probably not caring at all about drilling for oil."

"Okay, let's say this is the true motive behind Winston's drive to bribe Alex's father, blackmail his daughter and ultimately attack Alex. Doesn't he know that no secret stays buried forever? Look what I have already uncovered in just under a week? And now with you back home and onto him, how the hell does he think he can get away with all of this?"

"I don't know but my father does."

"Grandpa? What does he have to do with all of this?"

"Your grandfather and Winston's grandfather were friends back in the day and yes, did some wildcatting back in the 1980s when the talk of oil was hot but as you know, it resulted into just a myth. Lockhart was a gambler and lost practically everything in bad investments and then the stock market crashed and that was the end of his empire. When his son took over he was practically starting over from scratch with hardly any capital to work with. He was a decent rival and played as amicably as he could but then I took over and relationships changed."

"I was very aggressive when I took over at the helm and although grandpa still mentored me, I had my own vision for the state of the company and pretty much did what I wanted. I was responsible for a hostile take-over on one of the companies that Winston was trying to acquire. When he won in court and stole those properties causing the farmers to go bankrupt, I was convinced it was a personal attack and I never stopped trying to get those lands back. A few months ago, right before my birthday, I succeeded. He was outraged. I didn't care. I laughed in his face and threw him out of my office."

"I was too caught up in my work and everything that happened after between your mother and me, I got careless and stopped paying attention. I should have known he would try something to get back at me never knowing he would go after Alex or her father to get what he wanted. I guess I shouldn't be surprised."

"Dad, are you fucking kidding me right now? Shouldn't be surprised? Of course, it would make sense for him to seek revenge against you. You fucked him over. He waited out his time and instead of going after you which has been proven to fail and fail again. He decides to go after me by putting my girlfriend in the hospital with two god damn brain bleeds."

"I know and I'm so sorry. We will get to the bottom of this, I promise you."

"I need a drink and a shower, or maybe just a drink and keep them coming."

"One shot and you are going up to your room to sleep. I know you want to get drunk enough so you don't feel the pain you are feeling right now but that is not going to help Alex. She needs you to be there and you will after you get some rest, okay?"

"She has to make it, dad? I love her."

"I know you do. Come on, let's get that drink."

When my father went back to bed, I continued drinking. I know I shouldn't have but it was either getting drunk or killing Winston and if I were to do that, then I would need a whole hell of a lot of liquid courage. After my fourth drink, I knew I was toast and passed out.

"Rogan, wake up," I groaned while my head pounded into the pillow. "Rogan, you need to wake up and get over to the hospital." I sprang up too quickly only to get lightheaded and grab my head.

"What happened? Is it Alex?"

"You dumb shit! I knew I shouldn't have gone to bed knowing you were still free to drink. Son, you need to get up," my father shouted into my ear.

"I'm up and I'll be ready in five minutes," I said as my stomach rolled and then I ran to the bathroom barely making it to the toilet. Once I knew I was done vomiting, I shouted, "better make it ten."

I felt like shit as my father drove me to the hospital. My eyes were covered by my aviator glasses shielding the sun and my bloodshot eyes. "Rogan, we're almost there. Here, take this and put a few drops in your eyes." He handed me a bottle of Visine.

"Dad, I get it, I look like shit," I said as I put the drops into my eyes. "Please spare me the lecture."

"You're lucky I'm not knocking you on your ass. The one shot I gave you was from your grandfather's private stock and it's not the cheap over the counter crap. One shot was all you needed but as always you take it to the extreme and down four more. You are lucky to still be breathing and not laying in a pool of your own vomit."

"Are you done?"

"Yes, for now, I am. Pull yourself together, we're here." I looked up as he parked his jag in front of the valet podium.

"Keep it close, thank you."

"Dad, you don't have to go in with me, I will be fine on my own."

"I want to be here for you and for your girl, so stop trying to get rid of me. Come on, rounds are about to begin and you need to catch up with her doctor." Dr. Bennett had left passes for me at the desk. After we got them, we took the elevator up to the fifth floor and quickly spotted the doctor walking with a group of other doctors.

"Dr. Bennett, wait up," I called out. When I reached him I asked about Alex. He said he was just on his way in to see her and for me to wait out in the hall until he was through with his examination.

"You want some coffee?"

"No, I'm fine. I just want Alex to wake up."

"I'll be right back. Stay out of trouble."

I paced the hallway back and forth until the doctors finally emerged from her room. Dr. Bennett came up to me and asked to speak with me privately.

"How is she? Any improvement?"

"There is which gives me hope. She's remained stable throughout the night and that's a very good sign. I want to keep her here on this floor until she wakes up. She will remain monitored 24/7 and I'm remaining optimistic that she will open her eyes soon. I find no other reason why she won't. It's frustrating, this I know but she sustained quite a blow to the back of her head. It's a miracle she's still breathing.

I also wanted to mention something that may have been missed last night in the ER with all the chaos getting her up to surgery."

"What is it?" I asked. My father was back and joined us.

"How's Alex?"

"She's stable. I'll tell you about it in a minute. Dr. Bennett was just about to tell me something."

"She was fully examined after blood and hair fibers were found on her."

"No! Stop. Don't fucking say it. Shit! I'm going to be sick."

"Rogan, what has gotten into you?" asked my father as he took hold of my shoulders to keep me in place. Dr. Bennett interrupted my freak out moment and reassured me what I was thinking did not happen.

"Are you sure?"

"Yes, I am. I should have gone over my findings last night and clarify what we found. I apologize for that. No, she was not sexually assaulted, but it also had to be ruled out. As I stated, she was found to have blood and hair fibers underneath her fingernails. I'm a doctor, not a forensic expert but if I had to guess, I would say she fought her attacker who now has a deep scratch probably on his neck."

"Can I see her?"

"Absolutely, you can go in."

"Thank you, Dr. Bennett."

My father continued to speak with him as I entered her room, closing the door behind me. She looked better this morning with some color returning to her face but I wouldn't be satisfied until I could look into her gorgeous azure colored eyes.

I brushed the few stray hairs away that had fallen over her forehead. "You are so beautiful, Blondie. Please wake up and come back to me. I haven't even taken you out on a date yet. I think we just skipped ahead and forgot about all the many firsts couples do when falling in love with each other. I know it matters and I promise we will have all those firsts together. You just need to wake up so I can begin showing you the world. I want to spoil you rotten and all I want in return is you beside me. You've given me something so special that I never knew was wanted but now that I have it, I'm going to hold onto it for the rest of my life."

"Rogan, I'm sorry to interrupt. I have to get down to the office for my meeting. Are you joining me?"

"Yeah, I'll be right there."

I waited until he closed the door and then I continued speaking to Alex.

"You sleep baby and get better. I'll be back as soon as I can. I love you." I kissed her warm lips and stroked her cheek. It pained my heart to leave her but what was killing me more was knowing the person who hurt her was out there walking free. After I finish with Winston Lockhart, he will be lucky to still have use of his legs.

CHAPTER
Eleven

"So, what's the plan here? Is Lockhart coming in today?" I questioned my father. "Are you going to answer me?"

"Rogan, I plan on dealing with Winston in my own way and that way does not involve you."

"The hell it doesn't! Why are you shutting me out?"

"You are too close and clearly very angry which makes you dangerous and unpredictable. I can't have you going off half-cocked and showing your hand to him. He's already proven that he has nothing to lose and will do anything to get what he wants and that's including attempted murder on your girl. For all we know, he may believe he succeeded in silencing Alex for good. What we need to know is what he was looking for at her apartment? And was it worth killing for?"

"Maybe he didn't intend to hurt her at all?"

"What do you mean?"

"I'm thinking she came home early and surprised him. She's tough, a survivor. She's had to be all these months grieving for her father and living under Lockhart's threats and blackmail. Yesterday morning we had a heart to heart and dad, she bared her soul to me about losing her mom at a young age and growing up without her.

They were a team for many years and maybe I didn't understand it when I first found out her part in all of this, but I do now. This piece of shit Lockhart preyed on Alex and the love and loyalty she had for her father. I think she had enough and fought back."

"On all accounts, it's looking that way but until he admits it, all we have is speculation. When you left yesterday, I got in touch with some of my contacts at the FBI along with Fleming. They know everything and currently have Winston on surveillance. A meeting has been arranged and he will be here today at noon. The office is wired for sound and whatever he says will be also heard by a team of undercover agents in the office next door."

"I have to be here. Please don't shut me out." I implored.

"I'm sorry but you have to go. Again, you are way too close to this and I will not have you involved. I want you to go and be with your girl. I will call you when it's all over and he's in custody."

"What if this was mom? Or Emily? Would you be so eager to just leave their fate up to chance at nailing their assailant to the wall?"

"That's not fair."

"Oh, but it's fair for Alex?"

"You are not listening, Rogan. This is why you have to leave. You are not behaving rationally, and your anger is going to trip you up with Winston. Please, just go back to the hospital and I will call you as soon as it's over."

"Fine, I'm out of here."

"Excuse me, Mr. Douglas, everything is ready in conference room B."

"Thank you, Alison. Are Ty and Paul out of the office?"

"Yes, I delivered your instructions."

"Okay, back to business. Let me know when Winston arrives."

"Yes, sir."

"Oh, Alison, one more thing. Check with security and let me know that Rogan has left the building and grounds."

"Right away."

I knew my father well enough to know he would have tracked my movements until I was off the property and away from interfering with today's meeting. Once I was far enough away from the property camera's, I parked my car out of sight and returned on foot using the back entrances and ones he wouldn't be looking at. I re-entered the building through the loading dock and took the stairs all the way up to the executive floors. I couldn't just walk out in the open and alert my father to my presence. I took the back stairs and was right in front of conference room B. I heard voices coming from inside so I knew the FBI was set to go. I ducked out of sight and hid in the adjoining bathroom between my father's office and the conference room. I hoped I would be able to listen the best I could without being detected.

This was for Alex. I knew if this went south and that bastard didn't implicate himself, I would take the matter into my own hands and not give a shit what happens to me. My father would disagree but I just don't care.

About fifteen minutes later, I heard doors opening and closing along with voices coming from my inside of my father's office. One was my father and the other was Lockhart.

"Okay, Douglas, what do I owe the pleasure of being summoned to your office?"

"I think you know but I'll try to talk slow so you understand."

"Someone is touchy today. Rough night?"

"Yeah, asshole, a great way to open the communication by taunting my father."

"Where's your young apprentice? Did the lad need a day off? It must be exhausting trying to keep up with his old man."

"Age doesn't have anything to do with it. I'm still in the game, Lockhart, and my son is just beginning. You on the other hand, well, time's up."

"You're wrong, I still have a lot of moves to make and plenty of chips to cash in. It's already underway and soon I'll have back what is rightfully mine."

"The mineral rights on the Harrington farm?"

"For starters. They're mine, Douglas, and I intend to acquire them back."

"So you can drill for imaginary oil you believe is buried deep beneath the earth? Yeah, think again. You will never get those rights back because they have all legally been transferred back to Harrington."

"No, you're lying."

"I can assure you that I'm not. You lose…again."

"I still have a card to play."

"And what would that be? The mole you planted down at the EPA?"

"Fuck! I can't hear anything." I have to get in there and without compromising my father's plan.

I slipped out of the bathroom and walked to Alison's desk. She looked up surprised to see me. Her hand was on my father's private number when I stopped her.

"Stay out of this, Alison. My father is going to know I'm in the building because I intend to walk into his office."

"You're playing with fire, Rogan. You need to let your father handle this."

"Not this time. This is my family's company and legacy that bastard tried to compromise. An innocent woman has been hurt at the hands of Lockhart. I belong in that room. Please don't try to stop me." She nodded and gestured for me to go.

I knocked a couple of times on the door before entering. "Hey dad, sorry I'm late. My meeting ran over and I got delayed."

He covered perfectly. "It's fine, you haven't missed much. Don't forget your manners, we have a guest." He pointed over to Winston who was smirking like the smug bastard he is.

"How do you do, Winston," I say shaking his hand, trying not to punch him in the jaw.

"Doing just fine. And you?"

"I'm great, thanks for asking," I replied and then looked at my father before handing him an envelope with the EPA seal on it. "Great news, dad, you will find in that report that we have received all green flags on the farms that were flagged. It seems it was a misunderstanding and Ed Fleming sends his deepest apologies to us. I've contacted Harrington, Stallings, and Jefferson who are all already at work on their farms. We did it, dad," I said excitedly, hoping to get a reaction from Lockhart.

"This is great news, wouldn't you say, Lockhart? I guess your little undercover operation didn't work after all."

"It's impossible, you're lying."

"Now why would I lie? Reports don't lie, at least the real ones."

"No! those properties belong to me."

"They never belonged to you. You are out of your mind if you believe otherwise. Face it, Lockhart, it's over. We know what you've done trying to sabotage our work and the officials you bribed to make it happen."

"You got nothing, son, and will never be able to prove it." I looked back to my father showing him I got this. I wouldn't have come in if I wasn't confident I couldn't rattle Lockhart. He's a pompous sonofabitch who hates to lose or be outsmarted. I just had to be better and bluff my way into making him reveal his part in all of this. I already knew he was the one that broke into Alex's apartment. You couldn't miss the deep cut on his neck just noticeable enough above his collar.

I pulled a flash drive out from my pocket and raised it up for both men in the room to see. Lockhart looked visibly uncomfortable and then I knew I had him.

"You see what I'm holding here, yeah take a closer look because it's your undoing. Is this what you were looking for when you broke into Alex Depry's apartment?"

"I don't know what you are referring to."

He stepped back, I stepped closer. Sure you do, and you were willing to do anything to get your hands on it, weren't you? It contains all kinds of information. One, in particular, is when you admit planting evidence to make one Ernest Depry look very bad in his department. When he wouldn't comply with your demands, you force his daughter to doctor a phony report to red flag our jobs, but you slipped up Lockhart because you didn't count on what did you call me? Oh yeah, the young lad going directly to Fleming's superiors to reinspect.

"Stupid bitch, I knew she had to be recording me."

I got you!

"Is that why you almost killed her?" He ran his hands through his hair and shouted out.

"She wasn't supposed to be there! I never wanted to hurt her. She came after me first."

"Is that how you got that nasty cut on your neck?" said my father. "She fought you, Winston, and judging how she's fighting for her life right now, I would say it was pretty hard."

He fell to his knees and began to cry as he continued to say that he never meant to hurt her or take it this far. I wasn't going to allow this piece of shit to cry over my girl. I reached down and hauled him up by his suit jacket.

"You didn't win and will never be able to hurt anyone again," I said and pulled back with everything I had to knock him on his ass. At that moment, the FBI charged inside and arrested him on a number of charges breaking federal laws.

We watched Lockhart be led away in handcuffs and once he was gone and out of sight, I released the breath I had been holding.

"Holy shit, that was intense," I said bending over to grasp onto my knees.

"Come here," was all he said as he stepped closer to pull me in for a hug. My father held on to my shoulders where I practically sagged against him. "How did you know to do that? You took a big risk back there."

"I know I did but I saw no other way."

"You always have a choice, Rogan, and fortunately for you, yours paid off."

"Dad, you know how much I respect you, right?"

"Yes, I do."

"Then you know I would never just go against you and not be sure about the repercussions of my actions. He put Alex in the hospital. Whatever he was searching for had to be pretty big to do that."

"Did she ever tell you she had evidence as a back-up?"

"No, she didn't. I guess I watch too many crime shows. I was just going on a bluff and used what Alex shared with me to at least show Lockhart I knew what I was talking about."

"It paid off and thanks to your quick thinking, Winston Lockhart is going away for a very long time. You did great and I have never been more proud."

"Thank you, dad, I really needed to hear that right now."

"No, you didn't. You just needed to believe it. If I ever made you doubt that, I am truly sorry. You are my son first and forever."

"Thanks, dad," I said and then I delivered a hard slap to his back.

"Hey, what was that for?"

"Just another way to say I love you."

"I think you've been hanging around grandpa too much."

"Is that a bad thing?"

"Never."

"You'll finish up here?"

"Yeah, go see your girl. We're praying for her."

"Thanks, dad. Will you do me a favor?"

"Anything."

"Will you tell mom that I'm sorry too."

"She knows but sure, I'll tell her."

CHAPTER
Twelve

I showed my pass and took the elevator up to the fifth floor. When I got to her room, it was empty and the bed looked freshly made. Panic seized in my chest as the air escaped my lungs. "Where are you, Alex?" I gripped my shirt and twisted the material between my fingers.

"Turn around, I'm right here," she said. I couldn't believe what I was seeing. Alex was up and in a wheelchair looking as beautiful as she can be. I lost all ability to speak and simply dropped to my knees and placed my head on her lap. I broke down right there not giving a shit how I looked. She came back to me.

"I can't believe you're looking at me right now. I thought I was going to lose you."

"Impossible. I'm too smart to leave you when I just found you."

"Hey, that's my line."

"It's our line." I took my girl in my arms and kissed her passionately with everything I had. "Wow, I'm going to feel that for days," she laughed happily.

"I was hoping you would say that because I want you to feel them for the rest of your life as my wife." I paused for a moment to study her beautiful face. She was speechless which just made me want her even more.

"I guess I know one way to silence you but if I'm being honest here, I would rather hear something else come from your enticing mouth like the word, yes."

"Was there a question posed somewhere? Or was it you just issuing another statement of fact?"

"I'm not sure I understand your question."

"It should be pretty easy. Since we've met, you have basically have stated what you've wanted and have had no issue with taking it. Today is no different. Do you hope for me to be your wife? Or you just know it's going to happen because it's what you want?"

"And I always get what I want? Is that how you see me?"

"In a way, yes. You're strong, passionate, and confident but not in a cocky way. We are so different. I've always played it safe and never once colored outside the lines until the night I met you at Raggy's. I was drawn to you with this fiery connection burning inside of me."

"I feel as if we have known each other for a lifetime but in reality, it's only been a few weeks. How is that possible?"

"Because it's right and somehow we were meant to find each other that night. What I do know is my heart and how it's led me here to be with you. I don't care about the logistics and how we happened. All I care about is that we did happen and if there's any confusion about how I feel about you, then allow me to clear it up right now."

"I love you. I no longer want to walk in this life alone. I need you beside me always. This is me standing before you, asking you to love and trust me to always love you unconditionally and protecting you forever. Alexane Depry, will you marry me?"

"Honey, if you don't say yes, I will." We both laughed when her nurse walked in. "Well? Don't keep him in suspense?"

"Okay, I won't," she said looking back at me with stars in her eyes. "Yes, Rogan, I will marry you. Yes. Yes. A thousand times yes."

I took Alex in my arms and cradled her body against mine. "I love you so much. I can't wait to make you mine."

"I think I already am."

"Yeah, you are but I don't mind reminding you." I kissed her again and again before placing her down back on her bed. "You look, tired baby, do you want to get rest?"

"I feel great, don't worry about me."

"Yeah, well you weren't so great when I found you. Do you remember anything about what happened?"

"Yeah, it's a little fuzzy but I remember. I left the office intending to go to your place, but I needed to pick up some clothes first. I should have left the minute I saw my door damaged, but I foolishly went inside and saw Lockhart flipping sofa cushions and dumping my bookcase."

"Do you know why he would risk exposure by going to your apartment?"

"He believed I had evidence on him, and he wanted to locate and destroy it before I could hand it over to the authorities. The only thing is, I didn't. A call came through my office yesterday and it was him checking for a status. I told him that I was out and didn't care what would happen to me because I had proof that would end this one way or another."

"He got angry and threatened me again and I hung up on him. He never called back and I didn't talk to him again until I found him in my apartment."

"Did you have any evidence on him?"

"No, it was just a bluff. My father loved poker and taught me how to fake out an opponent. I guess I never utilized that skill until going up against Lockhart."

"How did you get hurt?"

"I tried to run and he grabbed me by my hair and threw me into the wall. He hit me again and that's when I fought him with every self-defense tactic I knew. I was almost free and then he struck me to the back of my head and I don't remember anything else until you came for me. I remember hearing your voice and then I must have blacked out."

"Yeah, that's pretty much it. I was out of my mind with worry and baby, I thought I was going to lose you. You were bleeding so badly and I couldn't stop it."

"It's over now, right?"

"Yeah, we got him. My father and I confronted him and the FBI got it all on video."

"It's really over?"

"For Lockhart, yes. For us, it's just beginning. Rest up and get well so we can get on that, okay?"

"Yeah, bossy man, I'm on it."

Five days later I took Alex home to begin the first day of the rest of our lives. The doctor said she made a remarkable recovery and was very lucky. She called me bossy which wasn't too far from the truth. I had her moved out of her apartment after she agreed to marry me. The place was trashed anyway and the few personal things she had moved with her from her family home is now in our home. I wasn't planning on holding on to the apartment and already had my very efficient assistant, Cari working with my realtor to find me a home close to my parents' home. Emily and Gus weren't too far away either.

We were always a close-knit family and with Emily and Gus in married bliss and me on the way, all my mom was dreaming of were grandbabies. She and my father were taking bets on who would be first but I was in no hurry. I wanted to savor every minute with Alex before I had to share her. I know it sounds selfish but it's how I feel. Since our relationship was built on blind faith, what's one more thing like pending parenthood?

"You are too quiet over there, what are you thinking about?"

"Just you and all the wonderful things about you that I love." I lifted her hand to my mouth and kissed it.

"You are so charming when you want to be. For the record, I'm excited to begin our new life together as well. Your sister has been texting me non-stop to make her our wedding planner. Isn't she too busy for that sort of thing?"

"You would think so with her work schedule, but Emily is a queen at multi-tasking. She lives for this kind of thing and I know wants to help."

"Are you sure? Because I don't know the first thing about wedding planning and I'm still navigating the waters of suddenly being part of a big family. It was only me and my father for the longest time. Our life was pretty quiet back east and I didn't have many friends. It's just me, you know. I feel as if I'm an orphan with no past."

"Well, we know that's not true. My family already loves you and I love you, so you are not alone. If anything, you have too many people in your life, but I've been told that's a good thing."

"Okay, you win. Just give me some time to adjust to it all."

"I will. We can go as slow as you want. As long as you're with me, I'm fine with everything else."

I didn't want to go home until we finished talking and she felt more at ease. By the time we did arrive back at my building, my girl had fallen asleep. I parked the car in front and had the doorman take her things while I carried her inside. She had lost weight in the hospital and carrying her was no effort at all. She protested because she thought she was on the curvier side but hell no, the curvier, the better. She's perfect and I would never change anything about her.

"I can walk you know," she said as she buried her face in my neck.

She is so lying right now. She loves it and I love it knowing how happy it makes her feel.

"Will you please put me down?" She implored.

"I will once we are inside," I unlocked the door and continued to carry her through the apartment and up the stairs to our bedroom. "Okay, now I'll put you down. Get comfortable because this is your new home away from home until you are 100% medically cleared."

"I'm fine, Rogan, and my doctor wouldn't have released me if I wasn't."

"No, you have selective hearing. Dr. Bennett only released you to my care because I promised him that I would be home to take care of you and I will. I'm on leave from work, so you got me, babe."

"Okay, I promise to be a model patient."

"That was easy, I thought you were going to put up a fight."

"I guess the old me would have but that was before you. I want to feel as if I belong and that's never going to happen if I'm fighting it."

Alex was true to her word and was the perfect patient. I only caught her twice trying to make a break for it but Emily was the true conspirator. Wedding plans were a go with both my sister and my mom helping Alex out. Although she was offered a position on Ed's team, she declined and gave her notice. Her father's name was cleared and the ones that were working for Lockhart were fired and brought up on charges. Ernest's hold on his pension was lifted and Alex has moved the money into a trust to begin a scholarship fund in her parent's name. It was a great idea and she had my full support.

For now, I wanted her well and concentrating on our wedding. She had plenty of time to choose what she wanted in a career or do nothing at all. It would be entirely up to my girl and there was no rush.

"Hey honey, thanks for stopping by." My mom said as she gave me a warm hug and invited me in.

"No worries, mom, I have some time to kill while Alex is at her check-up. What did you want to tell me?"

"Okay, it occurred to me today that with all this wedding planning going on around you, you forgot one very important detail."

"Oh, yeah, what's that?"

"Alex needs an engagement ring," *I almost swallowed my tongue. Holy shit! I never gave Alex a ring? What the fuck is wrong with me?* "Okay, I see the panic in your eyes but mama is on it. I have the perfect ring for you to give to Alex."

"Mom, I can't believe I forgot a ring. And why hasn't she said anything about it? Isn't that a little weird?"

"In Alex's case, not at all. In the last few weeks, I have spent a great deal of time with her and she defines simplicity. This girl of yours is very special and I can't tell you how sorry I am for doubting her love for you."

"Thanks, mom, your blessing means the world to us."

"You should have had it from the start but better late than never. So, back to the ring." I watched my mom look at her left hand and smile.

I placed my hand over hers and said, "Dad did a good job with your rings,"

"He sure did and as much as I would love to hand down my engagement ring to you, I just can't part with it. It holds so many memories of our life together and the ring you present to Alex will too. Over the years, your father has given me many beautiful pieces of jewelry. I have so much of it, it's hard to choose what to wear on any chosen occasion. When I realized her hand was missing an engagement ring, I opened my vault and began going through my collection. This is what I chose for you." She opened the velvet box and inside was a princess cut diamond in the middle with a sapphire stone on either side.

"The diamond comes from a pendant that your father had given me for our five-year wedding anniversary."

"And the sapphires? Do they have a story too?"

"They do. On the day you were born, my mom gave me a birthstone tennis bracelet and the charm dangling from it was a platinum heart with two sapphires in your honor. I took my pendant and bracelet to a jewelry designer and he came up with this. Do you like it? I hope I didn't overstep."

"God no, mom, this is perfect. How will I ever thank you for doing this for Alex, and for me?"

"It was my pleasure and my way of welcoming my new daughter. I love you both and only want the best for you. Now, go home and make her happy by giving her this ring." After I picked Alex up from her appointment, we dined at the harbor club to celebrate. We were seated at my favorite table overlooking the marina. It was a gorgeous late day afternoon and the scene was set to present Alex her ring. We clinked our glasses together and toasted her recovery and all who helped get her here.

"I'm so ready to get married, Rogan, and now that I am healthy and cleared, there is not anything standing in our way," she said excitedly and downing the rest of her champagne.

"Well, there's one thing," I said. She looked at me with confusion and then smiled when she saw the ring box. "I was reminded today that I forgot a very important detail and I can't begin to tell you how stupid I feel for not giving you a ring sooner."

"You had a lot on your mind." She laughed and held my hand in hers. I slowly opened the box and took the ring out to place on her left ring finger. I placed a kiss down to her hand and then leaned in to kiss her lips.

"Will you marry me, Alexane Depry?"

"Yes, I will. Now if it's alright with you, I would like to continue this celebration at home and in our bed. Oh, and we will be very naked doing all kinds of naughty things to each other. Sound like a plan?"

Thank you, god, for bringing me this woman.

"I agree with your plan. Check please!"

EPILOGUE

One year later

"Babe, you've been in there for a while now, is everything okay?" I asked knocking on the bathroom door.

"I'm fine," she called out. "I'll be out in a minute."

"You said that twenty minutes ago. Come on, what's going on?" I knocked and knocked until she finally unlocked the door and walked out. Tears were streaming down her face. I held her face and pulled her in for a hug. She could never hide anything from me, her facial expressions were just so animated and showed all her emotions.

"Please, talk to me," I asked again.

She didn't say anything in return. She reached for something in her pocket and asked me to hold out my hand. When I looked to see what it was, I never expected to feel that happy about it. After we got married and took an extended honeymoon, it was back to work and moving into our new home. We talked about starting a family and sure had fun trying but we left it up to chance and continued living our lives.

My sister Emily found out she was pregnant while planning our wedding and now is a mother to my nephew, Max. My mom is in seventh heaven and now it's our turn.

"Are you okay," I asked my wife as she continued to cry but never stopped smiling.

"I'm amazing. It was a shock and I just needed to take some time to process it and hoped you would be happy about it."

"Are you crazy? I'm going to be a father! I'm over the moon." I lifted her up in my arms and twirled her around the room until I was dizzy. This is how she made me feel. I can't wait to have this baby with Alex. We lay in bed talking about how it will be becoming parents and the excitement building up inside me just made my heart burst from my chest.

"Rogan," she whispered my name like a prayer.

"Hmmm," I responded by hugging her tighter to me. She fit perfectly.

"I was a little nervous telling you about the baby." I shifted to where I was on my side so I could look into her eyes when I talked to her.

"Why on earth would you be scared? Did you think I wouldn't want it?"

"No, never. I guess I was just nervous because you always said that you weren't ready to start a family yet and you didn't want to share me with anyone else."

"Honey, you misunderstood what I said. Our relationship didn't exactly begin the conventional way. We hit the fast-forward button and jumped a few steps ahead but no steps that I will ever regret taking with you. It has been an amazing year loving and keeping you all to myself but that doesn't mean I don't have room for more. I'm already in love with our child. It's love at first sight on the biggest scale imaginable."

She nudged closer resting her palms on my chest. "How could you be so sure?"

"Easy. I'm sure because I am so in love with its mother. Every single time I look into your eyes, all I see is my love for you staring back at me. This is how I am so sure, it's because of you."

"Way to go making a girl cry. Oh, Rogan, I don't believe you could top what you just said to me. I swear you should be working for Hallmark." I laughed heartily and positioned her on top of me straddling my hips just the way I like it.

"As great as that sounds, I'm happy just reserving all the sweet words for you and you alone. Now we had some sugar, how about you giving me some spice?"

"Oh, my goodness, that was corny, but I love you anyway."

"Hey, what can I say? I can't always deliver the cry worthy lines all the time."

"Nine months is a long time to be pregnant. I'm sure I will be crying a lot. Just keep the tissues close-by."

"And the ice cream, we can't forget that."

"No way, that is a pregnancy requirement. Now let me ride you so I can work up an appetite."

"Yes, ma'am. And you say I'm the bossy one in the relationship."

"I guess then we are made for each other."

"We are without a doubt. We've been destined from the start. Alexane Depry, you changed my life and altered my thinking without even trying. I sometimes look at you from across the room and my breath hitches in my throat and I forget what I wanted to say because my heart finds it difficult to catch up with my brain. Your love is a gift. This baby is our reward. I will love you forever." Her tears were unstoppable as I made love to her worshiping and cherishing every inch of her beautiful body. I was a lucky man. Our life was blessed.

"You know, they say when babies sleep, we should sleep," I heard her say as she wrapped her arms around my waist and buried her face in my naked back.

"I can't help it, I'm so in love with our daughter. I told you it was love at first sight, just like it was with you. I feel as if I've been hit twice by cupid's arrow."

"I see your Hallmark training is paying off," she mocked in the sweetest way.

"Ha! You wish baby. Hallmark doesn't have anything on me. This is what the women in my life have created."

"I'm not complaining."

"Good, because if you haven't noticed the Douglas men are sweet talkers and we love on our women like no one else can."

"Did you learn your smooth-talking ways from your father?"

"Nope, my grandfather. He's the original Casanova in the family."

"I would have to agree. He loves to flirt."

"Have I said, thank you?"

"For what, Rogan?" she asked lovingly as she kissed a trail of soft kisses along my muscled back. I stared at our baby girl sleeping all swaddled in pink. I would never tire of sharing these special moments with our daughter. I happily sighed and then turned around to hold my wife and kiss her madly until she was dizzy.

"You asked me why I was thanking you and there's only one answer I can come up with."

"And what's that?" she dreamily asked.

"Everything. My life with you and our daughter is everything. Thank you, Alex, for giving me a life worth living. For the here and now and most importantly, what's next to come."

Our hands linked as we walked out of the nursery closing the door behind us. I kissed her again and lifted her into my arms, holding her as close to me as I possibly could.

"So, now what?" She purred like the sexy minx she is.

I winked and said, "Let's go to bed."

THE END

A NOTE FROM
the Author

Thank you, readers, for taking the time to read *Here and Now*. I hope you enjoyed it as much I loved writing not just one love story, but two.

The best way to thank an author is to write and leave a review on the site you purchased this book. Even if it's a line or two, it's the best gift I could receive in return. They are always welcomed and appreciated. Thank you for your support.

All my best,

Mary

Acknowledgments

"Writing is the painting of the voice" by Voltaire.

I love that quote. It makes me appreciate the gift I've been given to have a voice through my words.

Thank you, God, for giving me the ability to create my art.
Thank you, to my family who love me unconditionally.
Thank you, to my friends who never let me fall.
Thank you, to the talented professionals that make my work come to life.

Thank you, Joe Marron. My editor. You get me, and I love you for that.
Thank you, Julie Titus, @ JT Formatting, a forever friend who does incredible designing to bring my words to life. Thank you for making the insides of my book look beautiful.
Thank you, Francessca, @ Francessca's PR & Design. You are a cover goddess and I love everything you do.
Thank you, Mindy Guerreiros for always reading my work first and giving me the feedback I need to make it great. The book world

would not be what it is without your love and passion for books. Thank you for all that you do but most of all, our friendship and sisterhood.

Thank you, to my readers. You mean so much to me. Writing has become an essential part of my soul, and without it, I would be lost. Thank you, for sharing this incredible journey with me. I truly appreciate you reading and supporting my work.

Thank you, to my author friends who I've built deep friendships with over the years. We may not see each other as often as time would allow, but I appreciate your friendships and hold them close to my heart.

Thank you, to my blogger friends. You work incredibly hard for authors in this community. Thank you, for always sharing the love.

OTHER BOOKS BY MARY A. WASOWSKI

Forever Series:
Forever: Book One
Second Chance at Forever: Book Two
Our Forever Promise: Book Three
Happily Forever After: Book Four
Forever More: Book Five

Standalone novels:
A Changed Life
All Roads Lead Home
An Unfinished Life
Return to Kildare
Revive
You Belong to Me
Run
Broken Dove
Shane
Before We Knew
New Release in 2020

ABOUT THE AUTHOR

Mary A. Wasowski is a best-selling author who writes adult contemporary romance. Best known for her *Forever* Series, Mary loves creating sexy alpha book boyfriends for you to swoon over. When she is not writing her happily ever after love stories, she is an avid reader of all romance.

A romantic at heart, she shares her zest for life with her husband, Henry, and their three sons. Proud to be an indie author, she lives in North Carolina and works as a full-time writer.

Stay in Touch!
I would love to hear from you.
Please stay connected wherever you are.

EMAIL:
AuthorMaryAWasowski@gmail.com

FACEBOOK:
https://www.facebook.com/Author-Mary-A-Wasowski-332971356804341

TWITTER:
https://twitter.com/wasow6

INSTAGRAM:
https://instagram.com/authormaryawasowski/

www.ingramcontent.com/pod-product-compliance
Lightning Source LLC
Chambersburg PA
CBHW071249250626
47163CB00002B/392